Diana threw her arms arou... ports, leaning the side of her face against the beam. Her mind was still trying to catch up with the wild sensations that were coursing through her body. Nothing in her sheltered existence had ever stirred her like Romulus' kisses had. Stirred her, frightened her, and made her feel more alive than she thought possible.

With the proof of Rom's ardor still on her lips, she wondered how she had ever doubted that he loved her! She heard him again as he had gasped, "An honorable man would not have let himself need you as I do." She would never let him go now. No one and nothing would come between them. *His Pride will come between you*, an errant voice pointed out, and she knew it to be true. Romulus knew his blasted place.

She had to do something decisive now, or he might be lost to her.

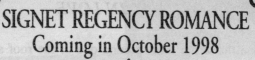

Keeper of the Swans

Nancy Butler

A SIGNET BOOK

SIGNET
Published by the Penguin Group
Penguin Putnam Inc., 375 Hudson Street,
New York, New York, 10014 U.S.A.
Penguin Books Ltd, 27 Wrights Lane,
London W8 5TZ, England
Penguin Books Australia Ltd,
Ringwood, Victoria, Australia
Penguin Books Canada Ltd, 10 Alcorn Avenue,
Toronto, Ontario, Canada M4V 3B2
Penguin Books (N.Z.) Ltd, 182-190 Wairau Road,
Auckland 10, New Zealand

Penguin Books Ltd, Registered Offices:
Harmondsworth, Middlesex, England

First published by Signet, an imprint of Dutton NAL,
a member of Penguin Putnam Inc.

First Printing, September, 1998
10 9 8 7 6 5 4 3 2 1

To Mom and Dad—who showed me the world
And to Elaine—who showed me the island

I have looked upon those brilliant creatures,
And now my heart is sore.
All's changed since I, hearing at twilight,
The first time on this shore,
The bell-beat of their wings above my head,
Trod with a lighter tread.

Unwearied still, lover by lover,
They paddle in the cold
Companionable streams or climb the air;
Their hearts have not grown old;
Passion or conquest, wander where they will,
Attend upon them still.

> —"The Wild Swans at Coole"
> WILLIAM BUTLER YEATS

I want a hero: an uncommon want.

> —"Don Juan"
> LORD BYRON

Chapter 1

It was definitely not good *ton* to flee your own betrothal ball.

But that didn't prevent Diana Exeley from slipping through one of the French doors that edged the ballroom of her sister's house and hurrying across the terrace. She had to get away—away from the heat and the noise, the crush of people and the cloying odor of overly scented bodies.

"Just a moment," she promised herself as she moved rapidly away from the bright light of the ballroom, toward the deeper shadows of the wide lawn. Though the rain had finally stopped—after a solid fortnight of downpour—the lawn and the surrounding willows were still dappled with moisture. A mist rose up from the grass, blending seamlessly with the wispy fingers of fog that reached up from the river.

Diana recalled the sum of money her sister's husband had laid out for her ball gown, so she dutifully rucked up the skirts of the silk and lace confection as she tripped across the wet grass toward the breakwater that fronted the river. Jutting out from that breakwater was an elegant boathouse with a narrow dock, and it was this shadowed refuge that beckoned to her.

She continued her flight until she reached the end of the dock. Resting her elbows upon one of the cobbled stanchions, she gazed out over the water, trying to calm the ragged beating of her heart. She hoped the sound of the river racing past would soothe her spirits—the Thames usually eased her, even when it was in wild motion, as was the case tonight. But her heart would not be soothed.

She knew she should have been pleased by the evening's events. As the daughter of an impecunious Yorkshire baronet, she should have been dancing with delight over her betrothal to a man of wealth and breeding. But Diana felt nothing but numb disbelief. Especially since the ramifications of that betrothal had not hit home until this evening, when her fiancé's many acquaintances, the cream of London society, had arrived at Mortimer House with the pointed intention of appraising her.

Diana wrinkled her nose. She did not want to have her every movement scrutinized by the *ton*; she had little care for that many-headed hydra. But it was clear that her future husband, Sir Beveril Hunnycut, did not share her distaste. She heard again his supercilious laughter, rising over the strains of the orchestra, as he bantered with his cronies beside the punch bowl. The sound had positively set her teeth on edge.

What had she been thinking, to allow herself to be coerced into marriage with a man she barely knew? Even if he did possess a tolerable fortune, and was nephew and sole heir to Baroness Hamish, the wealthiest landowner along the river. His position weighed little with her. But, unfortunately, the same could not be said of her sister, Helen, or her husband, James Mortimer. They had both worked very hard to procure this match for Diana. Not completely out of concern for her best interests, however.

James Mortimer had political aspirations which a man like Sir Beveril, who was a member of the Commons, could handily promote. Helen repeatedly reminded Diana that they both owed a great deal to James, and that requiring Diana to marry where it might do him some good was not a lot to ask. Diana thought that it was indeed a great deal to ask. But then Helen had always been prudent above everything.

Helen had met James at an assembly in York, while he was visiting relatives there. He'd been smitten by her dark beauty and had begun to court her almost immediately. Helen held him at arm's length while she weighed her options. James was a man of considerable wealth, but, alas, not nobly born. Although yet thirty, his manner was stuffy, and he tended to prose on about politics far longer than was tolerable. And he had neither dash nor style, qualities that were important to Helen. Diana had kept her own counsel on the matter. She doubted she could ever wed a man who had not won her heart. (A foolishly naive sentiment, she now thought, considering her present predicament.) When Helen made her decision at last—to marry her wealthy suitor—Diana saw it as just another instance of practicality over passion.

After returning from her bridal journey, Helen had written to Yorkshire, to insist that Diana visit her and make her comeout in London society. Diana had balked at first, unwilling to leave her father alone. It was she who saw to his comfort, prepared his favorite dishes, and distracted him when his arthritis troubled him. But her father had seen the wisdom of Helen's plan. He knew Diana would meet few marriageable men if she stayed in the East Riding. And so she found herself posting south only days after Helen's letter arrived.

Helen had made it clear that she expected Diana to seek a mate from the crop of influential politicians who went about in the *ton*. She had quickly scotched Diana's initial and horrified resistance to this scheme by pointing out to her sister that seeing Diana safely married would do a great deal to relieve her father—whose health was indifferent at best—from his worries over her unsettled future. And even without Helen's constant reminders, Diana knew what she owed her sister's generous spouse, who had not demurred at presenting her to the *ton* or at dowering her handsomely. It seemed she could do little to object to the Mortimers' machinations without seeming the veriest ingrate.

Diana had been surprised by the number of suitors who had flocked around her when she arrived from Bothys a month earlier. She knew herself to be past prime marriageable age, being nearly one-and-twenty, and she was not possessed of any particular graces or skills, other than the ability to dream bright, vivid dreams. Which was more of a liability, she often thought.

Sir Beveril had been the least objectionable of the men who courted her. He was not too old, not too prosy, and was accounted to be quite handsome, though she had never been fond of robust men. Helen assured her she would come to feel a proper affection for him, but Diana still harbored a great many doubts.

So far Beveril had been charming and courteous, and he'd even flirted with her at a champagne breakfast the week before. He'd raised her hand and kissed the palm of her crocheted mitten. It was a minor gallantry, but Diana had been flattered by the attention. The last man who had attempted any familiarity with her had been the young shepherd who lived on the hill behind her home in Bothys. The youth had not only been unconscionably forward, he had smelled unpleasantly of dung. After he had tried to kiss her on the mouth, he'd had his shepherd's crook jabbed in his ribs for his trouble. What Diana lacked in inches, she made up in spirit—she had a temper the size of Gibraltar. And a hard head to match, as Helen often reminded her.

Perhaps Sir Beveril would not make such a bad husband, she reflected. And he must truly care for her, to have proposed so soon after their first meeting. Diana scuffed one foot along the planking. Maybe it was time she put her foolish dreams of heroes behind her. They might have been tenpence a dozen in the stories from Greek and Roman mythology she was so fond of reading, but they were scarce as hen's teeth in the *ton*. Nelson was dead, and if he hadn't been, Lady Hamilton, for all her girth, would still have a hold on him. Wellington was married and, anyway, who wanted a hero who was never at home?

And who knew? One day Beveril might prove himself a hero . . . if he ever did anything in Parliament besides vote down reform bills or grumble about the prime minister. But somehow she doubted it—Beveril seemed to think that exhibiting a cleverly tied neckcloth was a major accomplishment in statesmanship.

She was so lost in her thoughts that she did not hear the sound of people approaching the boathouse. A woman's laughter fluted out across the lawn behind her, and Diana turned. A couple was strolling in the shadow of the willows, heading toward her refuge. She could have merely walked from the dock, and nodded a greeting to them as she made her way back to the ball, but she saw that they were walking with their arms entwined. She had no desire to interrupt a tête-à-tête. Nor did she want to answer any awkward questions—such as why she had needed to escape her own betrothal ball.

A rowboat was tied to the piling where she had been leaning; she'd heard it rocking against the dock. Usually the rowboats were kept in the boathouse, but in light of all the rain, which had caused the Thames to crest dangerously, one of them had been left outside. Earlier she'd seen the groundsmen using it to clear the debris, the branches and wooden planks, that the racing water had cast up onto the retaining wall.

Diana quickly scrambled down the wooden ladder and stepped into the boat, tucking her skirts around her to keep the hem out of the dank water in the boat's bottom. Taking hold of the nearest piling, she shifted the boat under the dock. She crouched there in the shadows, hoping to remain undetected, and thankful that the water in the lee of the boathouse was relatively calm compared to the wild stretch of river beyond her.

"I don't know how you can stand it," the woman was saying as the couple's footsteps echoed over Diana's head. "To be leg-shackled to a little country nobody."

Diana thought the speaker might be Lady Vivian Partridge, one of James's neighbors. She was a dashing widow with a question-able reputation. It figured she would be luring men out onto the rain-soaked grass.

"Oh, I'll endure it right enough," her companion responded.

Diana had a more difficult time placing his voice, especially since he spoke in a low, gruff tone.

"A month in the country with my wife, to satisfy the gossips, and then I'll be back in your arms."

"You don't sound very dismayed by the prospect of being with her." The lady's tone was peevish.

"A man's got to do his duty, Viv."

Ah, it was Lady Vivian.

"She's such an unschooled little thing," the woman continued. "No graces, no small talk. I shouldn't wonder if you're bored to tears inside of a week." She paused, and then added in a glib tone, "Not that *I'll* be bored, mind. You're not the only handsome man who lives along the river."

The man's voice deepened. "You stay away from that rascally knave, Vivian. You think I haven't seen you making sheep's eyes at him every time you chance to meet."

The lady sniffed. "What's sauce for the goose, my love, is cer-tainly sauce for the gander. You've no right to object to my little flirtations, when you are set on leaving me behind for another woman."

"Only for a short time, sweetheart. Now, hush."

There was a long silence, during which Diana assumed the cou-ple were engaging in a kiss. The man's voice then continued, a bit more raggedly than before. "You see, my feelings for you haven't changed, Vivian. But you know I cannot marry you, as much as I want to—your jointure barely supports your own expenses, and until my aunt pops off, which might be years yet, I need to get my hands on some blunt. The cents-percenters are hounding me to death, God rot them! The chit's brother-in-law has agreed to pay my debts in addition to her dowry. I know she's a bit gauche, but perhaps she'll improve once she's had a little town polish. And she's not a positive antidote, though I could wish she had more of her sister's looks."

Diana sat up suddenly, rapping her head sharply on one of the dock's crossbeams.

Sweet Lord above! It was Beveril! The man who had been kiss-ing the alluring Lady Vivian was her own fiancé. She rubbed one hand over her crown, wondering which was more painful, the ache in her head or the dispirited fluttering of her heart. It was too mortifying! They always said eavesdroppers rarely heard good of themselves, but it was still a blow to discover that Sir Beveril thought her gauche and unattractive. Not to mention how distasteful it was to hear oneself being discussed by one's betrothed and his mistress. And in such a disinterested manner, as though Diana were a leftover joint of mutton he was ordering up for dinner.

She attempted to block out the remainder of their conversation, which was not difficult, since neither of them spoke again for a long while. Over the brisk chuckling of the Thames, she could occasionally hear sighs and soft groans. She sat there, her chin resting on her fists, for what seemed like an hour, trying to tamp down her quivering feelings of betrayal and humiliation.

She couldn't possibly marry Beveril now. It didn't matter that half the husbands in the *ton* had mistresses, she would not be a party to such a sham marriage. It was far preferable to return to Yorkshire than to barter herself into a loveless, bleak future. Helen would be furious, she knew, and James would be disappointed. And her father would be upset that she had thrown away her one chance at a matrimony. But she would remain firm. Let them send her back to the East Riding. It was where she belonged. Not among the hypocritical members of London society, with their strict conventions and oddly loose morality.

"We must return, Beveril," Lady Vivian murmured. "Someone is bound to notice our absence. Oh, dear, my hair must look a fright."

"You look stunning as usual, Viv. Here . . . let me help . . . Lord, how I shall miss these golden curls."

"And you will help your wife do up her hair?" the lady asked archly.

Sir Beveril grunted and said disparagingly, "That wild mane? I've seen street urchins with better-tamed hair. There must be Gypsy blood somewhere in her family, by the look of her. But Mortimer's money is what I'm after, and a little thing like tainted blood isn't going to stand in my way."

Diana ground her teeth. She believed her hair to be one of her few good features. It was true it was a bit coarse and tended to curl more than was the fashion, but it was a vivid blue-black, and she always thought it set off her white skin and pale blue eyes very nicely. But Sir Beveril was clearly immune to any of her charms, save the financial ones. She had to get free of him, whatever it took.

She heard the muffled footsteps receding above her head as the couple moved off toward the house. Diana had every intention of following in their wake and announcing to the entire company that the engagement was off. But then reason prevailed. She realized with a sinking heart that such an act would create a scandal that neither Helen nor the benevolent James deserved.

Still, she was not to be married for another six weeks. Surely in that time she could convince her stubborn, single-minded sister that Beveril's unsavory character made him totally unacceptable as a husband, no matter how sterling his political connections. She purposely put Beveril's last pronouncement out of her mind. Even if *he* was totally unwilling to break off the betrothal, surely no one could force her into matrimony with the man. At least she prayed that was the case.

With a little *oomph*, she grasped the piling and guided the boat out from beneath the dock. But before she could grab the edge of the ladder, the boat drifted away from it, putting six feet of water between Diana and the dock. She didn't understand how it was possible, since the boat had been secured to the piling when she'd climbed into it. But then, as the current snatched at the craft and drew it farther into the river, she saw the sodden bow rope snaking along in the inky water. Somehow the boat had come untied.

Diana was unalarmed at first. Rowing along the shoreline was one of her chief pleasures at Mortimer House. But that was on sunny days when the river ran at a normal pace. Now the current was swift and strong, propelling Diana rapidly away from the dock. She groped in the boat's bottom for the oars and came up with only one. Scrambling to the stern, she tried using the single oar as a rudder, to steer the boat back toward the river bank. Instead, the craft began to slew in the water, gong sideways first, and then nearly turning completely around. Water splashed over the sides, soaking the skirt of Diana's gown, and as the boat rounded a bend in the river, Mortimer House was lost from sight.

Blind fear rose up in her now, gut-clenching, heart-thudding panic. She'd never seen the river as wild as it was tonight, white-capped and full of eddies. The little boat raced on, pitching wildly from side to side as Diana crouched in the bottom, holding onto the gunwales for dear life. The scenery that flashed past was unfamiliar, though she gauged she had to be somewhere near Hamish House, the home of Beveril's aunt.

At least there were no waterfalls to contend with—she knew the river ran a winding but level course up to London, where it widened enough for commercial shipping. Diana could just imagine her fragile craft ramming full speed into the side of an India merchantman, or an anchored man-of-war. All they would find would be the splintered remains of the rowboat, and a few of the silk roses that adorned her gown.

Diana was a capable swimmer, and she weighed the prudence of leaping from the boat and striking out for shore. But as hefty tree branches and ragged pieces of planking raced past her boat, she realized that even if the current did not wear her down, she risked being struck by one of those lethal objects.

"No!" she cried out into the night. "The river is my friend—it won't harm me!"

It was an odd sort of prayer. But as though the river gods had heard her, an island suddenly loomed up on her left. Frantically Diana thrust her oar into the water on the left side of the boat, keeping the paddle flat against the current. It was enough to shift her course toward the foliage that obscured the end of the island.

"Thank God!" she breathed as the boat was caught in an eddy produced by the jutting tip of the island.

She stood up and swung her dripping oar to the right side, trolling it back and forth to bring the boat closer to the shoreline. The trees that edged the water were coming closer, and Diana held her breath as the boat scraped over a submerged root. She was almost there . . .

The low-hanging limb was obscured by leaves, and Diana didn't see the danger until the branch collided sharply with the side of her head. With an inarticulate cry, she dropped her oar and reeled back. As she tumbled over the side, the boat immediately shifted away, and was thrust once again into the main current.

Diana plunged under the chill water, instantly dragged down by her sodden skirts. Now only half conscious, she groped for something to hold on to, trying to raise her head above the chopping waves. The hungry current was carrying her away from land, so she kicked out her feet with the last of her strength. Miraculously, her fingers grasped something solid. It was towing her now, through the water. In her disordered state she began to struggle, thinking it was the river again drawing her away from safety.

"*No-o-o!*" She cried out in protest and received a mouthful of river water for her trouble. Sputtering and flailing, she continued to resist.

"*Shhhh!*" The tugging would not let up.

"No!" she sobbed raggedly, still struggling against that firm hold.

But then the sloping riverbank rose up to meet her. She felt herself being carried forward until she came to rest on a hillock of swamp grass. Her head thudded to the ground, and as her consciousness gave way to the pounding blackness, she could have sworn she heard someone laughing softly.

"No!" she cried over and over in a thready, whimpering voice.

It wasn't fair. Everyone else at the ball was properly dressed, but somehow she had left home wearing only her chemise. Her hair was unconfined and it billowed down over her shoulders, partially obscuring a golden chain hung with large gold coins. A broad-chested man with curling blond locks jeered at her the instant she entered the ballroom and soon everyone had joined in. Their cruel laughter echoed in her ears.

She fled then, down the front steps and into the street. But disembodied hands caught at her, pulling her back, back to the scene of her humiliation. Eager fingers tugged repeatedly at the necklace of coins about her neck, choking her, cutting off her air.

"I cannot go back," she moaned, writhing against her pillow. "I will not go back!"

"*Shhhh.*" The soothing noise came from far away.

"Don't make me go back!" she pleaded hoarsely, before the cool cloth at her brow eased her distress.

Diana was hot and sticky all over. *I must be feverish*, she thought, remembering the time she'd been ill with the measles. With a great deal of concentration she was able to open her eyes. Not that she could see anything. The room before her swam sickeningly in double and triple images. And her head pounded as though a hundred blacksmiths were plying their noisy trade inside her skull.

Someone was moving in the room. She narrowed her eyes, trying to make out a form or figure. The shadow moved closer, and a low voice said, "I see you have decided to remain among the living." It was a man's voice, low-pitched and curiously soothing.

She opened her mouth to speak but nothing came out.

"Easy now. I've brought you some broth to drink." The man sat at the edge of her bed, levered her up from her pillow, and raised a porcelain mug to her mouth.

"No," she croaked, fretfully moving her head to one side. "It hurts too much." Even the tiniest motion made her stomach knot with nausea.

"But you must," the voice insisted. "I've put something in it to ease your pain."

"Are you a doctor, then?" She was squinting up at him trying to see what he looked like. To see exactly who went with that wonderful voice.

"Ah, no. But I've had some experience with stubborn creatures who will not eat."

"I'm not a stubborn creature," she grumbled.

"Then don't behave like one." There was a firmness to the man's tone that she recognized, in spite of her hazy grip on reality.

"Oh, very well," she said sullenly. "But I warn you, it's likely to come right back up again."

She clutched the mug, her fingers clasped over the man's as he guided it to her mouth. His hands were warm. Or maybe that was just because of the broth. She swallowed several mouthfuls, and then fell back onto her pillow. When the man stood up, she realized he was enormously tall. Probably a giant. A giant river god who had plucked her from a watery grave. One with an exceedingly nice voice.

The man came again later in the night, carrying a shuttered lantern, which he set down on the floor. Crouching in the shadows a few feet from her bed, he busied himself with some task. She couldn't move her aching head enough to see what it was that so preoccupied him.

"Are you the one who laughed at me?" she whispered. That laughter was the last thing she could remember of her ordeal.

"Mmm," he answered. "You looked like a half-drowned water witch. But it was mostly from relief that I laughed. I thought I'd lost you there at one point. You put up a rather good fight—in fact I've never seen anyone battle so fiercely to keep from being rescued. You're not a suicide by any chance?"

"I don't think so," she said weakly.

"Don't you remember how you came to be in the river?"

Of course I remember, she wanted to snap. But then she also remembered her fiancé kissing another woman. And her own feeling of mortification when he had discussed her so coldly. Once her rescuer knew who she was and alerted the authorities, Helen and a whole entourage of servants would come and whisk her back home. Back to the arms of the avaricious Sir Beveril.

"Maybe you can't remember just yet," he said musingly. "You took a nasty crack on the head. You're probably still a bit concussed."

"I can remember nothing," she said softly. "Except being in the water. It's . . . all so . . . fuzzy."

Yes, Diana thought, a convenient loss of memory would buy her some time. Until she could think of foolproof argument to convince her sister and James that she could never marry Beveril. She suspected the fact that he had openly belittled her to his mistress might not carry much weight with them.

The man rose, and then settled himself on the side of her bed. His hand brushed over her forehead, whisking back a few stray curls. "You don't feel feverish any longer; that's a blessing. Swallow enough river water and you're likely to end up with an inflammation of the lungs."

"Will I die, do you think?" she asked, wishing he would keep his hand there, upon her throbbing head.

"Not unless you drag yourself back to the river. Some suicides just keep on trying."

She was nearly too weary to respond to his sarcasm. "Next time"—she yawned—"poison."

"Hmm? Then I'd better go lock up the hemlock."

She grinned at him in the semidarkness and said, "Socrates?"

"Oh, have you remembered your name, then?" She didn't miss the wry tone of his voice.

"No, not my name," she said wistfully. "Perhaps it will return in the morning."

After he'd picked up his lantern and gone from the room, Diana swore she heard tiny, high-pitched voices whispering in her head. Maybe the man was mistaken . . . maybe she was still feverish.

Chapter 2

When Diana awoke again it was daylight. Her vision had cleared up and the pain in her head was now merely a dull throb. She boosted herself up into a sitting position. As the coverlet fell away, she saw that over her chemise she now wore a man's blue dressing gown. Her ball gown seemed to have disappeared.

Leaning back on her narrow cot, she took stock of her surroundings. Packing crates were piled everywhere, along with barrels and sacks of feed. There was an uncurtained window on the rudely plastered wall opposite her cot, through which she could see a bit of green treetop and a scrap of blue sky. It was not a promising setting; she might well be in some farmer's storage room.

But then she recalled the island where she had come ashore. Perhaps the man had been poaching on the island when he found her and had carried her back to his farm. Except that from what she remembered of their brief encounter, the man had not sounded anything like a farmer. And there had been something else about his voice, the hint of a foreign accent, as though he had learned English late in his youth, and had retained a touch of his mother tongue. But as to what that tongue might be, she hadn't a clue.

She forced her legs over the side of the bed and tried to stand. It was a good thing there was a pile of crates nearby—she had to grab on to them the instant she straightened up. Diana sighed in frustration. If standing upright was beyond her, walking was clearly out of the question.

She stood there for several minutes, waiting for the room to stop spinning. And waiting for the bizarre noise in her ears to cease. The *peep-peep-peep*-ing that went on and on. Then the weak, tentative pecking started on her fingers, where they clutched the top crate. She whisked her hand away instantly and fell backward onto the bed. The *peep-peeps* grew even louder.

"Good Lord," she muttered when she saw the source of the sound. The top crate was full of downy, pale gray chicks. And the one below it, as well.

Had the man put her in his barn? Had she spent the night sleeping with livestock?

There was the sound of whistling from beyond the room, then the door swung open and the enormously tall river god came in, carrying a tray.

"Had a good sleep?" he asked. She nodded, and he continued in a brisk voice, "Nothing like two days' rest to fix a broken head."

"Two days?" she moaned. "That's not possible."

"It's Monday afternoon. I heard you stirring, and thought it might be time to feed you again."

Monday afternoon! Oh, no! She put one hand over her face. Helen would be distraught.

"Have you remembered anything yet? Your name? Where you live? Why you were taking a swim in the middle of the night?" He set up a tray of food in her lap as he spoke.

"Nothing." She shook her head slowly.

What could she tell him? Once he knew her name, he would certainly return her to her family, and that was out of the question. She had only a vague recollection of the horrid dreams that had plagued her as she slept, but she felt positively ill at the thought of marrying Sir Beveril. Yet she needed to get some word to her sister—not her location certainly, but some reassurance that she hadn't met with foul play.

"One name does come to mind," she said haltingly. "Wilfred Bailey." She cocked her head and added musingly, "I have a notion he may be a lawyer." Bailey was James Mortimer's solicitor in London. If she got a message to him, she was certain he would relay it to her sister.

The man had crossed his arms over his chest. "And do you recall where this Bailey can be found?"

With his hand in everyone's pocket, Diana was tempted to reply. "In London, in Bishopsgate," she said aloud. "Perhaps I can write to Mr. Bailey, describing my person. He might be able to identify me."

Her host still looked dubious. Diana gave him a wide-eyed shrug of apology. "It's the only solution I can think of at the moment."

"I'll bring you some writing paper after you've eaten." He ran his knuckles along his chin. "But it's very odd—I've seen people with head wounds who got their memory back in fits and starts. But I've never met anyone who remembered the name and address of a *lawyer*, and yet didn't have a clue to their own identity."

"Yes," she said with a small frown. "It's most perplexing."

Diana tucked into the stew he had brought her, washing it down with a mug of cool cider. While she ate, he tended to the chicks, engrossed in his task as he lifted them, one by one, from the crate and fed them from a glass pipette. She took the opportunity to examine him while his attention was diverted.

All she had recalled after their first encounter was his melodious voice and unusual height. Now she noted that he was quite lean, though broad shouldered, and that his hair was an unusual shade of auburn. A dark, burnished red, the color of Indian mahogany, it fell in thick waves to the collar of his shirt. He was clearly not a man of fashion. Not that the style didn't suit him. As did the deep green buckskin coat he wore and the high leather gaiters. He looked more like a woodsman than any farmer she'd ever seen.

His face was in profile as he fussed over his birds. Diana thought the long, arched nose was a bit too prominent to be called handsome, though it nicely balanced his square, jutting chin. There were hollows beneath his cheekbones and his eyes were deepset. She could not make out their color, though.

"Are you a poultry farmer?" she asked as he closed the door of the top crate and moved down to the lower one. He swung around and gave her a look of thinly veiled distemper.

Hazel. His eyes were hazel—a rich swirl of green and golden brown. Flashing now in irritation.

"Great gods, ma'am! Do these look like chickens to you?"

Well, he was certainly on his high ropes. For a farmer. "I have little acquaintance with birds," she huffed. Now sheep, on the other hand, she knew. There wasn't a Yorkshirewoman born who couldn't tell a merino from a Cheviot with her eyes closed.

"These are cygnets," he said with deliberate slowness, as if to a lackwit.

"*Cig-whats?*"

The man rolled his eyes. "Baby swans."

"That's not what I'm eating, is it?" She eyed her stew with mock alarm. Then she saw the way he was cradling the downy creature—with great tenderness. Best not to rib him. "May I hold one?"

"They're not pets," he warned. "They'll be going back to the wild as soon as they're fit."

"Never mind," she said lightly, hiding her disappointment.

"Oh, here," he said, relenting. "But try not to handle her too much."

"Oh, it's a girl swan. A cygness, then?" Her eyes danced up at him as he set the small bundle on her lap. It hunkered down immediately, shaking its tiny tail as it burrowed into the coverlet with ungainly charm.

"She's very sweet. Where is her mother?"

The man's lean cheeks drew in even further. "Dead. I've three broods here, all orphaned. The parents work as a team, you see, and when one of them is killed, the other sometimes abandons the nest. This lot were orphaned by poachers." He spat out the word. "There are gentlemen who will pay a hefty price for a swan to grace their dinner table."

"I was only jesting . . . about the stew," she said softly.

"I know. You just touched on a sore spot, that's all." As he spoke, the man rubbed at the side of his face fretfully. "I am paid to look after these creatures. I patrol this whole stretch of river by myself and I can't be everywhere. Someone is taking the mature swans and leaving the cygnets to die."

Diana stroked her fingers along the downy back. The baby swan tucked in her short neck and made a soft cooing noise. "Poor little mite."

"You should have seen them when I brought them here last week. Nearly done in, they were. They've perked up considerably—tomorrow I intend to start them swimming. There's a pond on the island." His mouth drew up on one side. "Well, several now, actually, after all the rain."

"Oh, are we still on the island?"

He nodded. "I live here. It makes my job much easier, being in the thick of things, as it were."

"What is it called?"

He gazed down at the cygnet in her lap and shook his head. "I don't hold with naming wild creatures."

"No," she said, looking up at him with a grin. "I meant the island. Does it have a name?"

He shrugged. "Not that I know of. Here—" He scooped the

cygnet from her lap and replaced it in the crate. "You'd better rest now. When I return from my patrol, we'll see to writing that letter to Mr. Bailey."

Diana watched as he picked up her tray and went from the room. She had asked him everything but his own name. Maybe, like the island, he didn't have a name. Just "Tall River God."

Lud, she must still be addled. Or back in the fantasy world she had been obliged to put behind her in Bothys. She had soon realized when she went to live with Helen that her youthful dreams would never come to pass. Young ladies who were forced to wed for political reasons had no business holding onto their dreams. But nameless women who were fished out of the Thames could dream anything their hearts desired.

When she slept at last, Diana dreamed of a golden-eyed man with beech-leaf hair, who carried her from island to island with one stride of his impossibly long legs.

Romulus was glad the river was finally going down. He'd lost too many birds to the cresting water. The grebes who made their nests along the shore, and the peevish, territorial coots, were all endangered by encroaching floods. Even though the swans were his chief charges, he also kept watch over the other water birds: the tall gray herons, the small, hunched night herons, and the pipers that fed in the shallows. He freed them from poachers' snares, kept the village children away from nesting sites, and prevented the local population of cats and dogs from having them for dinner. Natural predators he allowed. He was not there, after all, to see nature confounded. He only wanted to see it respected.

The people in Treypenny thought he was addled—a grown man wasting his time with birds. He only went to the nearby village when Niall was away traveling with his people. Otherwise the Gypsy boy brought supplies to the island once a week. Everything Romulus and his orphaned swans could require.

But now he had a new chick to look after, and he was not happy about that fact. The balance of life always altered whenever something new was added to the equation. This woman—well, she was really more of a girl—had intruded on his solitude and he resented that intrusion.

The solitude was the best part of his job. He was wary of most people. His tolerance for foolishness was low and his temper was particularly short. He had been scrappy as a youth and had turned downright curmudgeonly as an adult. It was only after a stint in the army that he had learned to curb his temper. But then he'd gone through a hellish ordeal that had curbed a great deal more of his nature.

That nightmare had ended less than a year ago, and he still bore the scars. His nerves had settled, it was true—the tic in his cheek and the trembling in his hands had disappeared. But the villagers continued to treat him as though he were the gaunt stranger with the uncontrolled twitches and lurching walk who had appeared among them ten months before. And he did nothing to change their opinion of him.

The Thames was all he needed—it was his home, his source of peace. He often thought it was because he had been raised on the banks of another great river, one which also ran through a thriving capital city. The water beckoned him, like a prophet's burning bush. It spoke to him, soothed him, and refreshed him. But it had never before cast a black-haired water witch up on his island, practically at his feet.

He knew he should row the girl over to Treypenny, now that she had regained consciousness, and put her in the care of the magistrate. She was obviously well born—that ball gown she had been wearing would have fed a cottager's family for a year. But she was still unwell. And it wasn't much trouble to feed her—Niall had recently brought him a crate of supplies. And in spite of his resentment over her abrupt intrusion into his life, there was something about her that intrigued him.

While she had slept, restless with fever, she had repeatedly cried out in a childlike voice, "Please don't make me go back!" Romulus was not proof against such a heart-rending plea. He needed to discover what it was she feared so greatly before he made a decision of any kind.

Still, he'd best have Niall ask around tomorrow, to see if any of the young ladies in the district had gone missing Saturday night. Her family was no doubt in a proper state by now. Unless she'd run off and left them a note. Perhaps it was a runaway marriage which had gone awry, or some similar foolishness.

He sighed. Birds notwithstanding, women were surely the most flighty of God's creatures.

Diana awoke into darkness. The cygnets were silent—the man must have fed them recently. It was curious, though, that she hadn't awakened when he came in. But then he was a particularly quiet man. Had he watched her as she slept, held the lantern above her and looked down upon her face? It was unlikely—he was far more interested in his birds than in a sleeping girl with a tangle of black curls. Which was a pity.

Diana climbed from the bed and found she was much steadier on her feet. But she also found herself in desperate need of a privy. She tottered through the door and into a low-ceilinged sitting room, furnished with mismatched castoffs—two tattered arm chairs and a lumpy looking sofa. The stucco walls were painted a pale ochre, and against one of them leaned a tall shelf, brimming with a raggle-taggle collection of books. A branch of candles was burning on the mantel, and beside the hearth stood a surprisingly fine walnut desk.

She crossed the room and poked her head out into the narrow hallway. "Hullo?" she called softly.

"In here," a disembodied voice replied.

She made her way shakily down the hall to a brightly lit kitchen.

"Feeling better?" The man looked up, but did not rise from his stool, which was pulled up to a scarred pine table. He appeared to be holding a pair of long knitting needles in his hands. Diana realized with a start that there was a bird's body at the end of the needles.

"Yes, much better," she said as she drew closer. "What sort of bird is that?"

"Gray heron," he responded, as he unwound the bandage that was wrapped around the bird's left leg. "Got himself caught in a wire snare two weeks ago. Here"—he motioned with his chin— "hold that cloth over his head so he won't struggle. I need to remove the splint and see if his leg is mending properly."

Diana did as he asked, standing at his shoulder as he worked. It was a pleasure to watch his hands, so deft and sure, as they carefully removed the wooden splints.

"Will he be crippled?" she asked.

"Too soon to tell. I'll keep him here if he can't return to the river; I've a pen out back for such cases."

"Speaking of out back . . ." she said haltingly, "is there by any chance a privy?"

He turned his head and looked at her as though she had asked to have the Royal Barge brought around.

"Well, don't tell me there isn't."

"Well, there is. I'm just surprised you were so plainspoken about it."

He finished up with the bird, replacing the gauze bindings, and then motioned Diana to follow him. He went down a set of stone steps and into the lantern-lit back yard. Two adjoining net-covered pens stood off to the left; the nearest one contained a basin of water and a pile of hay.

"The privy's out there," he said, pointing beyond the pen. "Just past the woodshed. Take the lantern down from the wall so you can see where you're going."

When Diana returned to the pen, the man was inside, trying to soothe the frightened bird.

"He's very agitated tonight," he said, looking up. "A positive sign that he's mending, I think."

"Perhaps I can ease him," she said as she went through the wood-framed doorway.

She crouched down beside the heron, smoothed the flapping wings, and then took the long neck in the crook of one arm. With her free hand she began to stroke the bird's breast, humming softly at the back of her throat. The heron gradually stopped fighting and she soon felt the narrow body relax.

"There," she said, rising to her feet. "I think he'll do."

The man was looking at her like she was, in truth, a witch. "How the devil did you do that?"

Diana grinned. "My aunt used to have a parrot. He had fits sometimes, and that's what she did to calm him down. He was very high strung, but he liked the humming and stroking."

"I daresay he did."

The heron was now stalking awkwardly around the pen, but he seemed much less perturbed.

They returned to the kitchen. While her host put his tools away, Diana let her gaze wander around the room. Except for the small hearth and the soapstone sink, it looked more like an infirmary than any kitchen she had ever seen. On a rack along one wall hung an assortment of pliers, shears, tweezers, and metal probes. Glass bottles, stoppered with cork and containing dried herbs and colored liquids sat in a tidy row upon a narrow trestle table. The contents of each bottle was labeled in a sprawling, backhand script. Beneath the trestle a collection of baskets held gauze, bandages and wooden splints.

"Who are you?" she asked as she settled onto a stool.

He looked up from the gauze he was rolling. In the flickering candlelight his eyes had taken on a golden cast. "The keeper of the swans," he said simply.

Oh, she thought with a shiver, *that is almost as good as Tall River God. The Keeper of the Swans.*

"And does a name go with that title?"

"Perrin," he said. "Romulus Perrin."

"Romulus, as in Rome?" she asked, propping her chin on one hand.

He nodded. "I was born there. I lived in Italy till I was nine."

Well, that explained the odd inflection in his voice.

"I don't suppose *your* name has by any chance returned?" he inquired as he sat down opposite her.

Diana shook her head. "Something is shifting around in my brain. I could recall it at any moment."

He cast her a look of unveiled skepticism, his dark brows lowering over those golden eyes.

"Perhaps I need a new name until that occurs," she mused, trying to distract him. There was a book lying face-down on one end of the table—the *Inferno* by Dante Alighieri. Nice, light suppertime reading, she thought, with a silent chuckle. "How about Allegra?" she suggested. "That sounds properly Italian to me."

He saw where she had been looking. His long fingers reached out and stroked the morocco spine. "*Beatrice* would be more fitting in that case, I think."

He'd given the name its lilting Italian pronunciation. Diana thought that if he ever said a full sentence to her in that rich, melodic language she would probably swoon.

She wrinkled her nose. "Too starchy. I think Allegra is a lovely name."

"Then Allegra it is. And will you require a surname as well?"

After a moment's thought she said, "What about Swan? Allegra Swan."

"Sounds like an opera dancer," he muttered.

She grinned. It did have a nicely florid ring to it.

"Well, if you don't like the thought of sharing your home with an opera dancer"—she watched in delight as his lean cheeks drew in—"then what about Heron? In honor of our surly friend out there."

"No, I think I prefer Allegra Swan," he said. "Though you don't look much like one."

"What? An opera dancer?" she teased.

He replied between his teeth, "No, a swan." His eyes scanned her openly. "You'd have to be stately and elegant, in that case."

Diana ignored his slighting comment. "As long as it's not Allegra *Partridge*," she said darkly.

"Are you always this glib?" he inquired, crossing his arms on the table as he leaned toward her. "You seem surprisingly at ease for a woman who can remember nothing of her past." His eyes narrowed suddenly. "How is it you were able to remember the aunt with the parrot?"

Diana nearly cursed aloud at her lapse. She'd have to temper everything she said from now on.

"So I did," she said musingly, her eyes wide. "But for the life of me I cannot recall her name."

Romulus muttered something under his breath.

"Truly," she said and gave him her most winning smile.

He continued to frown, which only accentuated the high, arched bridge of his nose, and the stern, stubborn set of his chin. "You'd better get that letter written," he said gruffly. "So I can row it over to the village in the morning. I'll find a farmer going to market to carry it to London. With any luck, your Mr. Bailey will receive it tomorrow. Ask him to post his reply to the Waterthrush Pub in Treypenny. If he is able to identify you, then I'll have you out from underfoot by Wednesday or Thursday."

Diana shot him a look of annoyance. "You are certainly anxious to be rid of me."

He returned her look with one of impatience. "My anxiety is for those who have misplaced you. Your family or friends. Hasn't it occurred to you that they will be overset with worry?"

Diana shrugged. "Perhaps I live alone. Some ladies do, those of a bookish inclination."

"Oh, and do you sit and read your dusty little sermons in a satin gown?" He motioned behind her to where her ball gown hung on a peg, dry now, but wilted and gray from its sojourn in the river.

"Mmm? Maybe even bookish ladies go out of an evening."

"Give over," he said crossly, hiking himself off the stool. "There's a deal more here than you are willing to tell me. But short of shaking it out of you—"

"If you doubt my story, you could always read my letter to Mr. Bailey before you post it." She cast him a look of open challenge. "You might get a clue or two from that."

"That would be pretty now, wouldn't it? Rifling through a lady's private correspondence. It's just that I can't credit how well you are taking all this. Most of the fellows I knew who lost their memories—"

"Oh, and did you know a great many?" she asked airily.

"In the war," he stated, his hands gripping the edge of the table. "In Spain. After an artillery shell exploded, it wasn't uncommon for the soldiers nearby to become disoriented."

"How long did it usually take them to recover?" she asked more gently. Something in his tone had made her lose all her pertness.

"Hours in some cases. Days in others. Rarely more than a week."

I have a week then, Diana thought with relief. *A week before his suspicions would be truly aroused.*

"You are very quiet, all of a sudden," he said, then added slyly, "Care to have a stab at the truth?"

Diana looked up to where he leaned against the trestle table. "I don't know the answers," she said earnestly. Well, that was true enough. "I need time for things to sort themselves out. And I'll try not to be a charge on you, Romulus. Perhaps I can even help you with your work."

"You are only hours out of your sickbed," he reminded her. "And females have no business being out on the river. Look what trouble you got into Saturday night."

"I wasn't out on the river on purpose!" she cried, sliding off her stool in agitation.

"Aha!" He jabbed one long finger at her as he said silkily, "And how, pray, do you know that?"

She glared at him. "Even a lackwit wouldn't take a rowboat out after two weeks of torrential rain."

"I take my boat out every day," he said. "But then I am used to the river in all its moods. But tell me again . . . you recall being in a boat? There was no boat nearby when I found you."

"I certainly didn't *swim* to this place," she muttered. "So there had to be a boat. But whatever events led to my being in that accursed boat, you can be sure I wasn't on the river voluntarily."

"Ah," he said with an infuriating drawl. "So you think someone is trying to do you in?"

Diana marched up to him. The top of her head barely reached his chin and he was not even standing fully upright. She angled her head back to meet his eyes. "I didn't choose to fall out of that boat on your island, sir. And after the way you have been treating me, I think it might have been preferable to drown."

He grinned down at her. "And I thought I was being the soul of hospitality."

"You can row me to the nearest village in the morning," she snapped, turning away from his irritating amusement. "I'm sure someone there will offer me a place to stay. In the meantime, if you would kindly point me to the writing supplies—I still need to contact Mr. Bailey." She went to the kitchen doorway and stood there, arms crossed, one bare foot tapping impatiently upon the stone floor.

Romulus was frowning when he moved away from the trestle and went past her into the hallway. He motioned curtly for her to follow, and after settling her at his writing desk, he stalked from the sitting room.

"Well," Diana muttered, as she dipped her pen in the ink pot. "He certainly is a testy old thing. Even if he is rather attractive when he gets cross. I wonder what he did in the war? I wonder what he's doing here on this island caring for baby birds? Oh, what does it matter? I'll likely be gone in the morning."

She turned her thoughts to her letter, which needed to be worded very carefully. It wouldn't do to give too much away. Lawyers were cagey sorts, far too good at reading between the lines.

"Dear Mr. Bailey," she wrote after some consideration, "a certain young lady, late of Bothys, is at present staying with friends in the country. It will be some time before she can again return to her family. Please assure those who are concerned over her disappearance that nothing untoward has occurred."

There, she thought with satisfaction. Bailey would easily deduce the identity of his correspondent, and he'd then assure Helen of Diana's safety. And if the insufferable Mr. Perrin was ungallant enough to open her letter, he would learn only that she had lied about losing her memory. But there would be no way he could use the letter to trace her back to Mortimer House. Not unless he went to London and accosted Bailey himself. And that was highly unlikely. He just wanted her gone from his island.

Once her missive was sealed with a clot of red wax, Diana felt much better. Although her relationship with her elder sister was heated at times, she did not wish to cause Helen unnecessary distress. She placed the letter on the mantel, and then went to examine her host's bookcase. The lower shelves held reference books and portfolio's wrapped with brown cord. The upper shelves contained leather-bound copies of the classics, and tattered volumes of the less ponderous poets. A collection of Pope caught her eye. Yes, she could imagine the wry, sarcastic Romulus Perrin enjoying his Alexander Pope.

She plucked the book from the shelf, settled into one of the chairs, and began to read, chuckling occasionally to herself. Every few minutes she glanced up at the mantel clock, wondering where her host had disappeared to. Surely there was not a grog shop on this little island. If he didn't return soon, though, she would be much too sleepy to apologize. Which was what she had every intention of doing. She couldn't blame Romulus for being suspicious—her acting skills needed a deal of honing, and she had muddled her performance dreadfully. But she hoped an earnestly worded apology would keep him from sending her away.

As she tried to concentrate on Mr. Pope, her thoughts drifted to her father, back home in Bothys with only his books and his aged servants for company. Dear, misguided Papa, who had thought he was acting in her best interests by placing her in Helen's hands. Diana knew she could return there, and receive nothing more than a stern lecture for being headstrong. But she didn't want to go back to Yorkshire.

She yawned and gave a weary sigh. No, Yorkshire no longer held any allure. She wanted to stay right here on this island, with Romulus. Because it was . . . because he was . . .

Romulus found her asleep in his favorite chair, *The Rape of the Lock* lying open at her feet. He retrieved the book and returned it to the shelf, wondering what a society chit could possibly find compelling in the caustic humor of the immortal Pope. He shrugged. Her tastes in literature were none of his concern. In fact his only concern was to get her the hell out of his life. Before he became even remotely attached to her.

It was the only way with foundlings. Once they were strong enough to survive in their world, he saw to it that they were set free. No matter that he might have begun to look forward to their company. Baby birds or society belles, both had to be returned to their proper homes. His island was only a temporary refuge.

He saw the letter lying on the mantel and took it up. If she hadn't baited him about it in the kitchen, he might be tempted to read it now. But he had more scruples than brains, he reckoned, as he slipped it into the pocket of his coat. Whoever she was, he'd learn of it soon enough. Young ladies didn't go missing from their families without setting off some kind of stir. And if she lived within five miles of this island, Niall would discover her identity. The Gypsy was a veritable terrier when it came to digging things up, and he knew enough to be discreet. Which was essential, since the naive creature sleeping across the room from him seemed oblivious to the fact that she had been compromised. The only way she could go back to her family with her reputation unsullied was if no one learned she had spent time with an outcast madman. Which was why he couldn't let her go off to the village tomorrow. That was his only reason for wanting to keep her there, he assured himself.

Diana felt herself being lifted and carried. She stirred slightly, and then burrowed her head into the folds of a neckcloth. "Mmm," she murmured. "Is it morning?"

"No," Romulus whispered, bending his head low over hers. "It's still nighttime."

"Don't put me in the boat," she whimpered in a waiflike voice.

"Shhh. I'm just putting you to bed. In your own room." He nudged open the door to the store room.

"With the cygnets?"

"Umm. With all the other lost chicks."

"Good," she mumbled into his shirtfront. "I want to stay with the cygnets. And the heron . . ."

"Yes, I think you're better off right here."

He was pulling the coverlet over her when she reached out to grasp his hand. "I'm sorry, Romulus," she said groggily, still more than half asleep. "Sorry I'm such a poor actress."

He squeezed that small hand. "I'm afraid Allegra Swan doesn't have much of a stage career ahead of her."

"*Mmm* . . ." She grinned up at him as if he'd said something outstandingly clever.

He moved away from the bed, not daring to glance back at her as she snuggled beneath the blanket.

She was little more than a child by the look of her, but the feel of her in his arms just now had whispered of not-so-childish endowments. That first night he had been too overcome with relief after he'd rescued her from the water—especially since she had fought him off like a creature possessed and had nearly drowned in the shallows—to take stock of the body beneath the wringing wet clothing. And once he'd carried her back to his lodge, he'd been too preoccupied with doctoring the bump on her head and with bundling her under a blanket, to pay any heed to her feminine charms.

But now he'd discovered there were distinct curves to her body, and soft, scented hollows. He'd liked carrying her far too much. In fact he'd like to do a great deal more than lift her up in his arms.

Christ! He'd have to set Niall on her trail first thing in the morning. Because it was imperative they find her family. At once.

As he closed the door behind him, Romulus gave a muffled groan. Not every threat to his peace of mind came in the form of floods and poachers. Sometimes it came in the sublime shape of a black-haired water witch with gentian eyes and a round, rosy mouth.

Chapter 3

Treypenny lay just beyond the river, screened by a stand of oaks. The village boasted a collection of ivy-covered store-fronts—a bake shop, a greengrocer, a small livery, and a pub called the Waterthrush.

Romulus tied his rowboat to a ring at the base of Treypenny's granite river stairs. The children playing above him stopped to watch, and then as he mounted the steps they began to chant, "Bo-geyman, bogeyman," in loud, piping voices. He made a lurching motion toward them, and they scattered like chaff, even the bold-est of them not wanting to get within range of his hands. It was too bad, for they might have seen the look of amusement shining in his eyes. Amusement and wistful pain.

As Rom made his way through Treypenny, the villagers gave him a wide berth. The women drew their skirts aside as he passed and the men refused to meet his eyes. He shrugged off their ill-concealed dislike and continued on toward the main road. He lin-gered there until an overburdened farm cart came creaking along.

"Heading into London this morning?" he called up after hailing the driver.

"Aye." The farmer spat a stream of tobacco juice onto the road. "Got a load of mangel-wurzels to sell."

"God help you," Romulus muttered under his breath, trying not to grin.

For a shilling the farmer agreed to carry Allegra's letter to the lawyer in Bishopsgate.

Romulus quickly put Treypenny behind him, and found himself in a better frame of mind when he came to the Gypsy camp. He spied Niall working with one of his horses in the field behind the caravans.

The field belonged to a family named Yorrick, who allowed the gypsies to camp there to spite their neighbors, the Talbots. The two families had been squabbling for decades over boundary rights, and the gypsy caravans were parked on the exact piece of property that was in contention. Until the Talbots proved their claim, there they would remain, with all the good will the Yorricks could muster. Niall had related this tale to Romulus with relish. There was nothing a Gypsy enjoyed so much as a blood feud.

When the boy saw Romulus, he broke off from schooling his horse, an arch-necked, piebald stallion. "What brings you ashore?" he called out, as he slapped at the beast's hindquarters and sent him pelting away.

"Trouble," Romulus said as he came up with the Gypsy. "Not the dangerous sort, mind, but trouble all the same." He briefly told the boy about his unwelcome guest.

Niall whistled. "Fished her out of the river, did you? Now that's not your usual catch. Pity I didn't find her."

"It's a good thing you didn't. She's a fetching chit—you'd have tumbled headlong into love with her."

Niall, who was just turned eighteen, had recently begun cutting a swath through the neighborhood's female population. With his snapping black eyes, curling ebony hair, and warm, olive skin, he was an exotic change from the tow-headed farmboys the local lasses had grown up with. And the fact that he sat his brown and white stallion like a minor deity, all haughty brow and wicked smirk, didn't hurt.

Niall remarked blithely, watching Rom with merry eyes, "Oh, and of course you wouldn't tumble." When Rom didn't comment, he scrunched his hands into his pockets and asked, "So what's to be done with her?"

"I need you to ask around. Discreetly, of course. She's clearly well-bred and I don't want to foster a scandal. Chat up the serving girls and the grooms. Someone is bound to know who she is."

Niall nodded. "It's hard to believe she can't remember anything."

"It is indeed," Rom replied with conviction. He'd mentioned nothing of his suspicions to Niall, that the girl was playing a May game with him. "And there's another problem—she needs some things to wear."

Niall's eyes widened as he said with quiet awe, "She was naked?"

Romulus snapped, "No, of course not. But her gown was ruined in the river. She's trailing my dressing gown behind her, at present.

Perhaps one of your cousins has a few cast-offs . . . I'd be willing to pay."

"Hang that!" Niall muttered. "You know we'll not take money from you. I'm sure I can find something to tide her over till you send her home. What's she like, then? Tall, short, or middling?"

Romulus sketched the air. "She barely reaches my chin. Slim as a lad . . . well, not everywhere."

The Gypsy boy's mouth twisted. "You surprise me. Now that's the first thing I'd have mentioned."

"I was just helping you to get an idea," Romulus responded quellingly.

Niall grinned. "I already have a fairly good idea. No, don't bristle at me. Are you rowing over to Hamish House this morning? If you take me across, I'll start making inquiries on that side of the river."

As Rom walked through the camp, the Gypsies greeted him casually. They mistrusted most of the villagers, but this man had befriended their leader's son and had proven himself an ally once or twice. They didn't exactly welcome him with open arms—it was more of a benign tolerance. At least on the part of the men. The younger women watched him with less benign expressions, looking up from their chores with hungry eyes. With his towering height, green-gold eyes, and deep russet hair, he was as exotic to these Gypsy women as Niall was to the farm girls. But Romulus knew better than to even risk a glance in their direction, not if he wanted to keep a long knife out of his short ribs.

Niall disappeared into his grandmother's caravan. Romulus heard the sound of voices, softly pitched and speaking in Romany, and then Niall emerged, carrying a few bright garments over one arm.

"Thank your grandmother for me." Rom nodded toward the caravan as he quickly bundled the clothing into his rucksack. "Come away now, if you want to cross over to Hamish House. I need to get back to my cygnets before noon. I've left my guest to tend them, and I want to see how she's faring."

As they left the pasture, Romulus caught his heel on a hidden root.

"Watch it," Niall cautioned as his friend righted himself. "You don't want to tumble, now, do you?"

Romulus shot him a look of irritation, but Niall merely tucked his hands again into his pockets and ambled down the lane, whistling a plaintive gypsy love song.

Diana was faring very well. Or so she thought.

That morning at breakfast she had insisted she was perfectly capable of looking after the baby birds. Romulus had given in, though his expression had been doubtful.

He was surely the most baffling man she'd met in her twenty-one years. Not only because he was a caretaker to wild swans, but because, while he was all consideration to his feathered charges, he treated her as though she was a mildly annoying gnat. Not that he was rude, just disinterested.

She drifted out onto the porch. By daylight the island was a revelation, a miniature Eden burgeoning with greenery and wildflowers. An herb garden, still shimmering with the morning dew, lay on both sides of a brick path. Beyond the garden, tall trees rose up, oak and beech and slender aspen. The river could be heard in the distance, its soft chuckling a pleasing counterpoint to the morning calls of birds. There was more than beauty here—there was peace and tranquillity. Last night she had wondered how Romulus could spend his days on a strip of land in the middle of the Thames; now she wondered that he could ever bear to leave it.

Feeding the birds proved to be a simple task if one had patience—she seemed to have a knack for it. After she had fed the cygnets, she set them down to wander over the floor. Each one headed in a different direction until every cranny contained a bundle of grey fluff. She was delighted by their antics, but when she tried to gather them up, they receded even farther into their hiding places, peeping in alarm.

She went running from the storeroom, praying that Rom had left some of their food in the kitchen, so that she could bribe them to come out of hiding. Unfortunately the open storeroom door proved too great a temptation, and when Diana returned, the cygnets had scattered throughout the house.

"That's washed it," she muttered, watching a downy gray tail disappear beneath Romulus's desk. "Now he'll never trust me with them again."

Crouching down in the center of the sitting room floor, she started peeping in what she hoped was an encouraging manner, having no idea what an adult swan sounded like or if they even made any noise at all. Two bolder cygnets approached her, but when she tried to capture them, they scurried out of range.

This was not going well at all.

"It's an embarrassment, that's what it is!" Sir Beveril Hunnycut stood foursquare in his aunt's softly lit drawing room and slapped at his booted shin with the weighted riding crop he carried.

Lady Estelle Hamish stopped pouring tea and regarded him assessingly. Somewhat past her fiftieth year, she was the very picture of a patrician matron, with a long, angular face, a high-arched nose, and a crown of elegantly arranged white hair. She leaned back on her brocaded sofa and said in a slightly chiding voice, "I'd think your concern would be for the young woman's safety, Beveril, not for your own feelings of pique."

He gave an exasperated grunt. "How can I not feel mortified? She went haring off from our betrothal ball without a word to anyone. Her sister is beside herself, as you might well imagine."

"And you say she took nothing with her?" She cocked her head. "That is most curious."

Sir Beveril nodded. "Her abigail swears not so much as a handkerchief was missing from her room. I am at a loss—the chit seemed biddable enough until that night. God only knows what got into her head. But that's what comes of forming connections to provincials. I'll . . . I'll be the laughingstock of the *ton*."

Lady Hamish looked thoughtful for a moment. "Has it occurred to any of you that she might have been abducted? She is, after all, sister by marriage to a very wealthy man. I've never met James Mortimer—you know I rarely go out in company—but I've heard he roused a great many people to anger when he shut down his mines in Cornwall. Perhaps a disgruntled miner carried her off, by way of revenge."

He waved away her suggestion. "Mortimer had to close the mines. There was no longer any profit in them. And don't tell me some poor miner came all the way from Cornwall to abduct a debutante. It doesn't fadge. No, the girl has run off and left me practically at the altar. Gad, I'll be months living this down."

She looked up at her nephew. "Was she so set against marrying you, Bev?"

The man's brow lowered. "She was prepared to do her duty— Mortimer assured me of it."

The white-haired woman shook her head. "I have always misliked these marriages of commerce, you know. That is why I swore never to marry a man of my father's choosing."

"And it's a pity," he said smoothly, reaching down to pat her hand. "For you are the best of women, Aunt Estelle. A man would be lucky to have such a wife."

"Don't talk fustian, Beveril," she said a bit sharply. She was fond of her only nephew, up to a point, but she also knew that Mammon ruled his life. "If I had married and borne a child, all *your* expectations would be in the dust. But I have been content with my life, even without a husband."

"Nevertheless," he said as he seated himself opposite her and took up a tea cup from the silver tray, "it must have been lonely for you. Never having loved anyone enough to wish for marriage."

Oh, I never said I haven't loved, she murmured to herself before returning to her nephew's problem.

"What is being done to locate Miss Exeley?"

"James wants to call in the Runners, but Helen is afraid of creating a scandal."

"Is it possible the girl has eloped?" the lady inquired.

Beveril grit his teeth. "What? You think she fancied herself crossed in love and ran off with her dancing master? No, that harum-scarum little creature had no romantic illusions. I'd swear to it."

And a good thing, Lady Hamish mused, in light of her nephew's most unloverlike behavior.

Once they'd finished their tea, Sir Beveril rose and announced he was off to Mortimer House.

She watched his departure with a pinched expression around her handsome eyes. Every bit of her younger sister's self-consequential nature had been bequeathed to her only son. And yet Lady Hamish sensed that there was some good in the man. She had hoped the young woman he'd chosen to wed might have curbed some of his more wayward tendencies. Now it appeared the girl was even more wayward than her nephew. Poor Beveril. Jilted by a provincial nobody. He, who had never been humbled once in his thirty years. Maybe the girl's disappearance would do him some good, though. Give him something to focus on besides gambling, drinking, and the all-too-available Vivian Partridge.

Beveril was walking toward the stables when he caught sight of Romulus and Niall coming up the drive.

"You there, Perrin!" He went striding over to them. "I've warned you before about bringing that Gypsy trash onto my land. It's bad enough the Yorricks allow it, but they, at least, are on the other side of the river."

"He works for me," Romulus said evenly. "And since I work for your aunt, he has a right to be here."

Beveril's florid complexion grew even redder. "Don't bandy words with me, sirrah! If you must go about with such filth dogging your heels, see that it is left at the gates of my home."

"Not yours yet," Romulus muttered darkly. "Not bloody yet."

"What was that?" Beveril glared and canted his head back.

Romulus knew that Hunnycut considered himself a fine strapping figure of a man, and he imagined it rankled Beveril no end that he had to look up to speak to his aunt's hireling.

"I was not aware," Romulus drawled, "that Lady Hamish had turned the running of her property over to you. I congratulate you." The hazel eyes that Diana found so soothing now blazed with a martial light.

Beveril nearly sputtered. "It's still hers, damn your insolence."

"Then I must wish her a long and healthy life," Romulus purred.

"As do I," Sir Beveril said, his hands clenching repeatedly at his sides. "But mark me on this, Perrin—the instant I do have the running of Hamish House, your employment will cease. I'll have you off that infernal island . . . with my foxhounds at your heels if necessary."

"But, then," Rom couldn't help observing to his departing back, "I doubt they'd survive the crossing." He grinned ruefully down at Niall. "God, I shouldn't let that pompous windbag get me so riled."

"You mean Sir Beef-eril?" The Gypsy chortled as they again moved along the drive. "Do you suppose he was born that ill-tempered, or do you think his nanny dropped him on his head?"

"Whatever the reason," Rom stated, "he's not the man I'd want running Hamish House. From what I hear, he'd soon run through every cent of his aunt's money at the gaming tables."

Niall nodded. "They say at the 'Thrush that he's deep in debt. Plans to marry Mortimer's sister-in-law for her dowry. Got to take some bumpkin into his bed and leave the delectable Vivian Partridge unconsoled."

A vague memory stirred in Romulus's brain and then lay still before he could place it.

"I wonder if that's what's put him in such a foul temper?"

"He's always like that, Rom," Niall observed. "I think he fears you more than he lets on. Lady Hamish favors you, you know. And Beveril doesn't want anyone getting too close to the honeypot."

"Then the man's a jackass," Romulus said through his teeth. "As though I stand to gain anything from her ladyship, except her good will. Beveril's a fool to even think it. Maybe he *was* dropped on his head."

They separated at the back of the house—Niall went sauntering off to the dairy to coax information from his latest flirt, while Romulus ducked through the low kitchen door. The cook greeted him with a smile.

"Mr. Perrin," she said. "Go right on in, sir. I believe Lady Hamish is in the drawing room."

Rom went up the back stairs which led to the central hall. Fine paintings hung along the paneled walls, and a Venetian mirror gleamed above a marquetry console table. He recalled the first time he stood in that hall, ten months earlier, a shivering, emaciated wreck, clad in a borrowed cloak.

Romulus had been convalescing at the Royal Hospital in Chelsea, his health broken and his nerves in tatters, when he first met Sir Robert Poole, the noted statesman and reformer. Poole had attempted to befriend him—with indifferent success. Then an acquaintance of Sir Robert's came to see Rom. The woman was not young, but handsome, stately, and obviously wealthy. She announced blithely that she had a position to offer him—caring for the swans that had bred for centuries on her estate. She had discovered that his father had been a river warden in Wiltshire, and that as a boy Rom had learned to look after water birds.

He tried to refuse, but she was quite steely for all her elegant manners. And so after endless weeks in the bleak confines of the hospital, Romulus found himself in Hamish House, the greatest of the great houses that lay along that stretch of the Thames.

For the past ten months he had reported to her of his work on the river. It was curious, he often thought, that although she never went out on the river, she was much concerned with the welfare of the swans and the other waterfowl. He'd have thought her an eccentric, but she was the least fanciful woman he'd ever met.

Their relationship gradually evolved from one of respectful servant and lady bountiful, to one of near equals. Lady Hamish saw nothing amiss in discussing the books she read or the news from

London with her river warden. Or of having tea with him in the garden on a sunny afternoon.

Romulus wasn't sure how it had happened, this friendship with the reclusive baroness. At first he kept to the island, rebuilding the abandoned lodge. During his weekly reports to her he never strayed over the boundary of servant and mistress. But one day, after he'd been on the island a month, her groundskeeper delivered a sleek skiff for him to use on his patrols. He had gone to her home to thank her and found himself lured into conversation. She had spoken with him for hours that day, inquiring about his childhood in Rome and his life in Wiltshire with his father. Happily, she never mentioned his years in the army.

He left Hamish House that afternoon perplexed beyond words. Loneliness, he reckoned, had driven her to seek the company of her nerve-rattled river warden. And so he accommodated her, visiting more frequently and bringing her gifts from the river—bird's nests and cocoons, hawk's feathers and river rocks with tiny fossils embedded in them. Small enough tokens, but she clearly valued them, as though he offered her a window on a world she chose not to visit, but longed for all the same.

In truth, Romulus still had not sorted out Lady Hamish's curious patronage. But it pleased him to offer a diversion to the gracious lady who treated him with such kindness. And it was, furthermore, most gratifying to be a burr under the saddle to her officious nephew, who had been at odds with Rom from the instant he had come to live on the island. Rom reckoned it just another of his failures with the human race and thanked Providence that he possessed a better rapport with wildlife.

"Romulus," Lady Hamish said with unfeigned pleasure as he came through the wide, arched entryway of the drawing room. "You've only just missed Beveril."

"Indeed, he met me in the drive, ma'am." His tone gave nothing away.

"I'm so pleased he took the time to speak with you. He could learn a great deal from you, Romulus, about many things." She shook her head slowly. "But he shows little enthusiasm, I'm afraid."

"Your nephew has too much consequence to care for the doings of servant, ma'am."

"Nonsense," she said briskly. "You are no servant, as I've told Beveril a dozen times. You are here only until you are well enough to return to the army or some other career. So tell me, how are you faring?"

"Fitter every day," he said as he seated himself in a wing chair. "The swans, however, are not faring so well. There's a poacher on the river." She leaned forward intently, as he continued, "Three adults were snared last week and their nests were abandoned. I'm looking after the cygnets, but I doubt all of them will survive."

"They might not have anyway," she pointed out. "Nature does take a toll, after all. I am sure you are doing all you can. Anyone will tell you, Romulus, the swans have never had a better caretaker."

He raised his eyes to her. "You know I begrudge the loss of even one bird to poachers. If the foxes take them, or the snapping turtles and the otters feed on the hatchlings, that I can tolerate. But not the poaching of one bird to serve at a rich man's table."

"My father served swan once," Lady Hamish mused in a distant voice. "Our bailiff at the time vowed he would leave our service if such a thing ever recurred. Papa was most distressed—he was, we all were, very attached to the man. The swan had been killed by accident, you see, caught in a fishing weir. But I think Papa regretted that meal for the rest of his life. We Hamishes take our swans very seriously."

Romulus grinned slightly. He had apparently caught the Hamish affliction. "I recall that Queen Elizabeth was also a great lover of swans," he said. "Had her flock branded by the Royal Swankeeper. At least that's one thing I needn't worry about. As much time as I spend around them, the adults are still quite testy—especially during nesting season. I wouldn't fancy wrestling one."

"No," Lady Hamish said, chuckling softly. "We haven't carried our obsession to that extreme. But tell me, how does your new houseguest go on?"

Romulus gaped at her in confusion. Allegra had been in his keeping for less than three days, and he was positive no one, save Niall, knew of her presence on the island.

She noted his bewildered expression and added, "The heron you rescued? Is he still refusing to eat?"

"Oh, the heron." Romulus breathed a sigh of relief. "Yes, he's eating and his leg is finally mending."

"Excellent," she said. "Now, I see it's nearly noon. Would you care to join me for lunch?"

Romulus refused her offer with as much graciousness as he

could muster. His other houseguest, the troublesome Miss Swan, had been left alone for far too long. He feared she would be growing bored with nothing to occupy her, save the feeding of the cygnets.

"Thank you," he said, rising. "But I need to see to my chicks." *All my chicks*, he amended silently.

Romulus berthed his skiff at the narrow stone slip that lay on the eastern side of the island, and then walked along the path to his lodge, brushing back the encroaching foliage with one hand.

The lodge sat in a grassy clearing, raised up four feet from the ground on an open stonework base. Romulus had put his soul into refurbishing the tumbledown house, re-bricking the damaged exterior, and reglazing the broken windows. He had painted the woodwork a deep, rich ochre and had planted an herb garden in the front yard, using leftover bricks to make a curving path to the front porch. The house now looked welcoming and snug. It also looked particularly unoccupied. The back door yawned open and he could see no one moving about inside. It was a warmish day, but he doubted his houseguest had had to resort to opening the doors, when the windows would have sufficed nicely.

"Allegra!" he called as he ran up the front steps to the small covered porch. He went into the hallway, and ducked briefly into the sitting room and the storeroom. The two stacked crates were empty.

"Drat the girl," he muttered as he made his way to the kitchen. He marched out through the open door and down the steps to the yard. "*Allegra!*" he shouted in a voice that would have done a sergeant-major proud. When there was no response, he continued across the gravelled yard, past the woodshed and the privy.

At the northern end of the island there was a shallow pond of perhaps thirty feet in length. It was overhung with willows and oaks, and was boggy at one end, where irises grew in profusion. As Rom came out into the open field where the pond lay, he saw Allegra kneeling beside the water on a large, flat rock.

"*What the devil are you doing with my cygnets!*" he thundered.

Diana nearly tumbled off the rock. She had been watching in amazement as the sixteen fluffballs paddled merrily back and forth across the water, and so had not seen Romulus bearing down on her.

"*I* wasn't the one who forgot to latch the kitchen," she called back heatedly, as she scrambled to her feet. Wasn't it just like the man to place the blame on her. "I only let them out of their cages. And I suppose I did leave the storeroom door open. But I didn't bring them out here. I swear it."

Romulus used the time it took him to reach her to settle his temper. He'd had every intention of taking the cygnets to the pond himself, but at least he had a crumb of an idea of what he was about.

"Then how did they get out here?" he asked meaningfully, once he reached her.

She bit her lip as she gazed up at him. Lord, she wished he wasn't so tall. "You mustn't have shut the back door when you left this morning. A few of them had gotten into the kitchen, and before I could stop them, four of them went out the door. When I ran after them, all the others came trailing along behind me."

The stormy expression on his face hadn't softened one whit, but Diana thought she could see the beginnings of a smile in the depths of his eyes.

"I didn't know whether to rescue some of them," she continued, "and risk the others finding their way to the river. Or to just keep following after them, until they ran out of energy."

"I gather they led you here?"

"It was the most amazing thing." Her eyes widened. "They marched right up to the water and jumped in, one after the other, as though they'd been doing it their whole lives."

She stopped to draw a breath. Rom no longer looked as though he meant to throttle her. Not that the thought of being under those lean hands didn't have a sort of charm. "I assumed one had to teach them to swim." She nodded to where the baby swans were cavorting effortlessly in the water. "But they don't appear to need lessons at all."

Romulus chuckled. "Haven't you ever heard the expression, 'like a duck to water'? It's no different with swans."

He lowered himself onto the flat rock and stretched his legs out before him, crossing them at the ankles. Tipping his face up to her, he said more gently, "I'm sorry I railed at you, Allegra. It took the wind out of me when I saw they were gone from the house. I wanted to be here when they had their first swim. This is my first crop of cygnets in a very long time. Seeing them go into the water is . . . well, it's a treat."

"You are a very strange man, Romulus Perrin," she muttered, settling down beside him.

"I expect the people of Treypenny would wholeheartedly agree with you."

"Why? Do they know how you wax rhapsodic over swans?"

"I daresay it wouldn't surprise them," he replied with a frown. "Nothing I do surprises them. You see, they think I am mad."

Diana drew back. "Mad? As in addled?"

He nodded. "I was rather . . . um, battle scarred, when I first came here. And I wanted nothing to do with the people in the village. You may have gathered, I have little patience for fools."

"I suppose you think me a fool," she said softly, plucking at the fringed belt of the dressing gown. "I don't blame you. It was wrong to take the cygnets out of their cages without asking you first."

He mumbled his agreement, but then settled back on his elbows to watch his brood paddling about in the calm water. Several of them had climbed onto the grassy bank of the pond to preen their downy feathers, but they were keeping well away from the humans on the rock.

Diana had a sudden thought. "But how will you catch them now? I doubt they will let either of us get near them. Or is it time to return them to the river?"

Romulus shook his head. "No, they'll be with us a while longer."

Diana smiled to herself. She liked very much that he had said "us."

"And as for catching them," he continued, "you've just got to know how a swan thinks."

At that moment, Diana would have rather known what a swankeeper thought, especially about her.

He was sitting only a hand's span away from her, and his right elbow, in its green buckskin sleeve, was angled near her hip. She was tempted to rest her head on his broad shoulder as they reclined there in the bright sun, but feared he would toss her into the pond for such a familiarity. So she contented herself with watching him, shifting back a little so he would not know he was being observed.

The sun played over his russet hair, picking out the gleaming bronze strands that lay among the darker auburn waves. She saw the fine texture of the tanned skin on his face and his hands. And at the V of his throat, where his shirt gaped open slightly. She admired the firm muscles in his outstretched legs and the sheer breadth of his shoulders.

The *ton* had never seen his like, she mused. Dressed in an elegant suit of clothes, clad in topboots and a caped greatcoat, he would be nothing less than breathtaking. Ladies would throw themselves under his carriage wheels to gain his notice. Gentlemen in droves would go into fatal declines, envious of his impressive stature and admirable physique.

But he was not a gentleman, in spite of his cultured voice and refined manners. Gentlemen did not toil for their bread, at least not overtly. No, Romulus Perrin was an aberration—a common man who possessed a rich spirit and a masculine beauty that were anything but common.

"Were you a soldier before you came here?" Diana asked, needing to distract herself from the powerful lure of the lean body stretched out beside hers. "You mentioned the war last night, and you just now said that you were battle scarred."

As he turned to answer her, his elbow brushed against the side of her breast. At that moment, Diana thought she might just slither off the rock and into the pond. Anything to douse the fire that had leapt through her at his fleeting touch.

Oblivious to her distress, he replied gruffly, "It was some time ago. I don't like to speak of it."

"Then you are not like other military men," she pronounced. "I've met dozens of them in London, and all they ever do is rattle on endlessly about this skirmish or that battle."

"I see your selective memory is returning," he observed with a wry glance.

"I . . . that is . . ." Diana knew she was in for it now. Unless she used her mistake to her advantage. "Yes!" she said gleefully, "my memory is returning . . . a little. I can clearly recall conversing with a member of the King's Rifles in Hyde Park. Isn't that remarkable?"

"I rejoice," Romulus drawled, as he furled his long legs and climbed to his feet. "Now, I believe our charges have had enough swimming for one afternoon."

He went striding off, and Diana didn't know whether she was to bide or follow. She decided to stay beside the pond and keep an eye on the cygnets. A minute later Romulus reappeared, carrying what appeared to be a butterfly net set on a long handle. He deftly scooped two of the baby birds from the surface of the water, placed one in each pocket of his coat, and then turned back toward the house.

"Now watch," he called to her over his shoulder, just before he disappeared from sight.

The remaining cygnets paddled around for several seconds, and then, as if by an unspoken command, one by one they flipped out of the pond and went scuttling off along the path toward the house, marching in a straight line like camels in a caravan. Diana had never been more astonished in her life.

"How did you know they would do that?" she asked Romulus breathlessly, as she came into the storeroom in the wake of the last cygnet.

After he had lifted the bird into the lower cage to join its brethren, he drew Diana over to the stacked crates. "That one"— he pointed to one of the cygnets in the upper crate—"and that one"—he indicated one in the lower—"They are the largest, the leaders. Baby swans instinctively follow that leader. Whether it's the female or the cob or just an oversized sibling."

Diana peered into the shadowed cages. For the life of her, she couldn't detect the slightest bit of difference in any of them. "Those were the two you captured first?"

He nodded solemnly, and then gave her a crooked grin.

"Well, you needn't be so smug about it," she complained. "But I will admit, there's a deal more to swankeeping than I would have thought." An idea began to formulate in her head. "Romulus. . . ?"

"Hmm?" He had turned away to latch the two cages.

"Would you consider taking me out on the river with you tonight? To see the swans."

"Absolutely not!" He spun to face her, and she saw the humor had disappeared from his eyes, as though a shade had been drawn down. "It's totally out of the question."

"Then you're still angry with me for letting the cygnets out?"

"No, of course not. I'm sorry if you're bored in this house with nothing to entertain you, but I can't allow you on the river. Besides, you are barely recovered from your fever."

"Indeed, I am recovered," she insisted. "And I'm not bored in the house. Not at all. But it would please me enormously to go out on the river. Just once. I promise I won't be any trouble."

He scowled. "It's a foolhardy notion. I can't imagine why it would interest you."

"I want to see what you do, Romulus. This is all so new to me."

She detected a slight softening of his stony expression. "Please, just show me a few of the nesting sights."

"Let me think on it," he said as he moved into the sitting room. Diana followed close on his heels, rather like a cygnet herself. She'd follow him anywhere, she knew. If only he'd let her.

"Here," he said, passing her his rucksack. "I've a young friend among the Gypsies. He was able to find you some clothes . . . I can't take you on the river in my dressing gown—you'd scare off all the wildlife."

Diana disregarded this last remark as she dug into the sack and proceeded to pull out two muslin blouses, one yellow and one pale blue, and an embroidered skirt whose ground color was the deep violet of pansy petals. There was also a flounced petticoat and a patterned kerchief.

She looked up at him in wonder. "I am overwhelmed. And I'm sure I can pay your friend, once I get my own life back. From the looks of that ball gown, I must not have been a pauper."

"The Gypsies won't take my money, Allegra. I doubt they would take yours."

Her brows knit. "I thought Gypsis liked money. At least that is the common conception."

"Aye, and not a false one. But even more than silver, they like a good trade. I traded them something a while back, and they think they still owe me for it."

"What did you trade?"

"Enough questions," he said sharply. "You rattle on fit to break a man's earbones. Come and have your lunch. Then, if you take a proper nap, I might consider bringing you out in my boat tonight."

Diana could barely stand to close her eyes. She stretched deliciously on the bed, her arms crossed behind her head.

Romulus was taking her on the river!

She, who had scoffed at trips to Vauxhall Gardens and outings to the Tower Menagerie, who had belittled Astley's Amphitheater and been unimpressed by the assemblies at Almack's, now shivered with anticipation at the prospect of sitting in a rowboat with a man.

Ah, but what a man. Surly, sarcastic, short-tempered and altogether divine.

She grinned at the cygnets. "You are very lucky," she observed, "he is a wonderful swankeeper."

She ticked off all his fine qualities on her fingers. "He is wise, gentle, very patient—at least with you, if not with me. He is skilled in doctoring and knowledgeable about so many things. He is even friendly with the gypsies, which I find remarkable."

There was an abrupt, single knock at the door. "Stop talking to my birds," Romulus growled through the wooden partition. "They need their sleep as much as you do."

"And," Diana whispered to her fuzzy companions with a wry grin, "he is the soul of consideration, don't you think? I doubt I will ever meet his like again, no matter where I travel."

Somehow that last observation deflated Diana's high spirits. She knew in truth that there were few men like Romulus Perrin in the world. She counted herself lucky just to have met him. But she knew when the time cam to leave him, she might not think herself so blessed. He had already crept far past her guard. No, that wasn't precise—she'd never had her guard up with him at all. She hadn't needed to. She had trusted him implicitly from the moment he had lifted the cup of broth to her mouth.

Unlike the men she had met in the *ton*, he never made her feel self-conscious or tongue-tied. Quite the opposite, in fact. She had been in his company wearing no more than her chemise and his dressing gown, without ever blushing for her lost modesty. And she had chattered away to him without reservation. Perhaps a bit too freely, she thought, recalling her numerous slips. It was dashed difficult keeping her past from him, when she longed to tell him everything about her life. How unhappy she had been since coming to London. How much she missed her father and the bleak, beautiful moors of the East Riding. Things that she dared not share with him, without admitting full knowledge of who she was and where she belonged.

But at least he was no longer pressing her for her name, as though he were willing to be part of her arrant charade. Yesterday he couldn't wait to be rid of her, but today . . . today he was going to take her out on the river. She was going to see the Thames through his eyes.

She gave a huge yawn and rolled onto her side, wondering as she drifted off to sleep whether the keeper of the swans might be in the market for an apprentice.

Chapter 4

Off to the west, the setting sun was sending streamers of fiery red through the gunmetal clouds that edged the horizon. High above the river the sky had darkened to a rich gray-blue, like the wing of a rock dove, iridescent with new stars.

Rom handed Diana into his boat. As she stepped over the side he gazed in fascination at the bare feet revealed by the raised hem of her Gypsy skirts. He'd forgotten to get shoes for her, he realized. Her ten perfect toes teased him from beneath her petticoat as she settled onto the stern seat.

He pushed off from the slip with one oar, then settled in the center seat and began to row. He couldn't take his eyes off Allegra, who was lounging back, her elbows braced against the stern. She had drawn her hair off her face with a brightly colored kerchief, and the dark curls tumbled over her shoulders in charming disarray. Her skin glowed like alabaster in the waning light, especially where the wide-necked gypsy blouse displayed a tantalizing glimpse of high, firm breasts. The sight of her bosom, with its delicate muslin covering, was almost more than mortal man could withstand.

"*Birds!*" Romulus muttered to himself. "Keep your mind on the birds!"

He kept the boat close beside the edge of the island, out of the currents that ran amidstream. Low-hanging branches dangled just above their heads as the boat coasted along. It wasn't until they were past the island, and in the center of the Thames, that Diana saw how at home he was on the river. With easy sweeping strokes, he sent the skiff toward the western shore, plying the oars so smoothly that the boat cut through the water with barely a sound. He made it appear so effortless, as though the strong current was no more than a ripple on a pond.

She was impressed by his skill and his strength, more so when she recalled her own clumsy efforts with her brother-in-law's rowboat. She had deemed herself such a capable little boater, as she clunked against the breakwater, or slewed her craft around in a circle.

"So quiet, little witch? Thinking of spells to cast on my birds, so they will not fly away from us?"

Diana gave him a reassuring smile. "Just some spells to keep the poachers away. But I am feeling a trifle jealous. You handle the boat so well."

"This is my life, Allegra. Rivers and boats. I've been tending to waterbirds since I was a boy."

"Even in Italy?"

As he nodded, a thick lock of hair fell forward over his brow. Diana resisted the urge to lean forward and sweep it back from his face.

"My father worked for an Italian nobleman," he explained. "The Conte d'Ancona. He kept swans at his villa and many ornamental ducks. And peacocks. Thank God we didn't have to look after *them*."

"Why? I think peacocks are quite elegant."

"Elegant and prissy and ornery as a tinker's hound. And they make the most Godawful noise, especially late at night, when a boy needs his sleep."

Diana laughed as he raised one hand to the darkening sky and pointed. "Look—"

Two large white birds were flying overhead, one slightly ahead of the other, their wingbeats creating a haunting whir as they swept through the air.

"Wild swans," he breathed as he raised the oars and let the boat drift. "A cob and a pen, I suspect. And recently paired, by the look of things, as they have no cygnets to tend."

"Newlyweds," Diana said wistfully, as she watched the birds disappear around the bend in the river. She lowered her eyes to Romulus. "When do they usually pair off?"

"They normally do their courting in February," he said in a voice he hoped was matter-of-fact. He wasn't sure how prudent it was to discuss mating rituals with Allegra, considering how frequently his thoughts of her wandered in that highly provocative direction. "It's a delicate dance they perform out on the water," he continued. "The cob postures for his chosen pen, and she acts demure and shy, but then in a week or so she lets him come closer.

Sometimes while they are courting, they swim toward each other and touch the tips of their bills—so that the arch of their necks forms a perfect heart."

Diana smiled at the image. Swans were frequent harbingers of romance in mythology—Aphrodite, the Greek goddess of love, had a swan as her insignia. And then there was the tale of Zeus, who, disguised as a male swan, had taken the unwitting Leda as his consort. Diana had blushed when she'd read that story as a girl, wondering at the strangeness of such a conquest. She blushed now, in the shadow of the river trees, as she thought of being taken by a princely man disguised as a swankeeper.

"I expect that's why swans have been the emblem of lovers since the time of Homer," she remarked, trying to distract herself from her wayward thoughts.

"There's another reason," he said. "You see, swans mate for life." He then added dryly, "Though they do dance around each other every year at mating time, even when they are already an established pair."

"That's very reassuring. And wise of them not to let their affection for each other grow stale."

Romulus smiled as he again set the oars in the water.

Diana was surprised to discover that the river at dusk was teeming with life. Overhead the swallows and bats skimmed and darted, feeding on the insects that hovered above the water. Every so often a trout or bream would rise up to feast on those same insects. She could hear the clean splash of their sleek bodies breaking the surface as they returned to the water. Once, as she and Romulus neared a bend in the river, something large shifted back from the bank, and then went leaping away. A deer, she thought, having a drink in the shadowed safety of the oncoming night.

As if he understood her enchantment with this unfamiliar world, Romulus said very little. He kept the boat parallel to the shore, letting the current do most of the work. From the island, the river seemed mysterious, dark, and remote. But being on the Thames with him had given Diana a view into its secret heart; she'd seen the flow of life as well as the flow of water.

She knew that he watched her intently at times and tried not to let that fact fire her imagination. He was merely her teacher, one who was pleased that his lone student was so taken with her first lesson.

She pointed to something small and dark in the water, swimming near the shore.

"Coot," he said. "The white bill makes it easy to spot. Watch that mallard that's coming toward him."

"Oh!" she cried out as the coot darted across the water and snapped viciously at the mallard drake.

"Very territorial," Romulus said. "And very protective of his family. See the babies near the tussock of grass." He levered the boat so that it drew up closer to the shore. Sure enough, seven baby coots were bobbing along behind another adult.

"But they're so tiny," she said. "I wonder they can even walk yet, let alone swim."

Romulus grinned at her. "For waterfowl, swimming and flying are the important things. Ah, look, over on your right." Again he shifted the boat so that they approached an odd-looking bird with a pointy beak.

"Horned grebe," he said.

Suddenly the bird submerged, disappearing right under Diana's startled eyes. "Whatever is he doing?"

Romulus held up his hand. "Wait . . ."

Nearly a minute had passed before the bird reemerged with a long river eel wriggling in its mouth.

"Rather talented divers, the grebes. Not as daring as cormorants, however—"

Diana stopped him in midsentence with a laugh. "Enough, enough. I can't take in so much at once."

"I thought you were one of those bluestockings who lived for your studies?"

She chuckled. "Well, even if I were, I doubt I ever studied birds."

"A sad lack in a lady." His eyes narrowed in mellow humor, and his wide, mobile mouth was slanted into a crooked grin. "And one we can easily remedy. After supper I will show you my collection of bird books. I assume from your choice of Mr. Pope last night, that you are an eclectic reader."

Diana was about to reply that her father had acquainted her with every book in his well-stocked library, but she caught herself in time. That would have been a most difficult lapse to cover up.

She merely shrugged and said lightly, "Who can say what my taste in books is?"

"Who indeed?" His voice oozed sarcasm.

Diana poked him playfully on the shin with her bare foot, but her tart response to his drawling words died in her throat when she caught sight of his eyes. He was looking at her as a starving child gazes at a rich man's table. With longing and hunger and boundless hope. She sat there in breathless anticipation, less than three feet from him, wishing they were anywhere but in the restrictive confines of a rowboat.

He leaned forward, leaving the oars to drift upon the water, and lifted her foot from the planking, wrapping both hands around her ankle. He never took his eyes from her face as he stroked one finger along her instep. His flesh was warm against her skin, but she felt a shiver ripple up her spine.

"I'll have to see about getting you some shoes," he said.

"I like going barefoot," she whispered hoarsely, wondering what had happened to her voice.

Any reply he might have made was cut short as the boat bumped against a submerged log. Romulus let her foot slide from his hands and reapplied himself to the oars.

Diana felt the intimacy of the moment quickly dissolve. She longed to reach out and touch his face, to thank him for sharing this night with her. For sharing his special place.

"Thank you," she started to say, but realized he was no longer heeding her.

He raised a finger to his lips, motioning her to silence as he angled the boat toward the tall water weeds that grew along the shore.

They had for some time been traveling on an uninhabited stretch of the river. Before them spread a shadowed wilderness of swamp grass, reeds, cattails, and mallow. Five yards inland the trees began, oak, ash, and maple, growing among stands of cedar. The flat light of dusk lent the scene a hazy, unreal quality.

Romulus leaped from the boat and tugged the bow up onto a ledge of moss. He leaned over the side. "Stay here," he whispered, his mouth soft against her ear. "There's someone moving up ahead in the grass."

Diana shivered again from that brief contact, wishing that duty had not called him away at that moment. She sat where she was for several minutes, listening intently for any sound of movement. A night bird called in the trees overhead and another answered from farther upstream.

She wondered if poachers ever carried guns and worried that

Romulus might be in danger. Perhaps he had a pistol tucked in his rucksack or in his coat pocket. Was it legal for a river warden to shoot a poacher? She found it hard to reconcile the man who handled the cygnets with such fond tolerance with someone who could kill a poacher, even for menacing the adult swans.

When she could stand the waiting no longer, she climbed from the boat. After securing the boat rope to a sapling, she went forward into the high grass, which in many places reached above her head. It was nearly dark now, and she feared to lose her bearings in that dry, rattling maze. As she struggled onward, the sharp fronds of the reeds sliced against her bare forearms. There were occasional places that squished beneath her bare feet, which she prayed were patches of mud and not slugs or submerged bullfrogs.

Diana searched for several minutes without catching sight of Romulus. She was thinking of returning to the boat, when she saw a light moving through the high grass some distance beyond her. It flickered sporadically in her vision like a wandering firefly. As she moved toward it, someone grabbed her around the waist and tumbled her sideways. A hand slid over her mouth before she could cry out.

"I should have known you wouldn't stay put," Romulus growled into her ear. "Now lie still." She nodded against his hand. "And don't make a sound." Again she nodded. He drew back his hand.

"What is it?" She hissed the question at him.

He rolled his eyes in exasperation—even in the darkness she could see it. "The poacher. He's up ahead. Checking his snares, no doubt. Now stay here. I need to get closer."

He slid away from her, moving noiselessly through the reeds. Undeterred by the threat of the poacher, Diana followed after him, mainly because she didn't like lying there on the swampy grass at the mercy of every mosquito and gnat on the river.

The wavering light had moved even closer now. A wiry man clad in dark clothing came hurrying into the small clearing in front of her. He carried a shuttered lantern which cast a wobbling light as he scuttled toward the trees. A large white creature dangled from his other hand.

"*Oh-h-h!*" Diana's voice echoed out over the clearing as her hands flew to her mouth. The partially lit figure stopped for an instant at the sound of her ragged cry, and then raced for the cover of the trees. Romulus sprang up from the grass directly in front of her and took off after him.

Diana ran, too, thrusting the tall reeds away as she hurried into the clearing. Romulus and his quarry were gone, but the lantern lay on its side where the man had tossed it, casting a skewed light. He had also discarded the swan. It was staggering pitifully in the beam of the lantern, flapping its enormous wings in panic as it lurched from side to side. Diana saw that one of its legs was horribly mangled, as though the man had hacked at the limb to free it from the wire snare.

She quickly knelt beside the bird, her hands fluttering above it in confusion. She didn't want to touch it, didn't want to increase its already palpable fear. It raised its head to her, neck snaking forward, and hissed, opening its vermillion beak halfway.

"You're safe now," she crooned. "He'll take you back to the island. I promise you'll get well again."

She was crying now, the hot tears streaming down her cheeks. A shadow loomed over her and she started back in alarm. It was Romulus.

"Go back to the boat," he ordered in a ragged, breathless voice. "Now."

"But I can help you," she said as she scrambled to her feet. "Let me help."

Romulus was gazing down at the swan, his eyes hooded. "*Now*," he repeated without looking up.

She turned and started back toward the boat. When she reached the first clump of tall grass she spun around. "Please let me—"

Romulus was kneeling over the white bird, and there was a knife in his right hand.

"*No!*" Diana cried as she flew back to him. "No, please, Rom! I promised . . . *I promised*."

He looked up at her, his face as white as the glistening feathers of the swan. "Do you want to see this?" he snarled.

"No," she whimpered. "But there must be something you can do. As you did with the heron. A splint, a bandage. I promised you would make him well."

He shook his head, his eyes two wells of darkness in his pale face. "I am doing the only thing I can do. And the longer you stand here arguing with me, the longer this poor beast has to suffer."

She turned and fled. Went crashing through the grass, heedless of the sharp blades slicing at her arms. The only blade she could see was the one in Rom's hand, as it drew the life's blood of the great white bird.

After struggling along through the dark reeds, she eventually found the boat, floating a little offshore. She tugged it closer by the bow line and slid over the low gunwale. Crouched in the bottom of the boat, she let her tears overtake her, sobbing out her pain against one raised knee.

"*I-I promised . . .*" she stuttered out into the night. Because Romulus could do anything. Because he could solve anything. He was a healer and a rescuer. But tonight he had become a killer.

Her tears had subsided by the time he returned to the boat. She couldn't see his face, but as he climbed onto his seat she could feel the tension rising from his body. She wanted to apologize for alerting the poacher, but knew this was not the proper time. Before he pushed off, he reached his hands over the side and into the water.

Blood, she realized. *He's washing off the swan's blood.* She was nearly sick at the thought.

He rowed them back to the island in grim silence, his powerful shoulders clenching and unclenching as he sent the boat against the current.

"Go to the house," he ordered as he drew up beside the slip. "I need to check the other side of the—"

Diana didn't wait to hear the rest of his words as she turned with a low sob and ran off into the darkness. She couldn't go to the house, couldn't bear to face the sixteen orphans. Would the death of the swan tonight mean that there would be more orphans in the morning?

Without a conscious destination in mind, she paced rapidly along the path until she came to the pond. In the moonlight, the flat granite rock looked like obsidian, cool and hard. She stretched out upon it, letting the night air soothe her troubled spirits.

How ironic—that she'd thought Romulus daft for caring so much about the swans. But he wasn't daft. And now she cared as much as he did. It had wrenched her heart to see that majestic animal injured and in distress. And she understood why Romulus had had to end that distress—there were some things even a tall river god couldn't put right. But that realization pained her as much as the death of the swan.

Romulus Perrin couldn't save the swan from the poacher, and he wouldn't save her from Sir Beveril Hunnycut. That knowledge tore at her insides. Because in her heart that was what she was hoping he would do. That he would offer her a chance to stay with him, to work with him and learn from him. About the river, and the birds. About life and the harmony of an existence without trappings. And about love.

She rolled over and away from the beguiling moonlight. Was that what she truly wanted? To learn about love from a man who was a recluse and an oddity? A river warden who was mistrusted by the villagers, who was friends with the Gypsies? She breathed a prayer of apology to Helen as she said aloud, "Yes. Oh, yes."

For the second time that night, Rom's shadow loomed over her, but this time she did not start back in fear. She merely sat up, gazing at him with wide, worried eyes. He knelt down beside her, raising one of her hands from the surface of the rock. She could have sworn his fingers were trembling.

"You didn't need to run from me, Allegra," he said in a gruff whisper. "I am not angry with you." He shook his head when she started to protest. "The poacher would have gotten away regardless—he had a horse tethered to a tree. I want you to understand that."

"I cried out," she said bitterly. "I gave away our position."

"It doesn't matter. I know who he is now. I got a good look at him before he tossed away the lantern. All it needs is for me to accost him in the village and put the fear of God into him."

"You're not going to turn him over to a magistrate?"

He shook his head. "This matter is between the poacher and myself."

She said earnestly, "But he needs to pay."

"I'm not interested in vengeance, little witch. I just want him to stop killing my birds."

She shook off his hand. "Then you have a heart of stone. I would like to see him festering in a jail cell for years and years."

Romulus drew back from her as though she had struck him. "Don't wish that on any man, Allegra."

"But didn't you see what he did to the swan?" she cried. "He practically butchered it."

"No, I butchered it," he said softly. "The poacher merely crippled it."

Diana groped in the darkness to take back his hand, holding it between her palms. "I'm sorry. I didn't mean to lash out at you. But I've never watched anything die. Especially not something I cared about."

"How can you care?" he asked. "Yesterday you didn't know a baby swan from a hen's chick."

"But now I do know the difference," she murmured. "And now I must care."

"You are a very unusual girl, Allegra," he said with a sigh. "And I'm sorry you had to be there tonight. Sorry that it ruined everything . . ."

"No," she said sharply. "I'll never forget how it felt to be on the river with you." Her eyes were raised to his. "Never," she whispered.

Romulus held her gaze for a moment, afraid of what he read there and even more afraid of how much he wanted to respond to the yearning expression in her eyes. He rose to his feet abruptly and pulled her up after him. Her body swayed dangerously close to his.

"Go back to the house now," he said, shifting away from her. "I really do need to go out on the river. There are some nesting sites on the other bank I want to check."

"Will there be more orphans, do you think?"

"I hope not. I believe that was a cob he trapped tonight. With any luck it was one that had already lost its mate. Will you feed the cygnets for me while I'm gone?"

"Of course. And I'll make sure they all stay where they belong." She gave him a tight smile, and then turned for the path to the house.

"And where do you belong, my witch?" he murmured as she was lost in the tangled shadows of the trees. "Where in blazes do you belong?"

Romulus found the rowboat on the eastern bank of the Thames. The current had lodged it beneath the trunk of a dead oak, which lay canted out beyond the shore. He'd lit his lantern then, to see if he could identify the boat. Many of the estates along the Thames marked their rowboats and pleasure barges with their livery colors. This one was no exception. It bore a Greek key design painted in scarlet and gold along its outer gunwale. "Mortimer House," he muttered. James Mortimer's barge bore the same design on its sides.

And if he was still doubtful that this was the craft in which Allegra had come down river, the sight of a tattered, white satin rosebud caught in one of the oarlocks convinced him.

So she had come from Mortimer House. It needed only that he
row upstream and tell them of her whereabouts. Perhaps she had
been a guest at the house, maybe even a friend of Beveril's intended. Then something stirred in his brain, and he recalled her
comment of the night before, *As long as it's not Allegra Partridge*.
She'd said the name with distaste. And Partridge made one think
immediately of Vivian Partridge.

Even to those on the river who kept to themselves, as Romulus
did, it was well-known that Lady Hamish's nephew had been carrying on a less-than-discreet affair with the beautiful widow.
Romulus had seen her numerous times, riding with Sir Beveril
near Hamish House. Several times she had even stopped to speak
with Romulus, inquiring after his work, while Beveril sat his horse
beside her, bristling noticeably. Romulus had to admit she was an
exquisite creature. Not that he cared overmuch for Junoesque
blondes.

He made a tentative hypothesis. If Sir Beveril's provincial fiancée had somehow found out about Lady Vivian, it was possible
she might have fled from him in dismay. But the girl must be wits-
to-let to have taken a rowboat out on such a night. Maybe she really was a suicide, he thought with a mirthless grin. After all, it
was either kill herself or marry the pompous windbag. Not a pleasant choice, to be sure.

He vaulted over the side of his boat and into the thigh-deep
water. It took only a moment to free the rowboat from beneath the
oak tree. A tattered rope still hung loose from the bow and Romulus began to fasten it to the stern cleat of his skiff. It would be a
simple task to return the boat to its rightful owner, who would then
relieve him of his tempting, unwanted houseguest.

Simple.

With a sudden oath Romulus dropped the bow line. Placing one
broad shoulder against its stern, he heaved the boat up onto the
shore, flattening a clump of sawgrass. He then staggered onto the
bank and knotted the rope around one fist. He dragged the boat
into the tangle of bushes and tall reeds that edged the river and
then flipped it over, so its ash belly lay raised to the night sky. In
the lantern light its keel looked quite sound—it had made it
through the maelstrom without a scratch.

With his knife he rapidly hacked loose several lengths of leafy
vine and draped them over the hull, obscuring it totally. Not a soul
would suspect that a boat lay beneath all that greenery.

Yes, he mused wretchedly as he climbed into his skiff and pushed off from the shore, it should have been quite simple to return both rowboat and runaway to Mortimer House. But he knew that things were now no longer simple. Not since he had seen Allegra on her knees, weeping over the injured swan.

A world of complex feelings had surfaced in him at that sight. Anguish, helplessness, and the fierce desire to take her in his arms and comfort her. Her wide, tear-filled eyes had pleaded with him to make things right. And his heart had ached, knowing that he lacked the skill to mend the crippled swan. He had failed her, his water witch. As he had failed the others, the men whose dying cries still echoed in his dreams.

Romulus knew in his soul that he couldn't blithely row Allegra up the river and return her to Mortimer House. Whether she was, in truth, Beveril's fiancée, or merely one of the houseguests, she clearly feared returning to that place. Her unconvincing loss of memory was proof of that. He'd go on pretending he believed in her preposterous charade—he had committed to that lie when he camouflaged her boat.

He needed to give her more time. To let her trust in him grow, until she was secure enough to tell him the truth. Only then could he bear to let her go from his life. When Allegra was ready to leave his island, he would stand away. Until then, he would guard her and protect her with every fiber of his being. He vowed he would not fail her in that.

He rowed back to the island slowly, and with each stroke of the oars, his mind rebelled at the knowledge that she would only be temporarily in his keeping. Because he knew that even if she didn't ask to be returned home any time soon, there were others who would be searching for her. If she was Beveril's intended, he would likely have called in the Bow Street Runners. Rom feared it was only a matter of time before someone came to fetch her. He now regretted revealing her presence on the island to Niall, although the lad was the soul of discretion. One wrong word on the Gypsy's part, and Romulus would have half the gentry in the county beating at his door. And they would not take kindly to the thought of a gently-bred young lady being held in the home of a reclusive madman.

But Romulus was too used to going his own way to let that fear deter him. And he would keep his other thoughts at bay, the ones that whispered to him in the stark, lonely hours of the night. He would deny himself the vision of Allegra melting in his arms, of her sweet, rosy mouth raised up for his kisses.

She had shown him her heart, as she crouched there above the crippled swan. Compassion for the injured animal had shone in her eyes, and had touched a resounding chord deep inside him. She was no cold-hearted society belle, but a young woman capable of great feeling. That realization had shaken his world.

Here was a woman who cared about the same things he did— the river and the waterbirds, the wind in the trees and the moon on the water. He had been with her only three days and yet he had discovered in that short time that they were cut from the same cloth.

He'd always thought of himself a prudent man, not prone to flights of fancy or caprice. He knew his place in the scheme of things and had long ago grown used to his estate. But something about his black-haired foundling had lured him into longing. He now yearned for things that would always be beyond his reach, foolishly aching for a woman who was so far above him, she might have dwelled among the stars.

He brought the boat up to the slip, too preoccupied by his own thoughts to notice the slim figure waiting at the edge of the woods.

"I made some stew," Diana said as he came toward her. He stopped dead in his tracks. "I thought you might be hungry."

"A bit," he murmured, as he waited to let her precede him. He didn't want to get too close to her just then. "But you should be abed by now," he said. "It's quite late."

She didn't move from the path. The kerchief was gone from her hair and the dark curls wafted around her head, glistening in the moonlight. She laid one hand on his sleeve. "You were gone such a long time. I've been waiting here nearly an hour."

He gave her a wry look. "Then I expect the mosquitoes, at least, have had their supper."

She managed a weak grin. "I didn't mind. But Rom, please tell me—is there more trouble on the river?"

Yes, he wanted to groan. *There is a deal of trouble on the river. You are the trouble, little witch . . . I have perjured myself this night to keep you safe, and with no hope of reward for my crime.*

"No," he said, curtly, trying to tear his gaze from her pale face. "At least nothing I cannot handle." He began to brush past her.

"Rom . . ." She tugged at his sleeve. "I didn't really come here to talk about your supper."

"What then?" He tried to pull away but she held firm.

"It was you I was worried about, not the river. I thought you might need . . . someone . . . I mean, if you were upset about the swan dying."

"It happens," he muttered. "You get over it."

"Tell me then," she cried softly. "How *does* one get over it, without another to share the pain?"

He turned to her and let his chin rest for one instant upon her hair. *How, indeed?*

He knew in that moment that he desired far more from Allegra than her kisses. He needed the sweet balm of her compassion. In truth, she was not the only one who had been affected by the swan's death. But he dared not avail himself of the comfort she offered. As much as his spirit cried out for it.

Romulus knew a man could share his body with a woman and still walk away unfettered. But if he shared the secrets of his guarded, damaged heart with a woman like Allegra, he knew he would be bound to her indelibly. Then when she left him, as all his foundlings eventually did, it would cause such a wrenching tear in his soul as he'd never before endured.

Christ! The thought of losing her was already nearly unendurable. If he had any sense at all, he would toss her into the skiff and row her back to Mortimer House while he still had the strength of will.

But then he recalled his promise. He would offer her a sanctuary until she trusted him enough to confide her reasons for running away. He'd already seen the trust brimming in her eyes when she'd entreated him to save the swan. It couldn't be more than a few days before she revealed the truth. And in the meantime, he would damn well have to temper his feelings for her, starting this very minute.

"I'm fine, Allegra," he lied, drawing back. Her hands fell away from his arm. "Everything is fine."

Chapter 5

The Waterthrush, a Tudor-era assemblage of stucco and beams, was sparsely populated in the mornings. The public house did most of its business at the end of the workday, when farmers and laborers came in for a pint and a good round of gossip. But there were a few men, those with no settled occupation, who whiled away the daytime hours in the pub's cool, dark taproom, playing at checkers and cards.

Treypenny's ferryman, Wald Chipping, was one such fellow. He limited himself to drinking only in the mornings, praying he wouldn't be summoned to the river by the clanging of the bell beside the water stairs. Prudent travelers who wanted to use the ferry did so in the early morning, before Wald's daily imbibing began, or late in the afternoon, when he'd had a chance to sleep off its effects. At midday, Wald Chipping was as likely to overturn his passengers in the river as he was to get them across to the opposite shore.

There was also among the ranks of the 'Thrush's daytime residents one Argie Beasle, a wiry, shifty-eyed little squib. In spite of his air of poverty—the threadbare coat, dingy shirt, and greasy, slicked-back hair—he always had a supply of coins to spend at the 'Thrush. And his currency was as welcome to Joe Black, the pub's owner, as any other man's, even though his noisome presence in the taproom might not have been.

By way of profession, Argie claimed he rode up and down the riverfront on his ratty gelding, doing odd jobs for the landowners. But the local scuttlebutt was that he was more involved with the animal population along the waterfront than with the human one. Poaching was illegal, but it paid exceedingly well. Especially so close to London. But Argie always laughed off any hints that he might be engaged in such nefarious work, grinned with narrow-eyed amusement, displaying his broken, discolored teeth.

Romulus stood for a moment in the open doorway of the pub, letting his eyes grow accustomed to the dim light. Three men seated at a table stopped their card game to gawk. Perrin was infrequently seen on the streets of Treypenny, but he'd never, to anyone's knowledge, set foot in the 'Thrush. The cardplayers turned to Joe Black, to see whether he would serve the madman. He noted their look of inquiry and shrugged. He'd serve grass to bloody Nebuchadnezzar himself, if the barmy old king offered him good English pence.

Rom nodded curtly to the publican as he crossed the taproom to where his quarry sat.

"Beasle," he said in a deep, low voice, as he approached the table, "I need to have a word with you."

The man didn't even look up. "I ain't got nothin' to say to you, Perrin," he muttered.

"I'm not interested in your conversation, my friend." Rom leaned forward. "But you will be very interested in mine."

When Argie refused to raise his eyes, Romulus tipped out the contents of Argie's mug; the dark ale ran across the tabletop. Argie scrambled to his feet before the spreading liquid could saturate his breeches. Not that it mightn't have been an improvement, Rom thought. The little rat smelled like Portsmouth at low tide.

"Hey!" Argie whined. "You owe me for that!"

Romulus grabbed him by the throat, thrust him back against the paneling, and lifted him off his feet. "I owe you for a great deal, my fine fellow," he said, gazing into the man's darting, anxious eyes, which were now level with his own. "And you shall have every last thing that I owe you. Starting with this."

Rom leaned all his weight on the hand that held Argie off the floor. "Feel that?" he growled softly just before he decreased the pressure. "That's what the cob felt when I cut his throat. Not very pleasant, is it?"

"I don't know what you're on about. I swear!" Argie began to kick violently against the oak paneling.

"Not in here, Perrin," Joe Black admonished him from behind the bar. He'd been willing to allow Perrin to have his way with Argie, until his pub's decor was placed at risk. "I've only just cleaned up after the blasted cattle drovers from Dorset who stampeded through here last week. Take your business outside."

Romulus nodded curtly, and then half carried the struggling

man across the room and out the open front door. No one in the pub made any attempt to aid Argie.

There was an alley beside the inn, piled high with casks and crates. Romulus strong-armed his captive some distance down the alley, and then swung him up against one wattled wall.

"I swear I don't know what you want with me!" Argie cried piteously.

"You were out on the river last night. Poaching swans. I saw you before you threw down your lantern."

"I was here last night," the man protested feebly. "Here in the 'Thrush. Ask anyone."

Romulus shook his head. "I doubt they would lie for you. And maybe you were here, maybe before and maybe after. But at nine of the clock you were skulking through the river grass with a shuttered lantern and a poached swan. And I tell you this, Beasle . . . if you ever go near my section of the river again, I will spit you." Rom let his fingers drift meaningfully against the thin ribs. "I know where to stick a knife, so that you would take a week to die. There are places where I could hide a man's body. . . . There is sucking mud, Argie. Deep mires that can swallow a man whole. Think on that the next time you are tempted to poach one of my birds."

Romulus turned abruptly from the man, tossing him aside as one would discard a rag doll.

"So you'll spit me, eh?" Argie's tone had gone from whining to challenging in an instant. Perhaps that was because he now held a long, thin-bladed knife angled out toward Romulus. "Maybe I'll be the one doing the spitting." As he spoke, he feinted toward his adversary.

Romulus observed Argie with an expression of distemper on his lean face. "Don't" he muttered. "Don't give me an excuse to kill you."

"Ho, lads!" he called out. "This redheaded rogue thinks he can kill me—without so much as a blade."

Romulus heard the sounds of men behind him at the mouth of the alley, but he dared not turn around. As long as none of them came to Argie's aid, he knew he was in little danger.

"Put down the knife, Argie." It was the publican speaking in a round, soothing voice. "If you kill him, it will go hard with you. And what of your work for Lord Talbot? We both profit from that. Think, man!"

Argie made a rude noise and flashed a warning glance past Rom to the pubkeeper. Romulus almost laughed—by mentioning Lord Talbot, Joe Black had just given Argie's game away.

During Rom's first month on the river, Lord Talbot's head groom had approached him and had mentioned, ever-so-casually, that he might be interested in procuring the odd swan, at an in- flated price, of course, to compensate for the risk. The only reason Rom hadn't thrown the groom off the island, was because his hands had begun to twitch violently from the intensity of his anger. Lord Talbot's groom had shaken his head at his waiting boatman, remarking cruelly that a fellow couldn't do business with a "jib- bering halfwit." Lord Talbot had clearly taken his business to Beasle and Joe Black.

Argie was still making feinting motions with the knife, and Romulus thought it was time to end the farce. As the man lunged at him, Rom's hand flashed out and his long fingers closed hard over the bony wrist. In an instant he had twisted Argie's scrawny arm up behind his back, pressing on his fragile wrist bones until the knife dropped to the ground. Romulus swept up the knife and tucked it into his boot.

Argie wailed, "He's busted my arm!" as he cradled the limb to his narrow chest.

Romulus stalked from the alley—the men who had gathered there instantly cleared a path—and went up to Joe Black. He jabbed his forefinger into the startled publican's wide chest.

"Don't cross me," he snarled as the man wilted back. "Do I make myself clear?"

Joe Black licked his lips and nodded. "It weren't like you think—" he began. But Romulus was already out of earshot, his long strides carrying him in the direction of the Gypsy camp.

"I owe him," Argie muttered, while Joe examined his arm. "And I'll get my own back. See if I don't."

"It's not broken," the publican pronounced, releasing the weedy limb. "Not but that you don't deserve a busted wrist for pulling a knife on an unarmed man. Christ, Argie, have you got dung for brains?"

The little man squirmed away from him. "I'll get him, you'll see. Argie Beasle don't let no man use him ill. I'll find some way to make that redheaded cockerel pay. Some way."

Argie looked thoughtful for a moment, his eyes narrowed be- yond their normal squint, and then he turned to the ferryman. "Ho there, Wald, want to earn a few coins today? I have a yen to be out on the river."

The ferryman looked dubious until he saw the half crown in Argie's sweaty palm. "You can have my boat, an all, for the week," he said as he snatched up the coin with a wide grin. "I'm officially off duty, lads."

"You got to row me, Wald. Can't do nothin' till my arm mends."

"For this much blunt," Wald replied, "I'd tow you to London Bridge with the rope between my teeth!"

Joe Black left his two customers to sort out their questionable deal and returned to his taproom. He was beginning to rue the day he'd agreed to act as middle man between Argie Beasle and Lord Talbot. Even if the extra money had allowed him to give his eldest daughter a fine send-off when she wed. There were times a man danced with the devil at his own peril. Though Argie was less of a devil and more of a greasy, whining imp. He wondered if he should warn Perrin of Argie's incipient revenge. But then he recalled how effortlessly Romulus had disarmed the little bugger. No, the river warden didn't appear to need anyone's help.

After the cygnets were fed, Diana decided to gather some of the wildflowers that grew in profusion in the backyard. She had unearthed a blue and white pitcher from under the trestle to use as a vase. As she wandered along the edge of the yard, snipping off the stems of narcissus and cornflower with a knife she had appropriated from the kitchen, she was again struck by the mesmerizing beauty of the island. The wild vines that laced their way up the trunks of the towering trees were as untamed as the jackdaws and ravens that cawed raucously from their ariel perches. In this place, nature was unconfigured by the hand of man—with the exception of the rustic lodge and the outbuildings, the island appeared almost primeval.

Though she loved the bleak, treeless landscape of the Yorkshire moors where she had been born, this wild abundance of green foliage, with its vivid scattering of blossoms, spoke to her soul. Back in Bothys, she'd had to use her imagination to conjure up settings for her idyllic fantasies. Here, she merely had to observe the lush landscape that enfolded her, for dazzling tales to arise in her head. Tales of bravery and courage, of tenderness and compassion. Dark tales of loss and betrayal as well as thrilling ones of passion and possession. And every one revolved around the mysterious man who dwelled alone on this island. He had become the centerpiece of her life and her imaginings, and yet she was not certain how it had happened.

Romulus was a striking figure, to be sure. His melodic voice, with its slight hint of foreign shores, spilled over her like warm honey when he spoke. The flash of his golden eyes, or the tilt of his wide mouth set her senses spinning. And his physical splendor was matched by a nature that was compassionate and wise. But he was a man of secrets, who guarded his emotions behind a perpetual shield of gruff sarcasm. She needed to keep reminding herself of that fact. She dared not feel anything more for him than gratitude.

"Hang gratitude," she muttered as she plunked the flowers in the pitcher and set it on the table. Secretive or guarded or armed to the teeth with sarcasm, Romulus had won her heart. Maybe precisely because of his secrets—a man who was an enigma was prime fodder for a young lady's errant imagination.

Once the flowers were arranged to her satisfaction, Diana wandered into the sitting room, where her gaze fell on Rom's disordered bookshelf. Here was a task that fairly begged to be tackled. Not that she had any intention of rearranging his books, mind. She knew from her father that some men balked at the least notion of order in their libraries. So she merely removed the books that had been shoved haphazardly onto the shelf and realigned them, so that they stood upright, with their spines facing out. By the time she reached the bottom shelf, the bookcase was looking quite tamed. She sat back on her heels, admiring her work.

"He's going to have your head on a platter!"

Diana turned abruptly. A young man lounged in the doorway of the sitting room, one arm raised up to the frame. She was alarmed at first until she saw the bright clothing he wore and the golden earring that glinted in one ear. This must be Rom's gypsy friend.

"My head?" she echoed. "Surely you are exaggerating."

He came toward her, frowning ominously. "I myself have been warned away from those books any number of times. Not that I can read, mind. But there are some topping pictures of horses in the brown one."

Diana climbed to her feet and held out one hand. "I expect you are Niall. I am Di—delighted to meet you. My name is Allegra."

She winced at her near mistake, but the Gypsy boy just continued to regard her outstretched hand with misgiving.

"Gypsies don't shake hands with ladies." He spoke so ponderously that she missed the twinkle in his eye. "At least not if they want to keep their . . . um, privates intact."

"Oh," she said, dropping her hand. "I was just being polite. And I should certainly like to thank you for these clothes." As she spoke, she moved forward into the pool of light that spilled in through the window.

"Jiminy," Niall breathed, as he took in her face and figure. Especially her figure. "He told me you were a fetching little thing, but I had no idea."

"Who told you what?" she asked in confusion.

"Romulus. He said I was likely to tumble into love with you." He grinned at her. "Would you mind very much if I did? You're far and away the prettiest girl I've ever seen."

"Ho, you should see my sister," Diana trumpeted. And then immediately cursed herself. *Oh, Lord, not again!* "I mean," she sputtered aloud. "That if I had a sister, which I cannot be sure I do, I expect she would be even fairer than I am . . . because she would be older, you see."

Niall took this nonsense in stride. Intellectual stimulation was not yet something he required from his conquests. "Lost your memory, did you? Rom told me all about it. Don't tax yourself on my account. I can't abide a lass who rattles on about her past." He motioned toward the storeroom. "Cygnets all bedded down?"

She nodded. "That's why I was straightening the bookshelf, since I had run out of chores."

Niall gave a sultry laugh. "Well, I can think of something a lot more fun than sorting through old books."

Diana looked at him dubiously. It wouldn't have surprised her to learn that women all up and down the river were like putty in this gypsy boy's hands. It wasn't only the rich, olive-hued skin, or the glistening black curls—there was something sensual in his posture and his movements, like a languorous, feral cat.

She drew herself up to her full height. "I'm sure I haven't any interest along those lines."

Niall touched a finger to her nose. "I wasn't suggesting sporting, my little prude. Only fishing."

Before she could utter a word of protest, he had taken her by the hand and dragged her from the house.

"Rom's got the best fishing hole on the river in that creek of his," he remarked enthusiastically as they crossed the yard. "The finny creatures come up to the edge of the boat and fairly beg to be taken."

"But I don't know how to fish," she grumbled as he hurried her along the path.

"It's like falling off a log," he said.

They stopped at a low rise which overlooked the inlet that bisected the island. Willow branches hung lacelike over the dark water and frogs chorused in the May heat.

"I've never been here before," Diana crooned. "It's beautiful."

Niall led her down the incline to a weathered work shed, which was nearly obscured by vines. Two boats, a narrow punt and a small dory, were beached beyond the shed. "Rom keeps his boating supplies in here," he said as he threw open the warped door. "Ropes, lines, oars. And . . . fishing poles." He drew out a long bamboo pole for each of them, put a handful of lead sinkers into the pocket of his buckskin knee breeches, and then stuck a few hooks in his shirt placket.

"Never put hooks in your breeches pocket," he warned her, and then cast a glance at her skirt. "Though I daresay *you* won't ever have that problem. Now let's dig up some bait."

"Niall," Diana said as they dug for earthworms beneath the base of an uprooted tree, "would you make a trade with me?" She recalled what Rom had said about Gypsies loving a good trade.

He eyed her meaningfully as he drawled, "Depends on what you have to trade." He ruined the studied effect of this languid, seductive statement by then crying out in boyish tones, "Look, there's a nice fat one!"

Diana dropped the squirming worm into the tin bucket. "It's not what you think, I'm afraid."

He gave a cocky toss of his head. "And how would you know what I think?"

Diana sniffed. "Something highly improper, I shouldn't doubt."

Niall nodded merrily. "And you'd probably be right, in the normal way of things. But Romulus is my friend, and friends don't poach on each other's territory."

Diana looked bewildered at first. Did Niall truly consider her Rom's property? She lowered her head over the worm can to hide her furious blush. Whatever had Rom said to the boy to give him such an idea?

"The trade?" Niall prompted.

Diana sat back on her heels. "If you teach me to fish, then I will teach you to read."

She saw the eagerness light his eyes, and then watched as it was immediately replaced by blasé unconcern. He shrugged. "It makes no difference to me if I can read or not."

"But you will let me try?"

"If it will please you," he said. "But I've a hard head, as Romulus will tell you."

Diana grinned. "Not any harder than mine." Helen would have happily vouched for her on that score.

By the time he reached the Gypsy camp, Romulus had walked off very little of his anger. He'd hoped the poacher was working alone, but hadn't been surprised to find the publican in on the deal. A contraband swan could fetch five pounds from a wealthy buyer. More than enough profit for two men to split.

He feared that even if Argie layed low for a while, the publican might simply enlist a new accomplice. Argie's reputation as a poacher had made him the logical suspect when the swans began to disappear. But if Joe sought out another man to snare the swans, it might take weeks for Rom to track him down.

If the scene in Treypenny hadn't already soured his disposition, the news from the gypsy camp would have. The Gypsies reported that Niall had gone off that morning and wasn't expected back until sundown.

Damn! He'd come too late to prevent the boy from making any more inquiries. Niall could be asking at Mortimer House this very minute. Pray God, he didn't let on that he knew anything about the missing girl. If Allegra's family suspected a Gypsy might have been involved in her disappearance, Niall's whole band could be placed in danger. Especially if Sir Bleeding Beveril had anything to do with it.

Romulus skirted the main street of Treypenny when he returned to his skiff. He didn't want to come across either Argie Beasle or Joe Black. But he met up with no one, not one single soul. It was as though a crier had announced his passage through the town and sent everyone scurrying for safety. Even the children who normally played near the river stairs were gone.

A dead gull lay across the center seat of his skiff, its limp wings lolling down on either side.

With an oath he cast the bird away, not caring that it landed in the water. The turtles would make short work of it. Especially since, by the smell of it, it had been dead for some time. Good old Argie had dredged up a gull carcass in a childish attempt to intimidate his foe. Rom wondered that such a pitiful creature had been so successful at poaching his swans. Just went to show that gain was rarely based on merit.

He did a thorough patrol of both sides of the river upstream from the island. The birdlife seemed relatively undisturbed. The only thing the least bit unusual he encountered was Wald Chipping, rowing his boat toward Richmond. The man had uncharacteristically cut short his morning session at the 'Thrush.

Rom called out as they passed each other, "No ferrying today?"

The boatman shrugged. "Got supplies to deliver." He motioned to a canvas-covered hump that lay in the bow of the boat.

Romulus continued to guide his skiff along the water, keeping an eye out for slimy water rats skulking in the tall grass. A pair of swans sailed serenely past, their downy brood paddling furiously behind them. Romulus stopped rowing and sat watching as the adults nudged the curious cygnets away from his boat. His own cygnets would be back on the river inside of a week. And with any luck Allegra would have admitted her true identity by then, and have gone back to her own people. And then he would have his house to himself again. It was not a heartening thought.

As he rowed beside his island, he heard laughter coming from the inlet. Angling his boat toward the source of the noise, he caught sight of Niall and Allegra, dangling fishing poles over the side of the punt.

"Hello, Romulus!" Allegra waved gaily. "Niall is teaching me to fish. He came to see you this morning, but you'd already gone off."

"How did you get here?" Rom asked the boy, who was grinning like a hound.

"Had one of the Yorrick's men row me over to the island. He was going out after eels." Niall turned to Diana. "I love eel pie. My granty makes the best on the river."

Diana made an unpleasant face. "I can't say I've ever tasted eel." She shifted her gaze to Romulus. "But the grebes like them, don't they?"

He nodded. "Though not in a pie."

It was giving him an odd sensation in his middle to see Allegra frolicking with the Gypsy boy. They looked to be of an age, and could have been brother and sister, with their straight, slim bodies and night-dark curls. Except that Niall was regarding the girl with less-than-brotherly appreciation.

"I think you should come in now," he cautioned them, more sharply than he had intended.

"But I haven't caught anything yet," Diana protested.

"Oh, very well," Romulus said as he turned his boat back toward the river. "Just see that you stay in the creek. I've got my downstream rounds to make."

"Well, he wasn't very cheerful," Diana complained as Romulus disappeared from view.

Niall gave her a conspiratorial wink. "He's jealous." She was starting to blush, when he added, "He loves to fish. But he's got to go off and patrol the river, while we stay here and fish the afternoon away."

"I'm surprised he cares for fishing," she said. "That he could harm any animal, I mean."

"A man who lives on the river would be daft not to fish."

"You don't think he's really daft, Niall, do you?" Her eyes had narrowed in concern. "Rom told me the people in the village think he is addled. But he's not, not truly?"

Niall shook his head as he rebaited Diana's line. "He's the oddest *gorgio* I've ever met. He frightens people, that's the truth, with his size, and with those cat's eyes of his. But he's not addled. In fact, he saved my life just after he came to live here. We became friends after that."

"He saved my life, too," she said with a sigh. "Pulled me out of the river before I could drown."

"He apparently makes a habit of that," Niall observed as he leaned back and draped one bare leg over the side of the punt. "There I was sitting on an old tree limb, fishing for my supper"— he made an exaggerated motion with his bamboo pole—"when the blasted branch broke and down I went into the water. I couldn't swim a lick at the time—I was sure I was done for. The next thing I know, this fellow plucks me out of the water by the collar of my shirt and drops me into his boat.

"He wouldn't let me go back to camp until I'd learned how to swim. He taught me right here in this creek. I was shivering like a pup, from the cold, and from fear. But he stayed on me until I could make it across from bank to bank. When Rom brought me home, my father was so overjoyed, he offered Rom half his horses for saving my life. But he wouldn't take anything. He asked only that I help him sometimes, bring him food and supplies and such. I was happy to do it. Even if he was the prickliest fellow I'd ever met."

"I thought he was your friend."

"Oh, he is. But that happened gradually. He was more of a nuisance in the beginning. I stole a bridle once, from the stable at Hamish House, and he made me return it to the lady who lives there . . . in person. It was the hardest thing I ever had to do. But the curious thing was, the lady wasn't angry. Just upset. She gave me one of her yearlings to break, by way of paying her back—as though working with a highbred colt was any sort of punishment." He chuckled.

"So you've met Lady Hamish."

Niall gave her a long look. "Rom works for her. Didn't you know?"

Diana shook her head. "He's never spoken of her."

"She keeps to herself, that one. Just like Rom. She rarely leaves her home and has few visitors." He added with a thoughtful frown, "Well, except for her perishing nephew, Beveril."

"I gather you don't like him . . . her nephew."

"Let's say that he has no fondness in his heart for Gypsies. Or for Romulus, either. The two of them circle around each other like peevish terriers whenever they meet. It's really quite entertaining."

Niall was watching her intently as he spoke. Diana immediately turned her attention to her fishing, fiddling with the line to distract the Gypsy's sharp eyes. His revelation had made her very uncomfortable. It was unsettling to discover Romulus was connected to Beveril, however remotely. She hadn't thought she would be endangering him by staying on his island. But what if he lost his position because of her? What if he was forced to leave his home and the river he loved because of a stubborn, foolish girl?

She wasn't at all surprised, however, to learn there was no love lost between Sir Beveril and Romulus. Her intended was surly and short-tempered with underlings—she'd seen how he treated the servants at Mortimer House. It was one of his less endearing qualities. He doubtless treated Rom in the same manner, like a lackey. And Romulus Perrin, in spite of his less-than-gentle birth, was a very proud man.

Diana had lost all interest in fishing and soon complained to Niall of a headache.

He poled the punt back to the grassy shore of the inlet. "I expect you're not feeling well enough to keep your end of the bargain," he said as he helped her from the boat.

She couldn't tell if he was disappointed or relieved at the thought.

"No," she replied stoutly. "You kept up your end of the bargain. Now it's my turn. I'm sure I will feel more the thing once I am out of the sun."

Diana led him into the sitting room and lit the candles on the desk. "Sit here, where you can see."

She went to the bookcase and tugged out the large, brown volume he had spoken of earlier.

"Now," she said as she opened it to a page that featured an illustration of a Bedouin on a delicate-looking charger, "see the words beneath the picture . . . 'The Arabian horse is one of the breeds of antiquity.' "

Niall frowned. "It's mostly gibberish to me."

"It won't be when I'm through with you." She looked up from the book and mused, "I wonder if I might have been a teacher in my other life."

"Rom said you are of the gentry—it's not likely that you'd bother with other folks' brats."

Diana smiled to herself. She had, in fact, bothered a great deal with other folks' brats. Last year she had started a school for the children of the sheepherders and millworkers who lived near Bothys. It had been an instant success. Until the landowners and millowners heard of her good work and, fearing what an education might do to their future crop of workers, pressured her to close it down. Her father told her she had learned a valuable lesson—that men of stature were quick to curb even minor threats to their power. But that was small consolation to Diana. It was not in her nature to back down from a fight.

Niall tickled her on the chin with the end of a quill pen, drawing her back from the irksome reminder of her failure. "I'd have stayed in school and gladly," he said, attempting to coax the troubled expression from her blue eyes, "if the teacher looked anything like you. But that was years ago, when we camped in London. There was a church lady who gave lessons at our camp, but she had a face like a prune. I'd say your face puts me in mind of a peach."

She rapped him on the knuckles, and then grinned. "Lesson number one—no flirting with the teacher."

As Niall gave her a slow, lazy smile, Diana was glad her heart was already well and truly given. The gypsy boy cast a powerful spell.

"Now sound out the letters, if you please," she said briskly.

Romulus watched them silently from the doorway of the sitting room. He stood hipshot against the doorpost, one hand resting against his waist, the other trailing behind him.

Niall was painfully attempting to read from a large book, while Diana coached him through the more difficult words. Their dark heads were nearly touching, and again Romulus felt that twisting sensation in his gut. If seeing her with his friend drew such a primitive response from him, he dared not think how he would feel if he ever saw her with Beveril. He misliked the idea of any man getting near her. Any man but himself.

He coughed and both heads shot up.

"I hate to interrupt this charming scene, but I need to speak to Niall . . . in private. Allegra, perhaps you could clean the fish we're having for supper."

Diana looked perplexed. "But we didn't catch anything."

He held up the stringer of trout that had been dangling behind the skirts of his coat. "No, but I did."

"Well, you've certainly put my efforts to shame," she said, eyeing the three trout with envy. She closed the book and rose to her feet. "But I thought you were out on patrol."

"I always carry a line and some hooks in my pocket."

"Not your breeches pocket, I hope?" she said with a merry glance to Niall as she crossed the room.

Romulus shook his head. "No, I learned that lesson the hard way. Now off you go. And, Allegra—"

She looked up at him questioningly as he handed her the stringer.

He nodded toward the bookcase. "Thank you for setting my books in order. I've been meaning to do it myself this age past."

She smiled in relief. "Niall said you would have my head on a platter for disturbing them."

He glanced sidelong at the boy, and then said smoothly, "Nonsense. It's just that he knows there are some things of mine he is not allowed to touch."

Diana looked from the tall man who still leaned against the door, to the gypsy boy who now sat glowering at him. The sitting room was filled with a strange, almost palpable tension. She hastily took herself off to the kitchen, abandoning her plans to eavesdrop on the two men. They were clearly at odds with each other for some reason and she liked them both far too well to want to overhear any discord.

"Was that necessary?" Niall said, once Diana was out of earshot. "You've made me look a proper sod in front of her. She no doubt thinks I've been pilfering things from your house."

"As long as *you* got the message," Romulus uttered as he settled himself in Diana's chair.

"In no uncertain terms," the boy snapped.

Romulus leaned forward and took up the book Diana had left on the desk. "You never told me you couldn't read. Don't you think I would have taught you, if you'd wanted to learn?"

Niall said sullenly, "What does a Gypsy need with books? I'm only letting her teach me to please her."

"Oh, and is that an issue with you?" Romulus inquired softly. "Pleasing her?"

"Oh, no!" Niall cried, leaping up from his chair. "Don't start getting all huffy with me, Romulus. I know you are cross because I remained here this morning, even though I knew you had left the island. I just wanted to meet this water witch of yours. But that's all there was to it, I swear."

"So you don't find her to your taste?"

"Damn it, Rom. A fellow would be blind not to find her to his taste. She is . . ."

"What?"

"Dangerous," the Gypsy bit out. "To both of us. I wish you had never fished her out of the river."

"It may surprise you to know I have recently had the exact same thought. No good can come of her being here, and yet I haven't the heart to send her away."

"You may change your tune when I tell you where she came from."

Niall had spoken the words with great portent, but Romulus merely shook his head. "I believe I already know that. Last night I found a rowboat from Mortimer House downstream from here, trapped under a fallen oak. Does that march with what you've uncovered?"

"Yes, it does," Niall stated. "That's what I came to tell you—the dairymaid at Hamish House said that Beveril was in a rare snit over something that had occurred at Mortimer House this Saturday night past. I got a ride up river with a tinker and had a chat with one of Mortimer's grooms. It seems that Beveril's intended, Diana Exeley, disappeared the night of her betrothal ball and has not been heard of since."

Rom's mouth tightened as his fingers stroked the edge of the book. "I feared that's who she was."

Niall's brow lowered. "And yet you will let her stay on? Knowing that Beveril will see you flogged, or worse, for keeping her from his hands? Or is that why you are doing it, Rom? Is this some twisted form of revenge on him for the way he has treated you?"

"He will surely think it the case, if he ever discovers my part in it," Romulus said. "But I am doing it for one reason only. Because Allegra—er, Diana—ran away from something that night. And until she trusts me enough to tell me what it was, I cannot in good conscience turn her over to her family."

"What if she never remembers? You can't hide her away forever."

"Oh, she'll tell me soon enough." His mouth quirked up slightly as he added, "Her memory is surprisingly flexible. But until that time, I want no mention made of her to anyone. In Treypenny, or along the river. Promise me, Niall. Promise that you will not breathe a word about her to a soul."

"My granty suspects something," Niall said with a chuckle. "Remember, she furnished the clothing for the girl. She said she thought it was high time a fine fellow like you took a woman to his bed."

Romulus growled. "And I supposed you said nothing to discourage that line of thought?"

Niall looked unchastened. "She's a salty old thing, my granty. Thinks everyone ought to be busy procreating."

"Then she is blest in her grandson, at least," Romulus noted.

The gypsy boy blushed and stammered, "I-I'm not such a dab hand at it, as you seem to think."

"That's a relief. I expect any day to hear you have been skinned alive by an irate farmer whose daughter you deflowered."

Niall shook his head as he said musingly, "Funny isn't it, how a

fellow gets a reputation without a shred of truth to it? Like the villagers thinking you a madman."

Romulus said softly, "There was some basis to that, Niall. Just
as there is truth to your reputation as an up-and-coming rake. You
may not be, as you put it, a dab hand, but women certainly fall at
your feet. I wager there's not a lass on the river who hasn't at least
made sheep's eyes at you."

"You'd lose your money, then," Niall stated. He motioned toward the kitchen. "Your water witch rapped me on the knuckles
when I tried to cozen her. Not that I had anything improper in
mind, you understand."

"Oh, I understand perfectly." Romulus found himself grinning.
So the black-eyed Gypsy's flattery hadn't teased so much as a
smile out of Allegra.

"Then you'll let me come again, Rom? I think she needs something to occupy her time while you are away on the water."

"What? She should waste her time teaching a Gypsy to read?"

Niall rubbed at an imaginary spot on his breeches. Without
looking up he said, "Perhaps it might be of some use. I could read
to my granty of a night. And do up the accounts when we take our
horses to the fair."

Romulus leaned to him and put a hand on his shoulder. "You
needed only to ask, Niall. And I expect she'll be a far more pleasant tutor than I would have been."

"I don't know about that," the boy said. "Not if she has at me
every time I pay her a compliment."

Niall left shortly afterward. As they walked to the inlet, Romulus told him about the death of the swan and his subsequent encounter with Argie Beasle. He asked Niall to relay back any
information he might uncover about the poacher's activities on the
river. Romulus reckoned that between his lessons with Allegra and
keeping an eye on the river rat, his young friend would be too distracted to get himself into any trouble with nervous fathers of sus-
ceptible daughters. At least for the time being.

After Niall rowed off in the dory, Romulus stood looking out
over the water for some time, wrestling with the problem of Allegra's presence on the island. Dangerous, the boy had called her.
And she was that. In more ways than one. Perhaps it was time to
shake up his houseguest a bit. See whether he could discover if the
high-handed Sir Beveril had anything to do with her precipitate
flight from home.

Chapter 6

After she had cleaned the trout, Diana wandered onto the front porch. It was too hot to remain inside the house. Not that it was noticeably cooler outside—the breeze had died and the tree leaves hung unmoving, wilting in the unseasonable heat. She sighed as she leaned against the railing, watching the dark clouds that lingered off to the west. After the trouble with the swan poacher, Rom had reverted to his former gruff self. Which was a pity, because he had been particularly attentive to her, there in the intimate confines of the rowboat. But then the swan had died and their easy camaraderie had been swept away.

If only she had not been born into the gentry, Diana thought wistfully, she might have been able to coax him into courting her. But Romulus knew his place in society—he was a laborer, a hireling of the great lady across the river. His honor would have forbidden any sort of liaison with a lady of quality. Perhaps he was even embarrassed by her obvious attraction to him. But she knew that even if he welcomed her attentions, he would never speak of his regard for her. He held his emotions totally in check—she had seen it last night when he'd been forced to kill the swan. While she had crumpled, he had remained aloof from his pain.

And yet she suspected Romulus was not indifferent to her. She amused him for one thing. Even when he acted cross, there was always a trace of laughter in his voice. And she was not too green to recognize the hunger that sometimes burned in his eyes—she had seen it last night while they were out on the river and again when he had returned from his patrol. He had only to touch her hand, for a spark of energy to flow between them—an intense quickening that might very well be desire.

But she knew a man could desire a woman without ever experiencing any of the more tender emotions. Could that be all Romulus felt for her—nothing but lust? Then what of his insistence on sheltering her? Didn't that prove he was driven by more than the needs of his body?

It was just another of the baffling complexities she'd had to deal with ever since meeting Romulus Perrin. Sir Beveril, at least, was somewhat less baroque in his inclinations—marry the rich man's sister, make love to the beautiful widow. Simple and uncomplicated.

She sat on the top step and took stock of her options. She could continue to let Rom hold her at bay, until she admitted defeat and asked to be rowed back to Mortimer House. She knew she had gained enough fortitude to insist that her betrothal be called off. Before meeting her swankeeper, she had been a leaf in a stream, borne along by the currents, resentful, but unresisting. Now she would set her own course and stand firm in the face of opposition. It wasn't the Middle Ages—brides were no longer carried protesting to the altar. But the thought of leaving the island put her in a panic. Not yet, her heart pleaded. Please, not yet.

There was a second option, one she had not yet mustered the courage to pursue. She could tell Romulus what was in her heart. Tell him why she had continued to pretend a loss of memory long after it held any credibility. But she feared any declaration of that sort would merely increase his distance. It was dashed hard loving a man who knew his place, especially when she believed his place was beside her.

She had no illusions about how society would regard such a mésalliance. Not that she cared a fig for that. But there was her family to consider. Could they ever accept him?

As she sat fanning herself with one hand, Diana had a gut-wrenching revelation. She had been a naive fool not to have realized it from the start. But she had been so instantly beguiled by the island, and by the man who lived there, that reality had faded quickly away. The fact was, in the eyes of society, she was compromised beyond any means of redemption. One night in Rom's house would have been enough to tarnish her reputation. She had been there for four days.

"Oh, lord," she moaned against her fisted hands. Why had she not seen it? She could never return to her sister's home now. Even her father might refuse to take her in, though he'd had little patience with the strictures of society. What a coil she had gotten herself into!

"You're looking rather glum."

Diana's eyes darted up. Romulus was standing at the end of the brick path that bisected the herb garden. He'd been such a long time seeing Niall off, she assumed he'd gone back onto the river.

"It's the heat," she sighed. "It wears me down." As if to prove her point she caught her hair up in one hand and lifted it from her nape.

She couldn't see the way his eyes darkened or how his mouth tightened as she arched back against the porch railing, holding the heavy mass of dark curls off her shoulders.

Sirens, he reckoned, could learn a seductive trick or two from Allegra.

"I expect it's more than the heat that has wearied you," he said as he came forward and settled himself on the step below hers. "Niall," he said, answering her puzzled look. "It must be up-hill going, teaching a Gypsy boy to read."

"No, not at all. He is very bright. A church woman taught him his letters years ago . . . I only needed to jog his memory a bit."

"At least one of you has a memory that's joggable," he couldn't prevent himself from observing.

She flashed him a look of annoyance.

"No, no, stop looking daggers at me, Allegra. I'll leave off baiting you. I'm just a bit testy—I had a run-in with our swan poacher this morning."

She touched his sleeve. "That's something, then. I hope you put the fear of God into him."

Romulus scratched his cheek. "Not so you would notice. Argie Beasle is a stubborn river rat and not easy to intimidate. And, unless I miss my guess, he's in league with the local publican."

Diana gave a little sign of dismay. "Rom, isn't there a magistrate in the district who could aid you?"

He shook his head. The last thing he needed was a magistrate poking around in his business.

"I'll just increase the time I spend patrolling the river," he said. "I might be able to enlist Niall to help me . . . *if* I can get him away from his latest flirt." His eyes teased her.

She looked away from him and said matter-of-factly, "Niall told me how you saved his life. I gather that was the mysterious trade you made with the Gypsies."

He nodded as he leaned back against the step, his long legs stretched out before him. "I may yet come to regret it—you've got to be careful who you rescue from the river. Not everyone pays you back in kind."

"And do you regret saving me?" she inquired. She'd asked it in a playful manner, but when he took his time replying, she turned to him with a look of concern on her face. "Do you?" she asked again, more softly.

He sucked in one cheek. "Perhaps it's too soon to tell," he said. "You've certainly made things interesting around here. And I'm not sure I mean that as a compliment."

Diana's lower lip trembled slightly. "I've tried not to be a burden to you."

He raised his hand, wanting to trace his fingers over her quivering lip. Instead he brushed a catkin from her hair. "Don't look so out of sorts, my witch."

"I wouldn't blame you if you did regret rescuing me," she said in a tremulous voice. "I fear I may yet cause you a deal of trouble. It's only just occurred to me, you see. I was foolish not to have realized it sooner . . . foolish and thoughtless. I see now that my being on the island places you in a very precarious position."

"What is this?" he said, his eyes lighting at the intent, serious set of her small mouth. "Has your past come flying back to you at last? Have I been harboring the wife of a jealous Islamic potentate?"

"That's the point I'm trying to make. I'm not *anyone's* wife."

"And how can you be so sure?"

"Because of the ball gown in your kitchen."

Romulus leaned forward as he tried to follow the convoluted train of her logic. "The ball gown?"

With conviction she replied, "There is not a married lady in the breadth of England who would allow herself to be tricked out in such an insipid gown. I do know that much."

Romulus grinned. "Yes, that ball gown rather does have 'young miss' written all over it. But unlike you, Allegra, I realized at once the . . . what did you call it? . . . the precariousness of my position. And I think there is only one course to follow."

"Oh?" She looked less than relieved. "I suppose that means you are sending me to Treypenny."

"That would hardly serve to scotch any gossip," he pointed out. "Just the opposite, in fact. I can imagine how the villagers would react to the sight of their local madman rowing ashore with a young lady in tow." He shifted to face her. "No, I've given it a lot of thought since you arrived here. And I've come to a decision."

"And that is. . . ?" she asked cautiously.

"I intend to row you across to Hamish House and put you in Lady Hamish's care—"

"No!" She had nearly shouted the word. That was the last place she could afford to go.

Beveril had been running tame in his aunt's home for weeks, a fact Diana had formerly attributed to her own allure. Now she knew his prolonged visit had much more to do with the charms of Lady Vivian.

"I certainly cannot go there," she added in a more controlled voice.

"Why?" His tone gave nothing away.

Her hands fluttered in agitation. "B-b-because she is a stranger to me."

"As I am," he remarked evenly.

She flashed him a stormy look and crossed her arms over her chest. "Well, if that's what you think you are, then perhaps you should send me away. But whether Lady Hamish takes me in or not, you will still be seen as the man who compromised me." She added purposefully, "I won't have your good name sullied, Romulus, not as a result of your kindness to me. And I certainly won't let anyone force you to marry me."

"You relieve my mind immeasurably," he murmured, looking away so she could not see him smile. "But there is a way to prevent that situation from arising. If I ask it of them, the Gypsies will say that they found you, injured and disoriented." He chuckled softly as he added, "They don't lie among themselves, but think nothing of fibbing to a *gorgio*. I will tell Lady Hamish that I found you with the Gypsies. Your presence in her house will lend countenance to the story, and so you will be returned to your family with your reputation for the most part intact. All you need do is say the word, and I will set things in motion."

She grappled with her feelings, knowing the sooner she left the island, the less chance there was that he would be implicated in her disappearance. Yet she sensed he was as loath to let her go as she was to leave.

"And when would you take me to Hamish House?"

He looked down at the toes of his boots and replied softly, "To-morrow morning." She gasped noticeably and his eyes immediately darted back to her face. "It's the only way, Allegra," he said, as his golden gaze held her. "There's no telling how long it will take for your memory to return. And we can't afford to wait."

"But you said it should return within the week."

"That's been my experience," he said. "But you should have recalled more of your past by now. For instance, what it was you were fleeing from that night."

"Why do you persist in this belief that I was running away?" she asked fretfully.

He responded in a low voice. "I have every reason to think it. While you were ill you cried out repeatedly in your sleep, 'Don't make me go back!' What else am I supposed to think after hearing that?"

Diana was about to dismiss those words as nothing more than the result of a fever-induced nightmare, when she realized he had just handed her an excuse to remain on the island.

"Yes," she mused, "I cannot precisely recall it, but there *is* something I dread returning to. And who can say? . . . Perhaps it was something at Hamish House that frightened me." That was certainly true. The avaricious, duplicitous Sir Beveril was enough to give anyone nightmares.

"*Think*, Allegra," he entreated her. "I cannot help you to face your fear, if you will not even speak of it."

Diana gave a long, drawn out sigh. Guilt was washing over her with every breath. Romulus was still trying to aid her, and meanwhile she piled up the lies, one upon the other. She had a sudden urge to tell him the truth, to reveal her own duplicity. It was apparent he had no illusions about her feigned loss of memory—he seemed more amused than angered by it. Her honesty would at least relieve his worry over her nameless peril. But there was nothing to be served by telling him about Sir Beveril. If what Niall said was true, there was enough hostility between the two men without throwing a runaway debutante into the mix.

He spoke into the strained silence that had grown between them. "I seriously doubt your fear has anything to do with Lady Hamish. She rarely receives visitors—it's unlikely you've ever met her. I wager it was someone close to you who was threatening you or forcing something on you."

"Why would you think that?" she said. "It might have been a stranger."

He gave her a tight smile as he shook his head. "You are a young lady of some wealth, by all indications. And such young ladies are kept well away from the more sordid denizens of the world. I doubt you were fleeing from a blackmailer or a vengeful moneylender."

She sniffed. "Perhaps I ran away from an overly familiar stableboy."

Romulus surprised her by laughing. "Oh, no, Allegra. I've seen how you handle the Gypsy Romeo. There's not a lovestruck moonling you couldn't dispatch with a flick of your little finger. It wasn't a stableboy that set you on the river, my girl. I'd say something of a bit more weight."

About sixteen stone, Allegra muttered to herself, thinking of her strapping fiancé.

She put her hands over her face and said through her fingers. "Does it matter so much why I ran away, Rom? Whatever it was, I will deal with it when I return home."

His voice rumbled softly near her ear. "I didn't want you to have to face it alone."

She drew her hands down and gazed at him in wonder. "Thank you," she said in a husky whisper. "But you have done enough, letting me stay here." There was a world of sadness in her voice as she added, "There are some things we have to face alone, Rom. You have been my bulwark, here on the island, but out there"—she made a sweeping motion toward the river—"out there, I must learn to fend for myself."

Romulus took up her hand and twined his fingers with hers. "No," he said gently. "Do you think I stop caring about my foundlings, once they are returned to the river? Do you think my responsibility ends when they are no longer in my home?" He drew her hand to his mouth. "Nothing can harm you, Allegra." His lips touched the base of her wrist. "Not while I have breath in my body. You need only get a message to me, and I will come to you. Any time, any place."

Diana's heart clenched in her breast as she bit back a choking sob. The warm touch of his mouth on her skin had sent a ripple of aching tenderness through her. She knew that those comforting words were the closest thing to a declaration of love she was likely to receive from Romulus. He was letting her go, but not severing the connection between them. She wondered if she could live her life without him, consoled by the knowledge that he was hovering in the distance, like a well-beloved guardian angel. It was not what she wanted, but perhaps it was all she was to be allowed.

"Thank you, Rom," she said hoarsely as he laid her hand upon the step. "I could not ask for more."

He leaned away from her and plucked up a stem of soapwart that grew beside the stairs. "So are you willing to go to Hamish House tomorrow?" he asked and then added slyly, "Or can you promise me a miracle cure by the beginning of next week? Say . . . by Monday?"

A resounding joy swept through Diana at his words. He was leaving the choice up to her! He watched her with a guarded apprehension; it changed to relief when she said, "Yes, I'd prefer to wait until then. For one thing, we haven't given Wilfred Bailey much time to respond to my note. He might yet send me a reply."

"I suppose that is a possibility." Rom's tone indicated that he had as much faith in Bailey responding, as of a man riding a rocket to the moon.

"And I do believe some fragments of my memory have returned. This morning I recollected that I had been a teacher . . . It came to me while I was showing Niall his letters."

"Hmm?" Romulus mused, stroking the soapwart along her forearm. "Were you a governess, do you think?" He craned his head up toward her, his eyes now lit with amusement. "Perhaps you succumbed to temptation and stole that elegant ball gown . . . and took to the river to escape your pursuers."

Diana shifted away from the soft caress of the wildflower and said stiffly, "I hardly think I am a thief."

No, Romulus was tempted to reply, only a less-than-convincing liar. "Sorry," he said. "I know you don't have the makings of a thief." He climbed to his feet and flicked the weed away. "Very well. You have until next week. But Allegra . . . come Monday, there will be an accounting."

As she tossed in her bed that night, Diana re-experienced the sensation of Rom's mouth on her wrist. Over and over, she felt the trace of his lips against her skin, until she was nearly mindless with longing.

She knew the truth now—Romulus did care for her. And he had vowed to look after her, even when she was no longer in his keeping. Surely such a pledge was not prompted by masculine hunger. There had to be other, finer feelings in a man's heart to spur him into making such a promise.

There had been no trace of lust in the gentle salute he had of-

fered, only tender affection. And yet it had sent her pulse staggering out of control. He may have been a stranger to her four days
ago, but he was now as much a part of her life as the air she
breathed and the sun on her face. And as much of a necessity.

And she suspected, recalling the shuddering breath he had taken
once he'd released her hand, that she had become such a necessity
to him. He had integrated her into his life and made her a part of his
world. But come Monday, she would no longer share that world,
and she pondered which of them would most mourn that loss. There
was no future for her on the island, and no bright prospect for her
anywhere away from it.

But she did have four more days to share with him. A great many
memories could be stored up in that time. And happiness needed to
be seized wherever and whenever it could be found—even if it was
of a limited duration. Paradise lost, she thought sadly. But not quite
yet.

"You are a sorry fool," Romulus murmured to himself as he lay
stretched out on his bed.

He'd had every intention of calling Allegra's bluff in the morning, hoping that the threatened banishment to Hamish House would
at last end her charade. And then he would have had some answers
to his questions.

But when he had held her hand against his mouth, when his heart
had started racing from the taste of her on his lips, all his questions
had become meaningless. And her calculated deception had become merely an amusing diversion. There was only Allegra. Nothing mattered but Allegra, here on his island, in his life. And so he
had lost all his resolve to send her away.

But before he set her free, he vowed, he would confront her and
admit that he had known all along who she was. Perhaps then she
would tell him why she had run away. Either that, or she would rail
at him for his own prevarication and tell him nothing. But he'd risk
it, all the same. It would be difficult enough to send her away, without believing he was returning her to some nameless threat. He
would have to steel himself to the inevitable. By Monday, Allegra
would be gone. And her problematic and all-too-enticing presence
in his life.

As he lay gazing up at the shadowed ceiling, he saw again the
provocative pose she had unknowingly affected as she drew her
hair up off her neck. He recalled the desire that had pulsed through

him, the clamoring need to lay her back against the steps and cover her slender body with his own.

He groaned as he pulled the pillow up over his face. If he didn't keep a rein on his feelings, she would be compromised in far more than name. He prayed he could hold out until Monday. It was four days away. Four bloody, long days.

Niall came the next day at midmorning. Diana was glad for the company, since Rom had said he'd be away until evening. The boy recalled a great deal of his earlier lessons and was even able to scratch out a few crudely written sentences under her watchful eye. She gave him a black crayon and some papers from Rom's desk to practice his letters; he crammed them into his breeches pocket before he set out for the river.

After he left, she led the cygnets out to the pond, carrying the two leaders, which Rom had marked with a tiny dot of ink on their downy heads. She envied them as they swam and played in the water. The weather hadn't broken—the heat and humidity bore down on her like a stifling weight, and the dark clouds again hovered on the horizon. She swore she couldn't recall a May to match it.

She waded into the shallow water, in an attempt to cool off, but the pond's bottom was slick with algae. She grimaced and quickly returned to the bank. She was pulling on the woven sandals Niall had brought her that morning, when she heard a rustling in the bushes behind her. Her head swiveled around in alarm. She was not about to let a fox or badger sneak up on her charges.

After twisting a low branch off a nearby tree, she went striding off in the direction of the noise, lashing at the bushes as she moved along the path. She was halfway back to the house, having discovered nothing more threatening than a pair of blackbirds, when she heard the frightened peeping of the cygnets. When she turned to run back to the pond, she nearly tripped over the first of them. There they were, all sixteen of them, scurrying up the path toward her, their little bills opening and closing as they cried out their dismay.

She sat down in surprise, and they tumbled right into her lap. She didn't know whether to laugh or cry. It was utterly gratifying to discover these small creatures had become so attached to her that they couldn't bear to let her out of their sight. Romulus was not, unfortunately, afflicted with the same need.

As she gathered in the last of her brood, she saw something that made her eyes widen. There was a footprint on the path. A small muddied impression. She shooed the cygnets away and scrambled to her feet. Lifting one foot, she carefully placed it above the print. It was only an inch longer than her foot. Rom's footprints were the stuff of legends, she recalled. Niall wore soft leather boots, but these were not smooth bootprints, they were more cobbled in texture.

Diana quickly herded her charges into the pen in the yard, and then returned to the spot on the path. She crouched low as she moved in the direction of the river, and was dismayed to find several more distinct prints. When she reached the tangled foliage that edged the water, she hid behind a tree and peered out. Near the tree there was a deep declivity carved into the muddy bank. It didn't take a lot of imagination to visualize a boat leaving that mark. In fact, Diana was not at all pleased by what her imagination was telling her—that the poacher had been on the island. The little river rat, with his little rat feet.

She bristled at the thought of that creature sneaking about on Rom's island. And though she'd always thought that mantraps, the large metal claws that could sever a poacher's leg, were vile things, she now wished that Rom had one stored in his shed. She was that angry.

She hurried back to the house, her face still set with fury. Wait until she told Rom that the poacher had had the temerity to cross the water and invade his territory. Halfway up the kitchen steps, she halted. No. She dared not tell him. Only yesterday she'd gotten her reprieve. But once Rom knew Argie Beasle had been on the island, he would send her away so fast her head would be spinning.

More lies, she thought, sadly, as she went through the kitchen door. More sins of omission.

It was late afternoon before Romulus headed for home. It had been a profitless day.

After his morning patrol, he'd taken a look in the 'Thrush. Argie Beasle was not in evidence there, and no one had seen him. Joe Black was also absent from his post, which only increased Rom's disquiet.

For the balance of the day, he hadn't been able to shake a vague sense of restlessness. He blamed it on the weather. The temperature soared and dark clouds loomed in the west, as though a storm was brewing. Now, as he made his way upstream, he saw that the clouds had blown over, and only a faint, ominous rumbling in the distance gave any indication that they had been there at all.

If he'd really probed the cause of his restlessness, Romulus knew, he could put a better name to it than the weather. It was Allegra.

For the entire day he had purposely kept away from the island, thinking the Thames would distract him from his disturbing thoughts of her. It hadn't worked worth a damn. He'd found the beauty of the river somehow flat. It had lost its ability to soothe and charm him, as though having shared it the one time with Allegra, he could no longer appreciate it alone. Every creature he stopped to watch reminded him of the quiet awe she had displayed that night, every bird in flight brought to mind her bright, wondering eyes.

He thought back to the time before the wild water had cast her up on the island. His life had been his own then. His river had been unaffected by her presence. Now her ghost seemed to float above every turning, beckoning to him. The spell of the Thames had been supplanted by another sort of witchery.

He toyed with the idea of taking Allegra on the river again. But after their encounter with the poacher, he knew it would be fool-hardy to place her at risk. More importantly, he didn't want to put his self control to the test. It was bad enough sharing the house with her, let alone a small boat.

Not that *her* behavior could in any way be faulted. The girl was guileless; there was nothing overtly seductive in her manner. And yet she captivated him like no other woman he'd met. But it wasn't only her effect on his body that drew him to her. It was her spirit and her humor. And the easy grace with which she had taken to life on his island.

He pictured her striding across the grass with her bright Gypsy skirt billowing behind her, laughing with her head thrown back. He had taken her fishing in the inlet last night at sundown, and he saw her again, poling the punt manfully back to the shore with her very first catch, an improbably large salmon. And then crouching beside the water to release the fish, once he had admired it properly. There was nothing like Allegra, with bits of bracken in her hair, and a sun-kiss of freckles across her nose, to steal a man's breath.

Every part of the island was her dominion. The house, the pond, the inlet, the cygnets . . . his heart.

Romulus began to row with determination, pulling hard against the current. He hoped the hot, sweaty work would at last erase her image from his mind.

As he passed the shallows near where Mortimer's boat lay hidden, he was distressed to see portions of the hull peeking through the scattered vines. "Deer," he muttered. They'd made a nice meal of his camouflage. He grounded the skiff and quickly re-covered the upturned rowboat, using some cedar branches which he knew would be less tempting to browsing wildlife. He stood at the edge of the water, wishing he had the courage to burn the boat. It was a taunting reminder of Allegra's true identity.

But it wouldn't matter in a few days' time. He could tow the damned thing back to Mortimer House, once Allegra had been returned home. But then maybe it wasn't wise to risk a visit there after he'd disposed of her. It would break his spirit to see her in that setting, wearing a stylish gown, surrounded by rich furnishings. He would surely seem the worst of buffoons to her, with his rough, woodsman's garb, his sun-darkened skin, and work-calloused hands. How ludicrous he would look compared to Sir Beveril.

Something inside Romulus rebelled at that thought. *Would Beveril truly be a better man for her? Could he possibly care for her more than you do, in spite of his refinements and his noble birth?*

The question still gnawed at him as he climbed into his boat and made his way back upstream toward the island. So lost in thought was he, that he didn't see the ferryboat hidden in the weeds across the river. He didn't see the two men who lay there in the grass, watching him with eager, satisfied eyes.

Romulus straddled the bench in the backyard and wearily tugged off his leather gaiters. Allegra called him a greeting from the open door of the kitchen and then went back to her cooking.

That prodding voice again rose up in him, repeating the things he already knew in his heart. He wanted to keep her here forever. It was as simple as that.

But she surely had some say in the matter. The fact that she dreaded returning home, did not necessarily mean she wanted to spend her life with him. He'd have to be daft to think it. She was stalling for time, that was all. He grew a little resentful at the thought that she'd been using him. And that he'd let her. He rubbed at his shins, where the leather had bitten into his skin. Perhaps in the next four days he could discover just where her loyalties lay. With him or with the perishing Parliamentary windbag.

He rose from the bench and went to the small soapstone trough that sat beneath the pump. Dousing himself with icy water, he washed away all the grime and sweat from his day on the river. Then he walked around to the front of the house and went in through the porch entrance.

As he tugged a clean shirt over his head and drew on his best corded breeches, he grinned at himself in the shaving mirror. A tall, auburn-haired scoundrel grinned back. *Not bad*, he thought as he tucked in his shirttails and knotted a cravat at his throat. That lean face and thick russet hair had ever drawn women to his side. Which was a good thing—because Romulus Perrin was going courting.

The kitchen was nearly intolerable from the heat of the hearth. Allegra's cheeks, as she turned to greet him, were flushed a deep pink. There was a smudge of flour on her nose and another on her chin. It was all Romulus could do not to kiss those marks away, wanting to taste her skin, hungry to savor the delicate line of her lips and the soft texture of her cheeks.

"Niall gave me his granty's recipe for eel pie—*and* he wrote it down himself," she announced proudly, lifting a crumpled paper from the table. "Apparently, he got the eels from the Yorrick's kitchen maid."

Romulus rolled his eyes. The Yorrick chit would be lucky if Niall didn't return the favor in kind. "I thought you didn't like eels," he said aloud.

"I've never tasted them. They do smell rather good, though." She motioned to the dutch oven.

The rich odor of baking pie was wafting through the room and Rom's stomach grumbled.

"Eel pie is a poor man's supper," he remarked somewhat gruffly. "Fit for laborers and Gypsies. It might be a bit . . . coarse for your taste."

Diana frowned. She understood exactly the meaning behind his words. "My taste might surprise you," she said tartly. "But if *you* mislike such rude fare, I can always serve you fish stew. That appears to be all you ate before I arrived here."

Romulus gave her a sheepish smile. "I might do better to ask for humble pie. I'm not being very gracious, considering you've been toiling away in this infernal kitchen."

"Yes, a little gratitude would be in order."

"Actually eel pie is one of my favorites," he said, leaning back against the edge of the table.

She eyed his pristine shirtfront and said with a grin, "And a good thing, since you have dressed for dinner. I only hope my meal does your efforts credit." As she spoke, she swiped a stray tendril of hair away from her forehead with the back of her hand, leaving yet another patch of flour there.

Romulus leaned forward, raising his hand to her face. "Stand still," he said in a low voice, as he stroked two fingers over her brow, removing the dusty white smudge. "I wager there's more flour on your face than in your pie crust," he teased as his caressing touch drifted down from brow to cheek.

Diana raised one hand to scrub at her chin.

He caught that hand firmly between his long fingers. "No, let me," he said. It came out like a sigh.

His green-gold eyes were holding her, as surely as the hand at her wrist. He had shifted away from the edge of the table, his upper body now angled down over hers. He slowly lowered his head, until his mouth was a hair's-breadth from her own.

The room had gone suddenly still, as though time had halted in its forward motion. There was a distant humming in Diana's ears. The heat that shimmered in the close space, making her lightheaded and weak at the knees, had nothing to do with the logs blazing in the fireplace. She gazed up at him, unable to breathe, as he drew his thumb over her lower lip, slowly, languidly. And all the while those gilded eyes held her captive.

"There," he whispered, his voice a husky rasp. "You look less like a morsel of pastry now."

When he drew back from her and swung onto one of the stools, Diana felt as though her insides had been scooped out. His touch made her feel replete, sated, but when that touch was withdrawn, there was nothing but an empty, hollow ache. *Sweet Jesus, why hadn't he kissed her?*

"I am a rather untidy cook," she said with a nervous laugh, trying to cover her disappointment.

He turned his gaze to the tabletop which was littered with bowls and pans, each one covered with the ubiquitous flour. At the center of the table, a crockery pitcher held a spray of pink flowers.

He cocked his head. "I see you have brought me campion today."

Yesterday, he recalled, the pitcher had contained clusters of narcissus and cornflower. Once again, Allegra had added something ineffable to his home, this house that he had never thought to adorn with a single blossom. "You'll have the island stripped bare before you are through."

Diana wrinkled her nose. "The island is overflowing with wild-flowers—I expect there are plenty to go around. And though I believe campion is accounted a weed, it does have a certain charm." She gave him a long, meaningful look as she spoke.

He flicked at one small blossom. "Yes, they are pretty enough. I am only surprised you find them so."

Oh, don't you see, Diana wanted to shout. *I like common wild-flowers. I don't mind eating rough Gypsy fare . . . I am not a sim-pering society chit who needs to sit on a satin pillow and be treated like a doll. I want a man who is of the earth, one who knows the ways of the wild things.*

How could he have spent time with her and not known what pleased her? Not known that he pleased her? She swore the next time he came close to her, as he'd done just now, she was going to throw herself into his arms. That would leave him in little doubt of her tastes.

But instead of railing at him, she merely sniffed and said, "Perhaps you are not as observant as you like to think." Then she turned back to her cooking, stirring furiously at the soup which bubbled on the hob.

So she didn't see the slow smile that crept along his wide mouth.

It was too hot to dine in the kitchen, so once the pie was baked, they carried their meal out onto the porch. Romulus brought the tea table from the sitting room and placed it between the two wooden benches.

In the meantime, in keeping with the festive spirit that the eel pie seemed to have elicited, Diana ran to her room and quickly changed into her blue blouse, after liberally sprinkling herself with cool water from the small basin that sat on one of the crates. Romulus had unearthed a small mirror for her, and she now craned before it to survey herself. The heat from the kitchen had caused her hair to clench into tiny ringlets. A street urchin, she sighed, echoing Beveril's words, surely had better tamed hair. Having neither pins nor combs to restrain it, she coaxed the curling mass back from her face with the bright kerchief. After slipping on the two silver bracelets that Niall had brought her that morning, she returned to the porch.

Romulus was just opening a bottle of wine.

"Is this a special occasion?" she asked as she slid onto her bench.

He looked up from his uncorking. "Eel pie is always a special oc-casion," he pronounced with a wink as he poured some of the deep red liquid into her wine glass.

Wine glass? she thought in bewilderment. They normally drank from porcelain mugs. Where the devil had he gotten wine glasses from? Or the elegant damask cloth that covered the table?

"You've certainly made this very elegant," she said as she lifted the glass to her mouth. "I don't suppose there's a footman hovering behind that rhododendron over there?"

Romulus shook his head. "No. Just the two of us. As always."

He'd said the words with such warmth that Diana was blushing in happy confusion before she realized that his pronouncement was not quite true. Earlier in the day there had been an intruder on the island, and she was still not certain how she could reveal the fact without precipitating her own exile. But she determinedly put all thoughts of poachers and intruders from her mind. Romulus was in a rare mood tonight and she was not going to sully it.

The eel pie was a complete success. After three helpings, Rom-ulus pushed his plate away with a groan. "You've outdone Naill's granty, little witch."

He then reclined on the bench, his wine glass held aloft between his fingers, regarding Diana with an amused, mellow expression on his face as she struggled through her second helping.

"It's so good," she mumbled, her mouth half full. "But I will burst if I take another bite, I don't think I've ever tasted anything so fine."

"But then you wouldn't recall it, even if you had," he noted with a grin.

After dinner, Romulus drew her into the sitting room. "I promised to show you my books," he explained.

"You did indeed," she said with a wide smile.

"Anything you fancy?" He had carried the wine bottle in from the porch and was refilling each of their glasses. Diana had only ever drunk ladylike ratafia, and Rom's heady claret was already making inroads on her senses. In fact, she couldn't recall ever feel-ing quite so happy. Or so content.

"Oh, I want you to choose," she said as she settled into one of the chairs. "They're your books, after all."

She watched him as he knelt before the bookcase's lower shelves. His hair curled over the high collar of his dress shirt, and she could see the sloping muscles of his back straining against the thin fabric.

"I hope you like birds." He looked up with an apologetic grin. Diana blushed that he had caught her practically drooling over him. "I seem to have very narrow tastes."

He pried out one of the large volumes, then sat in the chair beside hers. He began to leaf through the pages of illustrations, which had been etched in black, and then colored in rich, subtle hues. Eventually Diana's neck began to ache—she had to twist around in her chair to look at the pictures—so she slid onto the floor and sat up on her knees, her elbows planted on the arm of his chair.

"Better this way?" she asked tilting her face up to him.

She thought he shuddered. But he said nothing, only continued to turn the pages and explain about each bird in his rich, melodic voice. She paid special attention to the pictures of waterfowl, and pleased him when she was able to identify several of the birds they had seen on the river.

It wasn't long before the wine made her sleepy. Which was dashed unfair, she thought, since Romulus was being particularly approachable tonight. The second time her head nodded against his sleeve, he closed the book and stood up.

"Bed?" he asked as he drew her to her feet.

For one glorious, disordered moment, she thought he was propositioning her. But then he gently propelled her toward the storeroom door.

"The cygnets?" she cried softly. "I left them outside in the pen."

"Yes, and they will be fine. I intended to move them out there on Monday. I only left them in the storeroom to keep you company."

"*Oh . . .*" the word seemed to drift out of her mouth. She gave him a beaming smile. "You're such a clever swankeeper, Romulus."

"Yes, and I suspect you're a little drunk." His voice was dry, but his eyes held nothing but fondness.

She gave him an owl-like stare and drew herself up. "Yes, I am. A little. It feels rather nice."

"You won't thank me in the morning," he said reaching past her to push open the storeroom door.

She turned and stood weaving in the doorway. The two empty crates seemed so . . . well, empty. "Oh," she said mournfully. "I have to sleep alone."

Romulus made a muffled sound behind her. She couldn't tell if it was a chuckle or an oath. "Yes . . . but if it's a problem, I suppose I could accommodate you."

She spun around to him and almost lost her footing. He caught her before she fell. Caught her and held her tight against his chest.

Her eyes blinked up at him. "*You* will acco-mo-nate me?"

She was standing on tiptoes, trying to facilitate any urge he might have to kiss her. But even with her body stretched to the limit, her lips were still sadly remote from his.

"The cygnets," Rom said into her hair. "I'll bring in the swans to keep you company."

"No," she said darkly, with an exaggerated shake of her head. "They make too much noise. *Peep, peep, peep, peep . . .*"

"That's done it—" Romulus announced. "You're foxed." He swung her up into his arms and carried her into the room. He didn't precisely dump her onto the bed, but her descent was unexpectedly swift.

She lay there gazing up at him. "Aren't you going to tuck me in?"

His eyes blazed for an instant, then he stepped back from the bed. "It's a warm night—you'll survive."

Diana watched as he blew out the single candle on her makeshift vanity table, and then went swiftly from the room. With a delighted chortle she turned and smothered her laughter in the pillow.

Thank heavens for James's cousin, Ferdie Pringle, the worst tippler in the *ton*. She had been observing his intoxicated antics at numerous parties during the past month. And now it had paid off. Pretending to be drunk, she declared to herself, was a dashed sight easier than pretending to have lost your memory.

Not that she was completely sober—she'd never have had the nerve to behave in such a manner with Romulus if she'd been unimpaired. And she'd never have dared to be so brazen with him, drunk or not, if he hadn't been so unusually mellow all night.

How lovely it felt to be lifted in his arms. And to be carried to her bed. And how his eyes had blazed with desire when she'd asked to be tucked in. The image now thrilled her all over again.

Next time she'd make him do it without the wine.

Chapter 7

Many hours later Diana was abruptly awakened. She had managed to squirm out of her skirt and blouse before she fell asleep, and now lay on top of the coverlet wearing only her chemise. Rom had been right—it was a warm night. It was now also an extremely stormy night.

Thunder crashed directly overhead, shaking the house to its fieldstone foundation, while lightning flashed in bright prongs, briefly illuminating the room. The heavy rain was slashing sideways, in through the open window. Diana climbed from her bed, intent on shifting the boxes that lay in the path of the rain. As she brushed past the empty crates at her bedside, she realized the cygnets were outside in this fierce storm. She'd better rouse Romulus so that they could fetch them back into the house.

She walked rapidly into the unlit sitting room and nearly collided with him.

"Oh!" she yelped softly, reeling back in surprise.

He thrust past her, moving swiftly across the room, a tall shadow, shapeless and spectral. As the lightning flashed again, she saw that he wore only his knee breeches—his chest and legs were bare, the corded muscles and smooth skin exposed by the harsh white light. But that was nothing compared to the stark, glazed expression on his pale face.

"What?" she cried with a touch of panic in her voice as she reached toward him. "Romulus, what is it?"

"It's nothing." His voice was flat, toneless. "Go back to bed."

Shivering in the darkness, she watched as he came toward her, his hands clenched at his sides.

"*Go!*" he growled when he reached her, his head snaking forward.

The thunder resonated through the stucco walls of the room as it boomed repeatedly overhead. Romulus had his hands up now, fisted on either side of his head, as though to block out the noise.

Diana's hands sought his, but he swung away with an violent oath. "For Christ's sake, Allegra, go away! I don't want you here. Not now."

She had never been so frightened in her life. Not for herself, but for him, for his pain, for the unguarded torment he was experiencing. Was this the madness that the villagers had seen in him, this wild-eyed terror, that slashed at her heart? How in God's name could she help him?

He was heading for the hallway now, back toward his bedroom. She ran to block the doorway.

"No!" she keened. And then she said in a more rational voice, "It's only a thunderstorm, Romulus."

"Let me pass," he rasped ominously.

She mustered all her courage and shook her head. "No, you shouldn't be left alone."

He gave a low laugh and said in a voice laced with despair, "There is only alone, Diana. That's all there ever is."

He lifted her off her feet and set her aside. Her hands clung to him, her fingers digging hard into his flesh. He tried to swipe her away, but she held on even tighter.

"Not alone," she cried over the sound of the storm, shaking him with all her strength. "Not any longer."

He stood there wavering for several seconds, and then with an inarticulate groan he sank to his knees, carrying her with him to the carpet. She pulled his head down, cradling it in her arms, as she murmured endearments and soothing words against his hair. "It's all right, Romulus. . . . I'm here. . . . It's just a storm, love . . . just a noisy old storm."

In time the thunder and lightning ceased, leaving only a barrage of rain pelting on the roof. Once the tumult had died down, Romulus stopped trembling in her arms. He nestled his head deeper into her shoulder and tightened his hold around her waist.

"Now you know," he said in a reedy whisper, "why the villagers think me mad."

Diana let her fingers comb through his tousled hair. "In Yorkshire, once," she said evenly, "I saw a fellow who stands on his head for hours at a time. Now that is my idea of a proper madman."

He chuckled softly against her throat. "In Delhi they would call him a holy man." He drew his head back to gaze at her. "I'm not truly mad," he said in a voice fit to rend her heart. "It's the storms. They fill me with terror and rage. I usually take the skiff out and row off these fits . . . but I didn't want to leave you alone."

"Well, then," she pointed out with utter logic, "you can't really be mad . . . not if you had a care for me in the midst of your raging."

"Yes . . . I suppose that's true," he said haltingly. He shifted his position so that he was now leaning back against the wall of the sitting room, still holding her close in his arms. "But I sensed a storm was coming . . . I should have warned you about . . . this."

"I'm relieved it was the thunderstorm that set you off," she said. "And not my eel pie."

He lowered his head and touched his nose to hers. "You are very glib for a woman who has recently wrestled a madman into submission."

"Is that what I did?" Her hands were stroking over his chest, feeling the warm skin, the slight rasp of hair, and the steady, vital thudding of his heart. Her voice lowered a notch and lost any trace of humor as she added, "Romulus, you must tell me why this thing happens to you."

She felt him shrug. "That's not an answer," she admonished him gently. "To toss your own words back at you—I cannot help you to face your fear, if you will not even speak of it."

"You didn't heed me when I said it, as I recall," he drawled into the darkness.

"Ah, but you are much wiser than I am." She laid her face against his cheek and rubbed it slowly back and forth. "And I want you to be well."

"Do you?" he asked as his hand lifted to her hair. "Faith, I believe you do."

"Then tell me." Her splayed hands pressed against the heated surface of his bare chest. "Please."

"Yes," he said wearily. "Perhaps you need to hear it." He shifted her from his lap and rose to his feet.

Diana scrambled up, and then stood peering at him intently. His voice had gone cold again, and she wished she could see his face. "Shall I light a candle?"

"No," he said, as he moved toward his desk. "I've never spoken of this to a single soul. I need the darkness now, if I am to tell you." He opened the desk drawer and she saw the glint of something metallic. He unscrewed the cap from the flask and jolted his head back. "Brandy," he said as he turned to her. "It's what I came out here for. Even in this light I can see your disapproval."

She sniffed. "I can hardly disapprove of brandy, after the amount of wine I had with dinner."

"Have a look then," he said, handing her the flask. "Here is the beginning of the story."

She carried it to the window, where in the faint, watery light she could make out a design etched into the metal. Her fingers traced over the raised pattern. "It's an insignia of some sort."

"From my regiment in the army."

She took a quick drink of the fiery liquid, hoping he wouldn't notice. She forgot she was silhouetted in the window.

"You've turned into a proper little tippler," he said as he took back the flask and refitted the cap.

Diana blushed in the darkness. "I . . . um, wasn't exactly as . . . intoxicatd as I led you to believe."

"Another game, *bella*?"

Diana drifted over to him. "What did you call me?"

"Don't change the subject. You were a rather endearing drunk, if a bit over the top."

"So you knew I was . . ."

Romulus snaked an arm around her waist. "I always know when you are . . ."

"What?" Her head angled back. He was going to kiss her. She could feel it in her bones.

But then Romulus shook himself and abruptly withdrew his arm. "Sit over there." He prodded her toward the sofa. "If you want to hear this sorry tale."

She did as he asked, curling her feet up under her chemise. He stood a slight distance away, the fingers of one hand resting upon the back of his desk as he spoke.

"As you have surmised, I was a soldier in Wellington's army."

"What about before that? Before the army?" she asked.

"That has no bearing on this story."

"Humor me," Diana said earnestly. "What became of you after you left Italy with your father?"

She heard him sigh in the darkness. "We lived in Wiltshire. My father had come into some money from a distant relation and was able to give me a proper education. When I was seventeen, I went off to a university near Bristol. Afterward, I found work as an estate manager, near my father's home. I was all the family he had, you see, and I wanted to be near him. Two years later, he . . . he succumbed to a wasting illness. I needed to get away from England then. Spain seemed like a decent substitute for Italy . . . even if there was a war going on. With my inheritance, I purchased a lieu-tenancy in the artillery corps." He drew a long breath. "But I dis-covered fairly quickly that I was not cut out for carnage."

"I don't believe anyone is," Diana observed.

"No, you're wrong. Some men look forward to fighting, to the glory of battle. But in spite of my distaste for war, I remained in the service, even got promoted to captain. I stayed in because of my friends in the regiment—a group of young officers, aristocrats every one, who had been at Oxford together. In the general way of things, I would have given them a wide berth, but they hounded me and had at me, until I was drawn into their ranks. It's surpris-ing they gave me the time of day, considering what a crusty fellow I am."

"Most surprising," she agreed dryly.

"They were an idle, pampered lot, lounging about the mess tent with their claret and card games, full of pranks and silly amuse-ments." He stopped a moment. When he continued again his voice held a distinct measure of awe. "But they were the bravest soldiers I've ever seen, Allegra. The best leaders of men and the best com-panions in the field. They taught me not to judge people by their trappings."

"But were you so different from them? You'd been to univer-sity, you'd traveled abroad."

Romulus scoffed. "We were worlds apart. They were sons of noblemen, I, the son of a river warden."

Diana heard the bitterness in his voice and understood its source. Romulus Perrin had somehow risen above his humble be-ginnings, but he was trapped between classes, neither yeoman nor gentleman.

"They apparently didn't feel there was anything lacking in you," she said a bit sharply.

Romulus grunted. "War does that—bonds the unlikeliest people together."

"But what became of them, these friends of yours?"

There was a long silence. Diana thought Romulus had lost his train of thought. When he continued, his voice was clipped. "We were captured by the French—at Albuera. My guns had been left unsupported by cavalry, and a French rout cleared out what was left of the infantry. We had a damned Sunday soldier from the Horse Guards leading our action. He didn't know a field maneuver from a filet of beef. But it's a moot point. He was shot off his fine, blooded stallion just before we were taken."

"What happened then?"

"Prison," he said simply. "French prison. Which means maggoty bread and foul water, beatings and whippings. The injured soldiers were not tended, not given any doctoring except what I could supply."

She drew a sharp breath. "That's inhuman."

With a shrug he continued, "They have no reason to love us, the French. I daresay we treat our prisoners no better. Though I pray that will change someday."

"How long were you there?"

"Nearly six months. Many of the men died in that time."

Diana heard the chilling emptiness in his tone. "How is it you were able to get free?"

"I bribed a guard, and he allowed me to escape with the remainder of my men."

"Bribed him? How? I would guess you had no money."

"The guard had a family living nearby. One of his children was dying from typhus—it was rife in both the prison and the town. I told him I would nurse his little girl if he would arrange an escape for my men. He'd seen me caring for the soldiers who were stricken with the disease and thought I was a physician."

"Did you cure her?" she asked, already knowing the answer in her heart.

"I got her through the worst of it. She was young and had not been weakened by starvation and abuse as my men had. She survived, and afterward the guard engineered our escape. I speak passable French and so we managed to get to the coast. I contacted a smuggler in Dieppe, and he carried us to Dover."

"What a relief it must have been for you, to be home again."

He shook his head slowly. "I was not the same man who had left England three and a half years earlier. The time in prison had worn down my reserves. I was still in shock, I suppose. I had managed to save a young girl, but had lost every one of my friends from the regiment. One by one, those gallant souls succumbed to the deprivations of that vile place. After I returned, I discovered why my well-born friends had not been paroled, as is customary with wealthy soldiers taken in battle—it was mistakenly reported that they had died in the fighting. That damned mistake was the final straw for me . . . the final straw."

Diana's heart twisted at the hollow despair in his voice. He had done all in his power to save his men, and had even managed to get the survivors back to England. But it was clear from his tone that he gave himself little credit for his deeds. On the contrary, he seemed full of self-loathing.

"What of the storms, Romulus?" she coaxed gently.

"Ah, yes. The storms that turn me into a madman." His voice lowered. "The whole time I was in prison, I heard the cannons from that last battle, booming in my head. Over and over. Day and night. It was a death knell, Allegra. I knew I should have died there in that prison . . . with my friends. That's what the guns were saying, '*You. You.* It should have been *you.*'"

Diana leaned from the sofa to reach for his hand. "And that is why the storms drive you into a frenzy? Because the thunder sounds like artillery fire?"

"Bloody foolish, isn't it?" He tugged his hand back from her. "I've gotten over the worst of it. But when Lady Hamish found me in the hospital, I was a broken man. I couldn't sleep, could barely eat. I still don't understand how she could have offered employment to such a creature. And it's no wonder the people of Treypenny thought I was deranged." He added in a distant voice, "Sometimes I'm not sure they're far off."

"Don't they know about what you did in the war?"

"Why should they care?" he muttered.

She slid off the sofa and went to stand before him. He looked past her, out the rain-dappled panes of the window. Diana grit her teeth. "Because you are a hero, that's why. What sort of father did you have, who never taught you to be proud of yourself? For being courageous and strong. For helping others when they needed you." When he made no reply, she flung away from him in frustration. "I think you *must* be daft," she snapped over her shoulder. "If you can't see those things."

"Eleven men died, Allegra."

"And how many lived?"

"Eight," he said. "Only eight."

"I wager those men don't think 'only' anything. Or their families, either. And there was the little girl you saved. And Niall . . . and me. There, that's evened the score, hasn't it? Eleven lost. Eleven saved."

Romulus made no comment. Diana returned to him and twined her arms around his shoulders. She could feel him trembling under her hands. "You were a captain," she said softly. "You probably watched men die under your command in every battle."

"True enough," he whispered hoarsely.

"And yet you don't blame yourself for those deaths. The men in prison with you were soldiers, Rom. They took a risk every time they marched into the field, the risk of being killed outright or of being captured and dying in prison."

"It's not the same thing!" he snarled.

"It is exactly the same thing!" she stormed back, pummeling his chest with her fists. It felt like granite beneath her hands. "I'm sorry your friends died, Romulus," she cried hoarsely. "But you can't spend the rest of your life regretting something you couldn't prevent."

She recalled the bleak anguish that had dulled his eyes when he'd killed the injured swan. Another failure, another unendurable loss. She knew then why keeping the swans safe had become almost an obsession with him. The brave, aristocratic young men had died, and Romulus saw protecting the swans as some means of reparation—preserving their elegant beauty for a world he could never be part of.

"It should have been me." He repeated in a disembodied voice. "*They* had everything to live for."

Diana cried out fiercely, "No, *you* have everything to live for. Oh, but you don't want to be healed, do you? You'd rather hide away on this island, letting your guilt destroy you, while you shut out the rest of the world. It's a convenient place to escape to, isn't it?"

"You should know," he answered tersely.

She stiffened and stepped back. "No, I'm not here to escape. I stayed on until I could make a decision. Because, like you, I had a tear in my soul. A small one, I grant, compared to yours. But you fixed it, Rom. It is completely healed. And now I know what I must do."

"Then I congratulate you," he said in a cutting voice as he moved away from her. "And if you have any wisdom at all, you will heed what I have told you tonight. There are some wounds that are beyond healing. Some forms of madness that never go away."

"I refuse to believe that," she said heatedly.

"It doesn't matter what you believe. I know it to be true. Now I am for my bed. All this melodrama has worn me down." He brushed past her.

"What of the cygnets?" she called out, recalling the mission that had sent her from her room. Perhaps caring for the chicks would distract him from his pain. "They're still outside—in the rain."

He stopped and turned. "They're *swans*, for God's sake. Try to use your head once in a while, Allegra." Then he went purposefully from the room, finding his way in the dark like a cat.

Diana sank down into a chair. Her heart was weighted with sadness. She had gotten what she wanted, it appeared—a genuine hero. But one who thought himself completely unworthy of the title.

His story explained so many of the contradictory things about him. He was not a laborer by trade, after all, but had been an officer in Wellington's army, a man of stature and consequence. He had gone to university—which accounted for his refined speech and his appreciation of literature. And his painful recounting of his stay in the French prison gave her a complete understanding of why he was so loath to put another man behind bars, even one as detestable as Argie Beasle.

He had come to the island under Lady Hamish's patronage, not as a hireling, but to be healed. It was clear the river had worked its magic on Rom's broken body and his shattered nerves, but Diana feared it had done little to mend his soul. Not in the deep, dark places where self-recrimination and guilt resided.

She saw the glint of his flask lying on the open panel of the desk. Maybe if she drank herself into a stupor she could forget the searing pain she'd seen in his eyes, visible even in the darkness, as he'd told her his version of the story—the one where he thought himself culpable for so many deaths. If there was any justice in the world, she thought as she tipped the flask up to her mouth, one day he would believe her version. And then he might truly begin to heal.

Chapter 8

Diana awoke with a raging headache. Not that it was anyone's fault but her own. She had stayed in the sitting room after Romulus stalked out, finishing off the contents of his flask.

She climbed from her bed and dragged on her clothing with slow, studied movements. The house was quiet as she tiptoed into the kitchen. Romulus was gone, his rucksack missing from its peg in the corner. Diana set the kettle on the hob for tea, and then eased herself gingerly onto a stool.

She had made a decision last night, before the brandy addled her wits—she was not leaving on Monday. This island was where she belonged. It was her home. Somehow she had to convince Rom of that.

She was still gnawing at the problem when Niall came bounding up the back steps, whistling his usual tune. "No!" she cried out as he started to slam the door behind him. It was too late. It thundered home and she put her hands over her ears to shut out the booming noise.

Niall eyed her with a wry grin. "Been having a night of it, then?"

She nodded. "I drank too much wine with dinner. I . . . I don't think lessons are a possibility today."

He pulled up a stool. "I can't stay long. I only came to tell you we're having a celebration tonight. The Yorricks have won their court case and have promised we can camp on their land as long as we like."

"That's nice," she remarked halfheartedly.

"I . . . I was wondering if you wanted to come?"

Diana raised her head off her hands. "Me? Romulus doesn't even allow me near the river by daylight. I doubt he would let me traipse over to Treypenny."

"It's not till evening, our celebration. It was just a thought. He's invited, too, of course."

"I'll tell him," she said. "But you know Mr. Starch and Vinegar. No amusements for him."

"You two have had a row, haven't you?" Niall was moving to ward off the kettle's whistle before it sent Diana cowering under the table. "It was only a matter of time."

"What do you mean?"

Niall grinned over his shoulder. "I told you . . . he's prickly. And it must be playing fast and loose with his conscience to be keeping you here."

"*What?*" Her voice had gone suddenly cold.

The boy bit at his lip and looked alarmed for an instant. Then a smile eased over his face. "It's nothing. I was just rambling. Where does he keep the teacups?"

Diana was still looking at him with sullen suspicion. "*Niall. . . ?*"

He shrugged. "Don't pay me any mind. More hair than brains, my granty says. Here, drink your tea and you'll feel worlds better. Now I've got to be off." He turned for the door. "Oh, one more thing. I've got an important message for Romulus. You might want to write it down."

"I believe I can remember it," she said as she laid her head on her crossed arms and closed her eyes.

He gazed at her lowered head with great skepticism. She looked like she was still fairly jugbit. "Suit yourself. Tell him Argie Beasle has been out on the river with Wald Chipping. Thick as thieves they are. But that's not the worst of it—the Yorrick's boatman swears he saw Argie on the island."

Tell me something I don't know, Diana remarked to herself. "Yes," she said aloud. "I'll remember."

"And don't forget the celebration," he called from the top step. "My granty's perishing to meet you."

Niall closed the door noiselessly on his way out, which was a small blessing. It was balanced, however, by the curiously provocative statement he had made about Romulus. What had given Niall the idea that Rom was feeling guilty for keeping her on the island? She was the one who kept refusing to leave. And after last night's wrenching revelation, she had no doubt that he wanted to see the back of her as soon as possible. He hadn't yet discovered how stubborn a Yorkshirewoman could be. But he would.

Diana spent the early part of the afternoon floating in the punt, waiting for her headache to subside. It was midafternoon when she returned to take the cygnets to the pond. They were feeding themselves now on the grass in the pen, and when they weren't eating, they terrorized the heron on the other side of the partition, leaping up and peeping furiously against the netting.

As she led them along the path, she kept a watchful eye out for the river rat. As a precaution, she had taken Rom's walking staff from beside the door. And she had every intention of using it on an intruder.

The storm had driven away the fierce heat and the breeze which blew over the island had grown almost chilly. She would need to expand her wardrobe if she stayed on the island. A warm cashmere shawl would be her first purchase. If she'd had any money, that was. It occurred to her that James's handsome dowry would be quickly rescinded when he learned of her intentions to live with a red-haired madman.

Romulus found her reclining on her favorite pondside rock, half asleep in the sun.

"Allegra," he said softly.

She stirred and then sat up. "Hello," she said, blinking several times. At least he was speaking to her. That was something. But his face still appeared taut and strained.

"Are you preparing to repel a French invasion?" He prodded the walking staff with the toe of his boot. "You may be carrying this guardian of the cygnets business a bit far."

"I saw a fox," she lied blithely. "Over there." She pointed to the far end of the pond.

"That's odd," he said frowning. "In ten months here, I've never seen a single fox."

"Maybe he swam over," she offered helpfully.

He gazed out over the pond. "Then we'd best keep them inside tonight. To be on the safe side."

Diana rose and dusted off her skirt. Together they led the cygnets back to the house and settled them in their crates. As Rom closed the door, she said matter-of-factly, "Niall left a message for you this morning."

Rom's eyes narrowed. "Yes?" He drew the single syllable out.

"The Yorricks have won their case against the Talbots, so tonight the Gypsies are having a celebration." She stopped to weigh her next words. She was torn between her desire to visit the Gypsy camp and the fear that Niall would surely tell Rom about

Argie if they met up with him at the gathering. Finally she said haltingly, "He thought you might like to go there."

"Me?" Romulus frowned. "What business would I have at a Gypsy gathering?"

"It's not just the Gypsies. The Yorrick servants will be there, as well. Niall invited me, you see."

"Oh, I do indeed see."

"Don't get on your high ropes, Rom. I have never been to a gypsy camp. I thought it might be amusing."

His eyes darkened. "Foolishness, is more like it. And was that the only message Niall gave you?"

Diana gazed back at him with sudden disquiet. "Wh-what else would there be?"

Romulus uttered a weary sigh. "This," he said, pulling a tattered sheet of paper from his coat pocket. He handed it to her. "I found it down by the slip."

The message was scrawled in black crayon on a receipt from the general store in Treypenny. "rom," it read. "wld an argy ar wachng yu. argy has bin on th eyland. i tuld alegra, but she dint rite it dwn. nial"

Drat the boy, Allegra groaned to herself. Niall had properly let the cat out of the bag now.

She let the paper drop from her fingers. "I'm sorry I didn't tell you—it didn't seem—important."

He gave her a withering look. "You didn't tell me because you knew how I would react to this news."

"What does it matter if he's seen me?" she cried. "I'm dressed like a Gypsy . . . how could he know I'm not just some woman you brought here."

"I have a feeling Beasle knows exactly who you are."

"Then why don't you ask him?" she responded archly.

"I'd rather ask you," he growled. "Look, Allegra, the time for foolish games and playacting is over. Argie would like nothing better than to make trouble for me. The only way I can prevent that is to send you away."

She tipped her head back and looked into his green-gold eyes, searching for some sign of regret, some sadness over the fact that he was about to banish her from his life. All she saw was stern intent.

"What if I refuse to go," she said heatedly. "I am not a coward."

"Perhaps I am, where you're concerned. The gypsies can lie for you until the Second Coming, but it won't save your reputation if Beasle has seen you here."

She didn't dare tell him that he most likely already had. And in that case, Rom was the one who was in danger. He'd lose everything that mattered to him if it was discovered that he had sheltered her. Could she ask him to venture so much? He needed to remain here, she'd seen that last night. He still had a great deal of healing to do, healing that would not occur if he was sent away from the island in disgrace.

"Well?" he said gently. "Will you go peacefully or will I have to truss you up like a Christmas goose?"

"I don't want to make trouble for you," she said with a sigh. "But I am so afraid of losing this haven."

He looked down at her as he rubbed one finger over his upper lip. There was a softening in his eyes then, the hard determination replaced by a gleam of compassion. "Then there's something you need to see."

She trailed him into the backyard and watched in bewilderment, as he snagged the cloth that hung on the door to the heron's enclosure and entered the pen. The heron stalked away, and Romulus followed, speaking to him gently. He wrapped the cloth over the bird's head, then tucked him under one arm.

As he came out, Diana looked up at him with sorrowful eyes. Romulus chucked her under the chin with his free hand. "Don't look so sad, my witch. It's a happy day for our reluctant guest."

She followed him along the path, skipping sometimes to keep up with his long-legged stride. When they reached the southern tip of the island, he set the bird down on its side and carefully removed the splint.

"Come see," he said over his shoulder. "But don't go too near the water in case someone is watching."

Diana moved in closer. The heron's leg was now completely healed, except for a slight ridge where the break had occurred. Rom drew the cloth from the bird's head and then stepped away, pulling Diana back into the trees. The heron flapped his wings erratically, lofting himself awkwardly into a standing position. He took several tentative steps, cocking his head once or twice to gaze at his mended leg. Then after shooting a baleful look at the two humans behind him, he ran slowly forward into the shallows, lifting his wide wings to catch the air currents over the river. Diana held her breath, as for an instant the bird hung in midair. Then with a rush of motion he sailed out over the water, flying low, in long, graceful swoops.

Romulus leaned down and whispered. "That is the way of wild things, Allegra. They must return always to their true home."

"I'm not a wild thing!"

"Ah, but I think you are. Untamed and unfettered." His hands slid to her shoulders and tightened slightly. "A wild thing who hasn't yet learned to trust."

"I trust you, Romulus," she signed. It would be heaven to lean against him, to feel the vital strength of him along her back. But his hands held her away from him.

"Then tell me, little witch. Trust me enough to tell me what I've waited nearly a week to hear."

Diana thought she must be dreaming . . . could he mean that he wanted her to tell him of her love for him? But her illusions were shattered when he added, "Tell me why you lied about losing your memory."

"Oh," she uttered, not attempting to hide her disappointment at that less-than-ardent question.

He waited, turning her so he could see her face. She stood there with a blank expression in her eyes.

"That's all? Just 'Oh.' You get high marks for brevity, my girl, but I'm not going to let you sidestep the issue. We've got to get this settled between us before we part."

"*No!*" It slipped out before she could prevent it. All her heartache was contained in that one tiny word.

He tipped her chin back with one finger. "Don't look at me like your world has just ended. Sometimes the closing of one episode only marks the beginning of another."

She shifted her head back from his touch. "If we are to part, then what does it matter if I lied to you?"

Romulus ran his teeth over his lower lip. "I . . . I was hoping you would make me a gift of your honesty before . . . before we had to say our farewells."

She felt the anguish begin in the pit of her stomach. It radiated out through her body until it reached every nerve ending. She had never known such pain. All the wise voices that had warned her that this idyll must end had not prepared her for the shattering numbness that would overpower her when that time came.

"I cannot speak of it," she said raggedly. "Except to say that I am sorry I deceived you."

"I'll row you to Hamish House first thing in the morning. But I'd like to hear from your own lips where your real home might be."

"My home is not along the river," she said with sudden intensity. "It is hundreds of miles from here."

He sighed. "More lies, Allegra? You came to me on the water, or have you forgotten? You couldn't have lasted more than a few miles in that maelstrom without overturning or having your boat's bottom stove in. I wager you live within four miles of this very spot."

"That is mere guesswork on your part."

Romulus flicked her cheek. "You forget, the river has no secrets from me."

Diana eyed him suspiciously. "And what of the secrets you keep from me?"

He refused to meet her eyes. "I bared my soul to you last night . . . or have you forgotten that?"

"Little good that did either of us," she uttered crossly. "Yes, you were honest with me last night. But you don't offer yourself the same courtesy. At least *I* am not so foolish as to lie to myself."

"No, only to others," he snapped. "Sweet Jesus, Allegra. I don't want to fight with you. These are our last hours together. What difference does it make now if either of us has lied?"

"None at all, now that you are determined to be rid of me."

"Ach, don't say it in such a way." He reached toward her, to comfort her, to soothe the hurt expression from her soft mouth. She ended up enfolded in his arms, her head pressed to his shoulder. Just one embrace, he thought, one blessed moment with Allegra held against his heart, then he would set her free. Forever.

But she had wrapped her arms about his neck and was clinging to him with all her strength. "Don't make me leave," she whispered urgently against his shirt. "I'm not sure I can bear it."

"I think you can," he said as he gently disengaged himself from her. "We've had a splendid time of it this past week. But you must go. We both know it is the only way. Those first steps may be a bit wobbly, my dearest girl, but you will fly."

At the moment she looked as though all she wanted to do was cry. He saw the first tears glistening on her lashes and knew if she shed even one of them, he would be lost.

"Now come along," he said with false heartiness. "We've still got the cygnets to feed."

Nancy Butler

"Yes," she muttered as she followed behind him. "More creatures who will be booted out of the only haven they've ever known."

"What was that?" Romulus had stopped on the path to wait for her to catch up.

"Nothing," she replied, gazing at the tips of her sandals. "Must be the wind in the trees."

Rom looked up at the oak and ash that rose above them. Not one leaf stirred in that wide field of green. He cast her a look of aching fondness before he moved off again. "Yes, I expect that's what I heard."

Diana insisted on feeding the cygnets alone. She needed some time to herself to calm the wretched confusion in her heart. If she stayed, she knew, he would be accused of compromising her and forfeit his position with Lady Hamish. But if she went home, she would lose him forever. She couldn't imagine Romulus coming to Mortimer House to pay court to her in his rude buckskin jacket and water-stained leather gaiters. Last night at supper he had worn neat, corded breeches and a fine lawn shirt, but even they fell far short of what the Mortimers would consider proper gentlemanly apparel. Helen would look shocked and scornful, and James would have him thrown from the house.

Her despair was mixed with a certain inarticulate anger that the sneaking Argie Beasle had been the cause of her imminent banishment. How infuriating that a miserable river rat had come between her and Romulus. And she could not think of any possible way to foil him. Not unless Romulus cast his scruples to the winds and asked her to stay with him.

Tell him, a tiny voice piped at her, as though the cygnets spoke in unison. *Tell Romulus you love him*.

She could do it, she thought. She could declare her feelings. This might be her last chance to say the words. But still the petrifying fear choked her. He loved her enough to have revealed the story behind his torment last night. The problem was, he didn't love himself enough to think he was worthy of anything. That had been the gutwrenching coda to his tale—he was still too racked by guilt to accept anyone's love.

Diana stifled her unprofitable meanderings and went to find Romulus. He had reminded her that these were the last hours they would spend together, and she was determined to savor every one.

He was in his herb garden, digging at the dirt with a small spade.

She settled on one of the porch benches and watched him in silence. He tended the small plot as he did all things, with pleasure and precision. He moved gracefully among the flowering herbs—like Pan among the hyssop blossoms, she mused.

She had a fleeting image of him years down the road, still tending to the swans and the island, still toiling in his garden. And still very much alone. She at least would be returning to her family. He'd made it clear last night that his father was all the family he'd had. Some new sorrow worked its way into her overburdened heart—sorrow for a man so inured to loneliness that he would let love slip from his grasp, rather than admit his need for her. It would take a mighty battle to shake such an admission from him.

Something was buzzing in Diana's brain, even louder than the bees hovering around Rom's lavender. The words he had spoken during the thunderstorm came ringing back to her. "There is only alone, Diana, that's all there ever is."

He had called her Diana!

She leaned over the railing, venturing the question even before it was fully formed in her head. "Romulus, how long have you known who I am?"

He didn't even look up from the mint he was pruning. "Since the night we went out on the river."

"How. . . ?" The word came out low and wavering.

He raised his eyes to her. Even from ten feet away she could see their rich golden gleam. "I found your boat—Mortimers' boat—downstream from here."

"It could have been carried away from the dock by the flood," she said impatiently. "It proves nothing."

He stood upright and fished in his pocket. "Here," he said as he came to the porch railing and held out his hand. "This was caught on one of the oarlocks."

She looked down and saw the wilted satin rosebud that had once embellished the hem of her ball gown. The salient fact that he had been carrying it about with him did not occur to her until much later.

He returned the rosebud to his pocket and crossed his arms upon the railing. "Niall learned of Beveril's runaway bride-to-be at Mortimer House. Then I knew for certain who you were."

Diana shifted away from the railing, turning her face from him. She needed to digest this startling bit of news, that Romulus had known her true identity—and that she was Beveril's intended wife—for three days and yet had continued to keep her hidden on the island.

That knowledge thrilled her beyond words. He had not only flown in the face of convention by doing such a thing, he had risked rousing the anger of his longstanding antagonist. The benevolent Lady Hamish would not have forced him from the island, she knew, but Sir Beveril would have had no compunction about casting Romulus from his home. Yet Rom had not let that threat deter him from keeping her there.

And now he had given her the means to shake him from his formidable reserve. Sir Beveril was the key. She prayed she possessed the acting skills necessary to deceive him this one last time, and the strength of will to strike at the area where he was most vulnerable.

He broke into her revery. "So I gather you are done with your playacting now?"

No, she responded silently, *I've only just begun.*

"I wondered why you allowed me to stay here for so long," she said stiffly. "Why you let me intrude on your solitude. Now I know the reason."

"Do you, Allegra?" His voice was no more than a sigh.

"It was because of Sir Beveril, wasn't it?"

"*What?*" His hands were now gripping the railing.

"Niall told me there is a great deal of enmity between you and Sir Beveril, that you dislike him excessively. Niall said you must be feeling guilty for keeping me here—"

"Niall should learn to keep his tongue between his teeth," Romulus muttered.

"You saw it as a way to mortify Beveril, didn't you, keeping me hidden away on this island?"

"I don't recall tying you to the bed to make you stay," he responded hotly.

Her eyes flashed at him as she rose to her feet. "No, you won me over with kindness. Or so I thought. But you were just using me as a pawn, to strike out at my fiancé. The longer I remained on the island, the more it would serve to embarrass Beveril."

"Sir Beveril doesn't need me to embarrass him," Romulus bit out. "He does just fine on his own."

"I don't hear you denying the accusation."

Rom's jaw tightened as he shifted his gaze away from her.

Diana pointed her finger at him and crowed, "Aha! I was right.

I see it in your eyes. It's clear that your care and attention to me were as much of a sham as my loss of memory."

"Allegra!" he cried. "Can you truly believe that?"

She nodded and crossed her arms over her chest. "I only wonder that you didn't take full advantage of the situation, once you had me in your hands. That would have served Beveril a pretty turn." Diana almost gasped at her provoking words. But then she steeled herself. This was raw combat, indeed, and like Romulus, she was finding she had little taste for carnage. But their whole future together was at stake. She added archly, "And I expect even a madman knows how to cozen a woman."

"I think you have said enough," he responded in a low, dangerous voice as he swung around the railing and came up the steps toward her. "You really don't have a clue as to why I let you remain here, do you?"

Diana tried not to wilt under his awesome scowl. "I can only surmise it was to tweak Sir Beveril."

"Then you are a bloody fool."

She drew herself up and looked him straight in the eyes. "Then tell me the reason. Tell me, Romulus."

He turned from her, his eyes hooded, his body tense. She saw the battle that was going on inside him, his rising temper warring with his need to stay aloof and detached. It was time to bring out the big guns.

She clutched at his shoulder and spun him to face her. "An honorable man," she began in a voice of ice, "would have told me the instant he knew my real identity. Not let me continue on with that foolish charade. An honorable man, one with no ulterior motive, would have forced me to go back to my family."

His response was a low growl. "An honorable man would not have forced you back, not to a situation from which you had fled, even at the risk of your own life."

"I didn't flee!" she wailed, forgetting to playact, as she thrust her hands into the skirt of her gown to keep from striking out at him in frustration. "I didn't risk my life to get away. That is some nonsensical notion you have taken into your head. I was hiding in the dashed rowboat to avoid Beveril. It . . . it came untied. I never meant to be on the river, never meant to fall in the water. . . . I certainly never meant to end up here."

"But you did!" he stormed, looming over her. "You did end up here. And I wish to bloody hell that the river had taken you, not

dropped you in a sodden heap at my feet. I thought you were fleeing from danger, and now it turns out it was nothing more than a
case of *bridal nerves*." He bit out the last words.

"Oooh!" she cried. "What a wretched thing to say!"

"You lied to me, Allegra," he continued in a frighteningly quiet
voice. "And played me for a fool. And if that wasn't infuriating
enough, you now have the gall to throw my hospitality back in my
face and accuse me of the worst sort of villainy. I'd thrash you for
saying those things if you were a man—"

Her eyes narrowed as she poked her chin in the air, "You
wouldn't dare!"

He held his clenched fists up close to her chin. "Aah! You tempt
me, Allegra—"

"*I'm not Allegra!*" she spat, pushing his hands away. "I was
never Al—"

He caught her wrists, twisting her hands behind her back. She
thrashed in his hold as she had done the night he pulled her from
the water, suddenly afraid of what her hurtful words had driven
him to. There was only anger in his eyes, spewing out in response
to her unjust accusations. Anger and pain, and yet, behind them
was a blinding hunger. He leaned over her and tugged her hard
against him, bringing the soft thrust of her breasts against his chest
and the rounded contours of her hip against his thigh. The more
she struggled the more she brought herself into contact with his
body.

For one instant Romulus held her gaze, and Diana saw all the
yearning she felt in her own heart reflected there. The next instant,
his eyes blazed again with heat. He butted her head back roughly,
his brow at her throat, and then quickly angled his mouth over
hers. He kissed her wildly, violently, taking out his fury on her
mouth. He tangled one hand in her hair, fisting it in the mass of
curls, keeping her head still so that he could have at her mouth,
again and again. Diana groaned against his lips, and Romulus
echoed her with a deep, crooning moan. It wasn't the declaration
she had been hoping for, but it thrilled her to the tips of her toes.
She tried to pull her hands free so that she could twine them
around his neck.

Romulus felt it the instant she stopped resisting him, and if he
didn't know better, he'd have sworn she was arching herself
against him. He could feel the rapid beating of her heart beneath
the rise of her breasts where they splayed upon his chest. Suddenly

his anger and pain were gone, burned away by the lush, potent feel of her in his arms. And then there was only the hunger left, the need to lose himself in her. But with that howling hunger came his conscience, loping along at its heels.

His hands were suddenly trembling where they touched her, quivering at her back.

"*Allegra*," he gasped against her mouth. "You *are* Allegra." His lips slid to her cheek as he gripped her shoulders. "You will always be Allegra to me," he breathed into her hair. He drew his head back.

There were tears now in her gentian eyes. This wondrous girl who had cried over the death of a swan, now wept over what she had suffered at his hands. He set her gently away from him and stepped back. She stood shivering, head tipped up, arms limp at her sides. Her eyes were clouded with shock.

"*No* . . . " was all she managed to rasp out in a plaintive voice. It nearly brought him to his knees.

"An honorable man . . ." he said raggedly, holding her only with his eyes. "An honorable man would have never let himself care for you . . . or need you as I do. But I am not made of stone, little witch. God help me, I am not."

He swung away to the top of the steps, and then said without turning, "I'll see that Niall comes for you in the morning. I'll . . . I'll keep out of your way until then."

Diana watched as he crossed the yard, his long strides sweeping through the tall grass.

"R-romulus!" she cried, with an edge of panic as she grasped the porch railing. "Where are you going?"

Again he did not turn to face her. "Fishing," he said in a clipped, controlled voice. "I am going fishing." And then he was lost in the trees that edged the clearing.

Chapter 9

Diana threw her arms around one of the roof supports, leaning her face against the beam. Her mind was still trying to catch up with the wild sensations that were coursing through her body. Nothing in her sheltered, guarded existence had ever stirred her like those kisses had. Stirred her, frightened her, and made her feel more alive than she thought possible. She touched one hand tentatively to her swollen mouth and wondered how Rom had lasted nearly a week without kissing her. How had she ever doubted that he loved her? Foolish, foolish girl!

It was as though she had been prodding a pile of ashes, thinking she would never see a spark. But it was clear now that the fire had merely been banked, and when it leapt into blazing life, it burned with enough heat to sear her very soul. His ardent words echoed again in her head—*An honorable man would not have let himself need you as I do*. With that declaration Romulus had freed her mind of all doubt and every shred of hesitation. She would never let him go. Nothing would come between them.

His pride will come between you, an errant voice pointed out. Diana wanted to argue, but she knew it to be true. Romulus knew his blasted place. He had admitted his need, had said the words she longed to hear, but she wondered if he had the courage to act on them. It seemed unthinkable that he still planned to send her away after kissing her so fiercely.

She let go of the porch beam and sank onto the top step with a deep sigh, her hands crossed upon her chest. Her heart was beating less wildly, though her thoughts continued to race. She now knew what Romulus felt for her, but he still didn't know of her feelings for him. She longed to fling herself after him and declare her love, but prudence advised her that he was too riled just now to listen.

As she sat there wrestling with the problem, she had a most telling insight. She recalled how the cygnets would scramble from the pond and come scuttling after her the instant she headed back to the lodge. Diana pondered, as she rose from the step and went into the house, if there was any similarity between proud men and baby swans. She prayed that was the case. In fact, she was banking on it.

She went into the storeroom and collected her few meager belongings. Crouching before the crates, she let her fingers trace over the downy heads of the cygnets. "Be well, my little friends," she said softly. "Grow big and strong, and keep away from the snapping turtles and the poacher's snares."

She cast one last look over the room. She had grown more attached to that cluttered space than she ever had to the fine, elegant bedroom at Mortimer House.

It took her only a moment to pen a note to Romulus. "Thank you for sharing your island with me. It was here that I learned the truth of what was in my heart. I hope that someday you will discover the truth in your own. I will treasure my memories of the river and of the most honorable person I have ever met, a man I have come to esteem beyond words—the keeper of the swans." She signed it, "Allegra."

She had toyed with the idea of revealing her destination in the note, but hesitated to be so obvious. She needed to spark some anxiety in his breast if he was to pursue her. When he realized she was gone, she knew he would fear for her alone on the water with night approaching. That should be enough to send him after her, but it wouldn't hurt her cause any if he found the note.

The mantel seemed the obvious place to leave it, but that spot reminded her uncomfortably of her other note, the one to Wilfred Bailey, supposedly asking for his assistance. Another of her facile lies to Romulus. She stood undecided for a moment, and then crossed the hallway and went into his bedroom.

She had never been inside his room—more's the pity, she thought, remembering his heated kisses. In the waning light, it appeared quite spartan. A simple pine bed with a military trunk beside it, a chest of drawers, a wooden chair near the window. No paintings hung on the walls, no rug covered the floor. The only embellishment in the room was a swan's feather, tucked behind the shaving mirror above the chest.

Diana wondered at the austerity of the chamber; it had an air of impermanence, as though its occupant intended to leave at any time. And yet Romulus seemed so grounded to his island, like one of the tall oaks with its roots sunk far below the soil. She crossed to the chest and reached out to touch the white feather. Perhaps the island was merely his nesting spot. One day, he would take flight and soar away from this place and find his true destiny. God, how she longed to be beside him on that day!

After carrying the folded paper to her lips, she placed it upon his pillow, letting her fingers linger in the slight depression where his head had lain. His rucksack sat on the trunk beside the bed—if he came in to fetch it, he would see the note.

With a determined step, Diana passed through the kitchen, trying to dispel the vision of a tall man who lounged against the table as he teased her about her cooking. Shutting the door gently behind her, she went down the steps and along the path to the river slip. She didn't like to take his patrol boat, but Rom was fishing in the punt and Niall had taken the dory. It would have to be the skiff. Something else he could add to her list of crimes, she thought wryly, as she untied the bow line and climbed in.

She set the boat against the current and headed for the southern tip of the island. The slight breeze was blowing again and Diana welcomed the cool air—by the time she was halfway across to the western shore, she had begun to labor at the oars. It was amazing to her that Romulus plied this boat up and down the river for miles in each direction and never seemed to weary.

Treypenny, she gauged, was half a mile or so upstream from the island, but she had no intention of going ashore there. She found a likely looking place on the bank, a short distance before the water stairs and grounded the skiff. It was a struggle to drag the boat up onto the grass, but she dared not leave it on the water; Romulus *would* have her head on a platter if she let anything happen to his patrol boat.

After she'd secured the line to a sapling, she took off one of her bracelets and hung it over the oarlock. A nice touch, she thought, as she set off across country. Not only a clue to her eventual destination, it also harked back to the satin rose Rom had found snagged on Mortimers' rowboat. The rose he carried about with him in his breeches pocket. It occurred to her then, with thrilling certainty, that a man who was so utterly besotted would not let her go without a fight. And if the river truly had no secrets from him, he would be able to follow her trail as though it was lit with a blazing torch.

*   *   *

It was near dusk when Romulus beached the punt. It figured that today, when he had no appetite at all, the fish would be taking the bait in droves. He had released everything he'd caught; he'd only been fishing to distract himself. A foolish endeavor. Maybe his evening patrol would soothe his nerves, he thought, as he made his way toward the slip. Perhaps being out on the Thames would remove the self-loathing from his soul, and the taunting vision of Allegra's tears from his heart. But he doubted it.

Romulus stood at the top of the path that angled down to the slip, his mouth agape. The skiff had vanished. He thought immediately of Argie Beasle. But even that little rodent wouldn't risk stealing his boat. Everyone on the river knew it was the property of Lady Hamish. An uncanny prickling had begun at the back of Rom's neck. He turned and raced full out toward the house, calling, "Allegra!" as he ran.

He searched the house, and then went out onto the porch. "Allegra!" he shouted again, trying to resist the alarm that was slicing through him. He went back to the storeroom. Her spare blouse was no longer hanging from its peg. He knew the answer then, with a sinking feeling in his gut. The chit had stolen his blasted skiff and run off home.

"How could you let her go?" he asked the cygnets, as if they were responsible for her sudden flight. "How could you let her go?" he repeated in a hollow voice as he walked from the room.

The house had never felt so desolate. It was what he had wanted, surely, but now that it had come to pass, he felt only an aching sadness. At Mortimer House, in contrast, there would be great joy. And Sir Beveril would be exultant at his fiancée's return. Rom grit his teeth. Best not pursue that line of thought.

But then his anxiety returned in force. Mortimer House was four miles upstream, against the current. She'd be lucky if she made it even as far as Hamish House. If she got into trouble on the river, it would take him hours to find her in the slow-moving punt. He'd best pole over to Treypenny and fetch back the dory, provided Niall wasn't larking about in it somewhere. Then he recalled the Gypsy celebration—Niall was not likely to miss out on any festivity that included young female servants.

He went to his bedroom and snatched up the rucksack. After a moment's thought, he knelt and opened his field trunk, where a loaded pistol lay. Pray God the little fool didn't land herself in any trouble that required him to use it. If he had any sense he'd use it on her. Put them both out of their misery then.

Sitting back on his heels, he tapped the barrel of the pistol on his palm. Why the devil was he in such a pelter to follow her? The chit knew how to row a boat and the Thames was the calmest it had been for weeks. She would be traveling through the populated portion of the river, and if she got into trouble, surely someone would come to her aid. Christ, if she made it as far as Hamish House, Sir Bleeding Beveril would escort her the rest of the way home. Maybe that was even where she was headed.

Let her go, let her go. The voice of reason pounded through his brain. *Let her go back where she belongs, to the life she knew before she came to your island.*

He purposely disregarded the words—he merely wanted to assure himself that she was safe.

He was turning for the door when he caught sight of a note on his pillow. With a sigh, he sat on the side of the bed and took it up, pressing it between his palms. He was afraid to read it, fearing the words of recrimination and distaste he would find written there.

As he unfolded it, his eyes were drawn to one phrase, " . . . the man I have come to esteem beyond words." Something twisted in his heart. He read the entire message and his head began to reel.

She had not run from him in fear and loathing. She thought him honorable . . . she esteemed him. His eyes shifted again to one line, *I hope that someday you will discover what is in your own heart.*

Sweet Jesus, what had he been thinking—to lecture *her* about honesty? How about some honesty on his part? The honesty of his overwhelming feelings for her. He thought she had fled from his untempered desire, because that was all he had allowed her to see. Not the love that filled him, or the admiration he felt for her stubborn pluck and her generous nature.

Allegra had been more honest with him, in spite of her pretended loss of memory. She had not disguised her feelings for him last night, when she cradled him in her arms during the storm. She had not hidden her heart out there by the river. He knew full well what he had seen shining in her eyes when she had pleaded with him to let her stay. That was honesty, indeed.

If he believed his love was unreturned, then letting her go was the only sane option. But he had seen that fierce, bright emotion in her face, and had know instantly that his regard for her was completely reciprocated. And knowing that, he had been a fool to drive her from his life. She was his life. The morning star, the sun at noon and all the planets of the galaxy shimmering down upon his night.

Allegra. He spoke her name aloud as he raised the note to his lips, unknowingly touching the spot she had kissed. Nothing would come between them once he had her again in his care. Let society be damned, let her family go hang. He had suffered enough in his lifetime, spent too many days in bitter regret. It was time to seek out the joy that was the birthright of every man, whether pauper or peer.

If there was a scandal, he would take her out of the country—show her Rome, and Tuscany, and all the places he had known as a youth. He had banked his army pay and most of his present stipend. They would not be wealthy, but he would find work. Wherever there were rich men with birds to tend.

But could she be happy with such a life? He took a moment to ponder this. He knew so little of her life before she had come to his island. Only that she was sister by marriage to a very wealthy man. Could she give up those trappings and luxuries to join him in an uncertain future?

He had a sudden vision of her sitting beside the pond, her legs bare beneath her Gypsy skirt. She was laughing up at him, a spray of wild violets in her untamed hair. He couldn't offer her riches, but he could give her another sort of wealth. The water and the wide sky, and all the creatures that dwelled in-between. For Diana Exeley, such a life might be sadly lacking. But in his heart he knew that for Allegra Swan, for the black-haired water witch who had so miraculously transformed his life, it would be enough.

"No," he vowed as he stood up and slung the rucksack over his shoulder, "I will never let her go."

Diana found it rough going.

She knew from Niall that the Gypsy camp lay a mile or so from the river, and she reckoned she'd reach it before dark. But as she twitched her skirt free of the dozenth patch of nettles, she realized that traveling a mile through rough bracken was not the same as walking that distance on a country lane. There were boggy places she'd had to skirt, and stubbled fields that were painful to traverse.

It was full dark when she neared the camp; the sky to the west was lit by the blazing campfires. She followed those beacons until she came to a wide field. Eight caravans were drawn into a semicircle, and a great many people were milling about in that open space. She could hear fiddlers playing a rhythmic tune and the steady beat of a drum keeping time to the music. Men and women were dancing at the center of the clearing, their shadows now and again obscuring the large central fire. The scene reminded her of a pagan revel, primitive and otherworldly. The haunting quality of the music, and the sensual movements of the dancers both disturbed and compelled her.

She struck out toward the caravans, hoping to locate Niall before her presence there could be remarked on. She passed a solitary caravan, which sat some distance from the others. An old woman was sitting in the open doorway, smoking a corncob pipe.

"Ye be comin' for the gatherin'?" she called out in a throaty voice as Diana walked by.

Diana turned back to the old woman. "I am looking for Niall."

She cackled softly. "They all be lookin' fer Niall. Every lass on the river be lookin' fer my gran'son."

"You're Niall's granty?"

The woman nodded, and then eyed Diana suspiciously. "That be my best skirt you are wearing, lass. Happen I'd know it in the dark." The old woman rose from her seat and tottered down the steps. She poked a bony finger toward Diana. "You be the lass that red-headed fellow's been keeping on his island."

Diana winced. So much for remaining undetected.

"Yes, and I think I must thank you." She drew up a fold of her skirt. "For letting me borrow this."

The old woman beckoned Diana closer. "Let me take a look at you, girl. I been wonderin' what sort of chit Romulus would bother himself with. You're a mite of a thing, ain't you?"

Diana nearly chuckled. She and Niall's granty were exactly the same height. "You weren't supposed to know I was on the island," she chided gently. "Niall promised to keep it a secret."

The woman gave her a narrow-eyed look. "You think that boy can keep a secret from his granty? No, no, he didn't break his word. I just know things sometimes."

"Gypsy magic?" Diana asked, her eyes bright.

"Gaelic magic, more like. My own granty was a Scot. Had a powerful sight, she did. Well, you'd best come into my wagon, girl. You won't stay a secret long, once the menfolk have a look at you."

Diana ducked into the caravan as the old woman called out to someone at the edge of the crowd.

"I've sent one of the lads to fetch Niall," she said as she came grunting up the steps. "Hope he's not off trimming his wick with one of the Yorricks' serving girls."

Diana blushed furiously. The old woman gave a dry laugh. Her face was brown as a nut, the papery skin covered with a maze of fine wrinkles from brow to chin and her thick white hair was braided into a coronet around her head. She wore so many silver necklaces about her raddled neck and so many bangles upon her birdlike wrists, that Diana wondered there was enough strength in that withered body to hold her upright. She had Niall's eyes, Diana saw, bright black and gleaming with good humor.

"I am called Gizella Yanni," the woman said, as she settled onto a padded bench that ran along one side of the caravan. "You'd best have a seat. My gran'son may take some tracking down."

Diana sat and folded her hands. She let her gaze wander over the caravan's interior, marveling at how much that small space contained. Baskets and leather bags hung from the roof, along with pots and dried herbs. Across from her were several open hampers, where bright clothing spilled out in splendid disarray. The walls were painted in gay patterns, the windows covered with chintz curtains. She thought a person could easily live in such a cozy place, and then realized that this *was* the woman's home.

She saw that Gizella was watching her, scrutinizing her with those bright eyes.

"You're a pretty thing, for a *gorgio*," she cackled, removing the pipe from her mouth. "He's a fool to have let you get away. But then the best of them are fools, when there's a tasty morsel under their noses."

Diana's head snapped up. "He didn't . . . that is, I wasn't . . ."

The woman shook her head. "No need to deny it. Not that I blame you for running off from him. He's a strange sort, that Romulus."

"The villagers think he is mad," Diana said softly. "But he is only solitary, you see. He keeps to himself and that makes people suspicious."

"And doesn't every Gypsy know about that. But tell me, girl, where will you go now?"

Diana squirmed a bit. "I was hoping you would let me stay here."

She pursed her mouth. "We don't like to get mixed up with the doings of *gorgios*. It's sure trouble."

Diana saw that her presence had once again brought the threat of retaliation down upon the undeserving. First Romulus, and now the

Gypsies. "May I stay with you, just for tonight?" she asked. "And tomorrow I will go home."

"Where is your home, child?"

"At Mortimer House." It was Niall who had spoken. His dark eyes were hooded as he observed Diana from the open doorway. He shifted his glance to the old woman. "She is James Mortimer's sister by marriage. And Sir Beveril Hunnycut's intended."

Gizella laid a hand on Diana's arm to keep her from leaping up. "Hold, girl. No need to take fright."

"But I don't need to tell you, do I?" Niall continued, moving toward Diana. "Your memory seems to have conveniently returned."

"It was never lost," Diana admitted in a low voice. "But *I* was lost. Lost and injured and confused." She looked up at him. "I'm so sorry now that I lied. I should have gone home the next day and faced my family. But I wanted . . . I wanted so much to stay on the island."

He crouched before her and took up her hand. "Silly chit. You needn't have bothered with the ruse—he'd have let you stay on regardless. He's like that . . . can't refuse a creature who needs help."

"I accused him of keeping me there to spite Beveril," she said mournfully.

Niall's eyes widened. "Oh, that must have sat nicely with him."

"I only wanted to make him admit how he felt about me. We had a dreadful row, and then . . . well, I decided it was best to leave. I'm sorry I came here, if it's going to make trouble for you."

"I think there's going to be a deal of trouble," Niall said ominously.

"Something's brewing," his grandmother agreed. "I feel it in my toe bones."

Diana tugged at Niall's sleeve. "I don't understand. Rom said you would tell my family I was staying here in the camp—to protect my reputation. Why would you do that, if it would endanger your people?"

He gave her a tight smile. "Once you were safe at home, then it wouldn't be dangerous to say we'd aided you. But if Beveril came here tonight and found you with us, he wouldn't wait for explanations before he had the law on us. We Gypsies have a bad enough reputation for stealing children."

"I'm not a child," she protested.

He laid one hand on her cheek. He suspected she was several years his senior, but he always felt like a seasoned man of the world around her. "You are a complete child, Allegra. Foolish and head-strong. How did you come here tonight? Alone and on foot? Yes, I thought so. With half the county heading here, and the men all full of drink and high spirits. You're lucky no one tumbled you in a hedgerow."

Gizella chuckled softly, and the boy gave her a quelling look.

Diana shifted her head away from his hand. "I didn't come by the road, I came across the fields." She pointed to the hem of her gown which was muddy and riddled with nettles. "I have that much sense."

He shrugged. It wasn't his job to keep watch over her. But where the devil was the man who had appointed himself to that onerous task?

"I can't believe Romulus allowed you out on the river alone. And at night, no less."

"She ran away," Gizella interjected matter-of-factly. "From that handsome, red-headed rogue."

Niall sat back on his heels. "If that don't beat everything! So Rom doesn't know you've come here?"

"No . . . he doesn't," Diana said haltingly, fighting off the misery that clawed at her insides.

It was hours since she'd left the island. Romulus had surely dis-covered the missing skiff by now. And if he went into the house, he'd have found her note. But it was clear he was not coming to the Gypsy camp. Perhaps he'd missed the beached skiff in the dark-ness, and was punting toward Mortimer House to find her. Or maybe he was sitting snug in his own house, reading Mr. Pope, and not thinking of her at all.

The boy rose. "How did you get across from the island? Not in the punt?" he added skeptically.

Diana sniffed and shook her head. "I took his skiff."

Niall's brows lowered another notch. "Great jumping Christ! He'll skin you alive—No, he'll skin me alive, because I'm sure he'll find some way to blame me for luring you here."

"You didn't lure me, Niall. I came here because I thought Romulus would follow me."

"What?"

Gizella gave a dry, whispery laugh when she saw the expression of bewilderment on her grandson's face. She poked him in the ribs. "You don't yet know everything about women, my little cockerel.

I figgered that out from the start. She ain't runnin' away—she's waitin' to be run to."

Niall ground his teeth. "Did you leave him a note then?"

"Yes, of course I did. But I . . . I didn't tell him where I was going."

Diana was wondering how her excellent plan had come to sound so idiotic. If Romulus really loved her, he wouldn't need to be teased into following her, he'd have brooked James and Helen and even Sir Beveril, himself, to get her back.

Niall rolled his eyes and muttered to his grandmother, "She thinks Rom's a gypsy, that he'll be able to see where she's run to in his tea leaves." He moved to the doorway of the caravan and stood looking out at the festive party that was going on in the camp. He wondered why he was not in the midst of all that merrymaking, instead of sorting out Allegra's tiresome problems.

He turned to her. "I'll have to take you to Mortimer House tonight."

"I refuse!" She sat upright on the bench and folded her arms across her chest.

Niall looked like he wanted to box her ears, but Gizella merely patted her shoulder. "You can stay here the night, child. Tomorrow you will know where you belong."

"I know where I belong," she cried. "On the island, with Romulus."

She was tired and hungry and Rom was not ever coming to get her. These people were being as patient with her as they knew how, but it didn't lessen the ache in her breast.

When Niall saw the tears coursing down her cheeks, his heart softened. He never could bear to watch a female weep. "Allegra," he said soothingly as he seated himself beside her. "You can't force someone to change their nature. Even I know that, and I'm still a sprat." He saw the amusement begin to surface in her eyes. "Rom's made no secret to me of how he feels about you"—Diana's heart leapt at his words—"but he's also given neither of us any reason to think he would ever act on those feelings. Do you understand? Just loving someone is not enough."

"It should be," she sobbed quietly.

For once, even Gizella had no comment to offer.

Romulus poled across the river in the punt, thankful that the water level had gone down enough for him to touch bottom. Still it was slow going, moving against the current for nearly a half mile. He was almost to the village—he could see the water stairs up ahead—when he spied his skiff grounded on a patch of grass. His heart lurched for an instant. It was on the wrong side of the river. If Allegra had been heading toward Mortimer House, she would have been rowing along the eastern shore.

He climbed from the punt and went to examine the skiff. The last rays of the setting sun sent a shaft of light through the trees, and Romulus caught sight of the silver bracelet dangling from the oarlock. A Gypsy bangle, one of a pair that Niall had brought her. He stood looking at it with a puzzled frown.

Something was afoot here—the boat on the wrong side of the river, beached where he would surely notice it, and the bracelet, so casually left in plain sight. It teased his brain that she might almost have been laying a trail for him to follow.

"Little fiend," he muttered fondly as he pocketed the bracelet.

Leaving the skiff where it was, he poled down to the water stairs. He vaulted up the steps and headed into the village. As he came even with the 'Thrush, he ducked inside. Even though he'd seen Wald Chipping's boat at the Treypenny slip, he wanted to make sure the man was accounted for. Sure enough, he sat in a chair near the entrance and—lo and behold—none other than Argie Beasle was sitting across from him. Both men looked down into their drinks as he crossed the taproom.

Joe Black blinked in surprise as Romulus came toward him. "What can I get you?" he asked genially, as though he and the river warden had not had words only a few days before.

Romulus didn't dare ask after Allegra, not with those two curs sitting within earshot, but after poling across from the island he found he needed a drink. Badly. "A pint of lager," he said in a low voice.

The publican drew him a tankard and set it on the bar.

"You headin' to see yer friends at the Gypsy camp," one of the nighttime regulars taunted.

"Mmm—" Romulus tried to shrug him off. He was not in the mood for baiting.

"They say there's girls dancing nekked in front of a fire. That what you goin' to see?"

"Stand off, Cleary," Joe Black said curtly to Rom's gadfly. "The man's got a right to have a drink without you breathin' your whisky breath all down his neck."

Romulus glanced at the publican in surprised appreciation. Joe Black motioned him a bit closer.

"Perrin," he said in a low voice, "you maybe got the wrong idea about me. I do have an occasional bit of business with Lord Talbot . . . sell him the odd barrel of brandy."

Romulus spent a moment chewing over this new bit of information. "Smuggled, I take it?"

The man nodded. "Yon little rat, Beasle, tells me when his friends in London come into a hogshead or two. I store them here at the 'Thrush. That is my only dealin' with Argie, sir. I'd never help to take a swan, and that's the truth. My missus and little girl would have my head, they're that fond of them."

Rom ran one finger around the edge of his tankard. "I haven't seen yon rat in here for several days."

"No, tonight's the first he's been back since you thrashed him. But I will tell you one thing, he's now in tight with the ferryman. You might do well to watch yer back." Joe Black stood upright and began to wipe a rag over the oak sheen of the bar. "And more than that I could not say."

Rom slid a gold coin across the bar and gave him a crooked grin. "More than that I could not ask."

Joe Black watched Romulus walk through the door and then gazed in disbelief at the coin on the bar. He'd never seen a golden guinea before—he was almost afraid to touch it.

Romulus went along the lane, taking slow measured strides. At a turning in the road, he ducked into the woods and began to backtrack. Sure enough, there were Argie and Wald, walking back to the village. They'd followed him a short distance to make sure he was heading away from the river.

Back in Treypenny, Rom kept to the shadows as he followed the two men through the village. They bypassed the 'Thrush, and made their way down the water stairs. After a prolonged conversation on the slip, which Rom wasn't close enough to overhear, they both climbed into Wald's boat.

Romulus knew, even under the waning moon, they would be able to spot him if he followed them in the dory. Instead, he crouched behind one of the granite columns on either side of the water stairs and tugged a field glass from his rucksack. He watched in surprise as the ferryman set his boat upstream, against the current. Whatever they were after, at least it wasn't his swans.

Romulus sighed with relief as the boat disappeared from sight.

He couldn't have gone after them while Allegra's whereabouts were still in doubt. Well not really in doubt. Old Whisky Breath Cleary had reminded him of the Gypsy celebration. It explained why the skiff was on the wrong side of the river.

It also explained why Romulus had a fair head of steam worked up by the time he got to the edge of the camp. Rom wasn't sure that Niall, the gypsy Adonis, understood how primitively possessive he felt about Allegra. He'd hate to come to blows with his friend over a shatterbrained runaway water witch.

Romulus could see the mass of people moving in the firelight. There was the sound of music rising over the wide field, that distinctive gypsy music he had always loved. As he neared the edge of the crowd, Rom caught sight of Niall. He called out his name over the din of the music. The boy turned. His mouth twisted unpleasantly as he approached Rom, and once they were face-to-face, he spat out an unfamiliar word. Romulus took its meaning all the same.

"Where is she?" Rom asked calmly.

"As if you bloody care!" Niall snarled back. He took Romulus by the shoulder and thrust him away from the caravans, back toward the lane.

"Steady on, lad," Rom cautioned, knocking his hand away. "I've not come here for a fight. I've come to find Allegra."

Niall put his hands on his hips and regarded his friend with a testy scowl. "Changed your mind then, have you? First you want her gone, now you want her back."

"Jesus, Niall, what's gotten into you? She took my skiff and grounded it near the village. I only want to make sure she's unharmed."

"Oh, she's not come to any harm on the river. Now on your island is another story."

Romulus ran a hand through his hair. "You're certainly prickly tonight. Been having at the wine barrel? I thought you wanted me to send her away. And that's what I was going to do, tomorrow morning as a matter of fact. She only anticipated me a bit. So I don't know why you're in such a state."

"You haven't seen her. She looks like she been pole-axed. She's in my granty's wagon crying—"

"Then you'd better take me there."

"You're not going anywhere near her. Why should I let you? You'll only hurt her again."

Rom took a step back and said grimly, "I gather she told you that I forced myself on her."

"No, she did not," the Gypsy bit out. "I was talking about her feelings. But I see now that you have left no part of her untouched. And after all your haughty speeches, warning me away from her."

"I don't intend to stand here taking abuse from you, Niall. How I behave toward Allegra is my own business. My own bloody business."

Romulus pushed past him and went striding off into the crowd. Several women caught him by the arm, trying to coax him into the dance, but he shrugged them off. He could see Gizella's caravan some distance beyond the noisy throng. He was nearly to the wagon when Niall caught up with him. The Gypsy threw himself upon the steps to prevent Romulus from entering.

"No," Niall cried. "You've been my friend, Rom. But so is Allegra now. I won't let you tear her apart."

Romulus regarded the youth's melodramatic posture with jaundiced amusement.

"Oh, get up, for God's sake. You look like the hero in some damned provincial playhouse. Do you think I came here to make things worse? Don't be an ass, Niall. The chit is everything in the world to me."

"You promise you're not going to hurt her?" Niall's eyes were still narrowed with uncertainty.

Romulus grinned as he effortlessly plucked the boy from the steps and set him on the grass. "I'd like very much to throttle her," he said with feeling. "But no, I promise she'll survive the encounter. Though I don't know if the same can be said for me."

Romulus knocked hard upon the Dutch door. "Gizella!" he called. "Open up."

The upper half of the door creaked open. The old woman observed him in silence for a moment and then shook her head sharply. "She won't see you."

Romulus could see Allegra sitting on the bench behind the Gypsy woman. She was purposefully gazing away from the door. Her shoulders were back and her chin was up—she looked like an etching of a Christian martyr about to meet the king of beasts.

He looked down at the old woman in entreaty, and she winked at him with one heavy-lidded eye. Then she opened the door wide, stepped past Romulus, and hobbled down the steps. He slipped into the caravan and softly shut both doors behind him.

"Thank you for sending him away," Diana said in a hollow voice.

"Don't thank her too quickly," Romulus uttered.

Diana's head pivoted around and her eyes widened.

"It appears you have been abandoned by your watchdogs," he said smoothly. He saw that indeed she had been crying—there were tearstains all down her flushed cheeks. The sight nearly unmanned him.

"Now what?" she asked sullenly. "Are you going to rail at me for taking your skiff."

"Later," he said as he knelt down before the bench.

"Are you going to lace into me for coming here alone?"

"Undoubtedly, but not right now."

She met his eyes at last as she said, "Then what do you want?"

"This," he said as he took her face between his hands and kissed her gently on the mouth. "For the rest of my days, Allegra, I want this."

She sniffled slightly and then smiled dreamily. As exciting as it had been to be kissed in passion on his porch, this tender, cherishing kiss in a caravan had a distinct charm.

She slid her arms around his neck and tugged his head forward until they were brow to brow. "I knew that," she whispered. "But I wasn't sure if you knew how much I wanted it, too."

"Then why wouldn't you let me come inside?"

"Only a man would ask that," she said with a sigh. "Just look at me, Romulus. I am nettles and mud from collar to hem. And my face must look like a pomegranate from crying."

"I like pomegranates," he murmured. And to prove it, he drew his open mouth slowly over her left cheek. Diana felt her toes curl into tiny fists.

"And do you like nettles, as well?" she inquired as her fingers traced over his collar.

"I'll overlook the nettles, as long as they remain on your skirt and don't wander onto your tongue."

"You think me sharp-tongued, then? A fishwife?" She baited him with a grin.

"I think you completely adorable, my witch. And as for your tongue—"

He traced one finger along her mouth, and then having opened it slightly, he brought his lips to hers and let his tongue wander into that moist cavern. It danced against her own tongue, flooding her with so many delicious sensations and making her so dizzy that she thought the caravan had tipped over and toppled her to the floor.

She actually was on the floor, she realized, once she came out of her languid stupor. In the midst of his long kiss, Romulus had lifted her from the bench and lowered her to the small patterned rug.

"What are you going to do with me?" she said, gazing up at him. It was the question she had been wordlessly asking him since he had first sat on her bed to feed her broth.

This time her tall river god gave her an answer. "Love you, Allegra," he said. "Nothing else seems to make any sense."

She touched a hand to his mouth. "And you don't think I am a scatterbrained goose?"

"Oh, I never said that," he teased gently. "But then you know how fond I am of waterfowl."

She chuckled. "God, how I envied those swans of yours. I am more of a wren, don't you think?"

He studied her a minute, thinking she was more lovely than any creature on God's earth. With her midnight hair and morning-sky eyes, her rose-red mouth and peach-blossom skin, she was a symphony of all that was fair in nature.

"You are neither goose nor wren," he said, drawing her against his chest. "You are the bright phoenix bird, who rises up from the ashes of loss and gives hope to those who have been too long without it."

Diana clung to him, all glibness gone. She was crying again, not for herself, or for her foolish illusions of love, but for Romulus, for the pain in his voice when he had spoken of loss and for the wonder in his face when he had spoken of hope. For all his skill at healing, she now knew he had not been able to heal his own wounds. But she could—she would make it her life's work if necessary.

"Ach, don't cry, my little pomegranate," he crooned, rocking her. "Niall will think I am beating you."

She laughed against his shirt. "I doubt he would object," she said. "I think he wanted to beat me himself when I arrived here."

"But I thought he invited you?"

"Not to run away, not to come here alone. He said I was lucky I didn't get tumbled in a hedgerow."

"The night is still young," Romulus drawled as he tipped her head back and kissed her throat. He moved to her mouth, murmuring against it, "And hedgerows are common hereabouts."

"Don't," Diana protested. "Don't make me laugh while you are kissing me."

"Can't do two things at once, hmm?"

"I need to concentrate," she said. "I don't want to be distracted."

"Sorry," he said, as he returned to his pursuit of her lips. She sighed deeply as he turned her head this way and that, trying out all possible angles, discovering that each one was perfect in its way.

There was a sudden thudding at the door. "Allegra! It was Niall's voice. "Are you all right? I don't hear anything."

Romulus shook his head. "You'd think the boy could use his imagination." She giggled into her hand.

"Allegra? I'm coming in if you don't answer me."

"Go find your own woman, damn you!" Romulus called out.

The top half of the door opened. Niall leaned his elbows on the bottom half and grinned. "Just wanted to see how things were progressing."

Diana shifted into a sitting position, adjusting the neckline of her blouse.

"My granty needs her caravan back," Niall stated amiably. "She doesn't like all the smoke from the fire—says it makes her cough."

"That's probably from her damned pipe," Romulus growled as he tugged Diana to her feet. "Anyway, we both know your grandmother is made of Toledo steel."

He flung open the bottom door and swept Diana down the stairs. Then he was off across the grass, towing her behind him. She cast a sheepish look over her shoulder at Niall, and was surprised to see him ushering a buxom young serving girl into the caravan.

"I think he did," she said breathlessly as he drew her swiftly away from the noisy crowd.

"Did what?"

"Get his own woman," she said with a chuckle.

Her blood was racing through her veins, and she felt as though her feet were skimming over the grass. Every hundred feet or so, Rom would stop his progress, catch her up in his arms and kiss her soundly. Then he would take hold of her hand and again propel her across the field.

"What are you doing?" she asked when he finally came to a halt at the very edge of the pasture.

"Looking for a hedgerow," he said with a grin that she could see in the dark.

"Truly?" she asked with undisguised anticipation.

"You'd let me, wouldn't you? Tumble you in a Gypsy field?"

Diana pondered this. "You'd have to do something first," she said cautiously.

"What? Marry you?"

"No," she said, trying to sound somber. "Take the fishing hooks out of your pockets."

She darted away from his hands, laughing as she ran. He let her get a good headstart and then easily caught up with her. When he wrestled her to the ground, she was still laughing, but when he kissed her, covering her body with his own, she was suddenly quiet.

Then she gasped as he stroked one hand over her breast. "My witch," he murmured just above her mouth. "*Strega mia della aqua.*" She purred her delight at his lilting words. "My entrancing water witch."

Diana tugged at his hair, letting her fingers tangle among the long, thick strands. "Romulus," she whispered. "My only, ever love."

He groaned softly as she pulled his head down to her mouth. She let her tongue dart against his and heard the sharp intake of his breath. He was like Toledo steel himself beneath her questing hands, hard and fit. But when he moved, raising himself slightly to slide his body along hers in an arching, aching caress, he was supple and fluid, like a sinuous jungle cat.

Diana had not known it could be like this between a man and a woman. That every heated touch could intoxicate, that every hungry kiss could stimulate, until they swirled together into a steadily rising need. Her body was longing for his touch, even as his hands explored her skin. Her mouth cried out for his kisses even as his lips melted against hers. No contact appeased her; she longed for some completion that was far beyond her ken.

It was only when he drew down the wide neckline of her blouse and laid his mouth against the rise of her breast, that she at last understood what it was she sought. As he raked his teeth over her flesh, her body began to shudder. And deep within her another sort of shuddering began. A twisting, burning, coiling ache of need. She moaned as her hips rose to meet his body.

"No," she gasped as he let his mouth drift to the tip of her breast. "Ah, yes!" she cried out as he flicked his tongue over the swollen bud. Again she arched up to meet the fire.

"This is a dream, Allegra," he breathed against her skin. "This is every beguiling dream I have ever had, even before I knew you existed."

"It's not a dream," she countered, in a low, throaty voice. "It is a storybook, filled with gallant heroes. It is every wondrous tale I've ever read and believed in."

"Then I'll be your storybook hero," he said into the hollow of her throat.

"And I'll be your beguiling dream."

Romulus hugged her tightly, and then shifted away from her. She was frowning slightly as he sat up.

"Are we finished?" Her body was insisting that there had to be something more.

He grinned and reached out to touch the side of her face. "I think I'd better be your storybook husband, before we go any further."

Diana gave him a relieved smile. "So there is a 'further'? You see, I am very naive about these things." She leaned forward and propped her elbows on his knees. "Someone will have to teach me, I expect."

Romulus chuckled softly. "I believe we can find some poor unsuspecting soul to do the job."

"He will need to be tall," she mused as he drew her into his lap and twined his arms around her waist. "And I do fancy red hair. Dark red, you know, like beech leaves."

"Not an uncommon color," he murmured against her ear.

"And his eyes should be green . . . and brown . . . and gold."

"It gets more difficult."

"His nose must be arched, and his mouth . . ."

"What about his mouth?" he breathed.

"His mouth . . . *his mouth*—"

Romulus demonstrated exactly what this paragon's mouth needed to be like. Hungry and demanding, gentle and coaxing. By the time he'd finished, they were both lying on the grass, shivering with desire.

"This isn't working," Rom groaned as he attempted to stand up and failed utterly. "Another five minutes and we won't need a parson."

"Maybe you would like to rail at me now for stealing your skiff," Diana suggested, trying not to grin—her river god looked positively bosky. Not that it wasn't entirely gratifying that she was the one responsible for his unsteady state. "I'd rather you got that over with before we go back to the island."

Romulus considered this. "The trouble is, Allegra, that even when I am furious with you, I still want to kiss you. You got a taste of that this afternoon."

"Well, then, don't get angry. Just read me a cutting lecture on my bad behavior. Icy disdain is much more effective than anger."

He rolled over and leaned back on his elbows. "Very well. But first, tell me why you were crying in the caravan. I suspect you wanted me to come after you. The skiff and the bracelet were hard to miss."

Diana nodded. "I left a trail a blind man could follow. Yet it took you hours to find me. It was very embarrassing to be sitting there with Niall and Gizella, thinking you didn't care enough to come after me. I thought you knew the river, Romulus, at least well enough not to row past your own boat."

"Unfortunately, I also know the river rats. Argie Beasle resurfaced while I was in Treypenny. With Wald Chipping, the ferryman. I got sidetracked in my search for you."

"What happened?" She drew up her knees and wrapped her arms around them.

"They cast off in Wald's ferry boat, and I feared they were going after my swan's. But they surprised me by heading upstream. Probably after rabbits or pheasant."

"Well that's a relief. Anymore questions?"

He plucked up a long stem of grass and began to chew on it. "Mmm. Maybe one or two. The thing I have been perishing to know, is what the devil you were doing in a rowboat last Saturday night."

"Oh, that. I thought I'd made that clear. I was hiding from Beveril."

"And why were you hiding from your intended husband?"

Diana bit her lip. "I think I'd better tell you the whole story."

"Hallelujah," Romulus said under his breath. He'd only been waiting for five days.

Diana rose and assumed an orator's stance. "I left my betrothal ball because I needed some air. These society parties are all very well, but there are generally far too many people crowded into a—"

"We've only got until dawn, Allegra," he reminded her drily.

She winced. "Sorry, but I thought you wanted to know *everything*."

Romulus motioned her to continue. "As you will, my witch."

"I left the ball and went down to the river, because I needed to think . . . I was very troubled over my upcoming marriage to Beveril."

"Ah. You begin to make some sense," Romulus interjected.

"While I was on the dock, a couple happened along. I hid in the rowboat so that I wouldn't have to answer any awkward questions."

"Like how you could bear to affiance yourself to a pompous windbag, you mean."

Diana disregarded this remark. "I was there for some time. The couple, er . . . well, they were doing what most couples do when they sneak off from a party." She stopped and gave Romulus a wicked grin.

"And did you discover the identity of this amorous couple?"

"Yes," she said. "It was Sir Beveril and Vivian Partridge."

Romulus gave himself a small nod of acknowledgment for having anticipated that scenario days ago.

"And you felt very humiliated there in your rowboat," he stated gently.

"Yes," she said, clasping her hands before her. "I have never been so mortified or so angry."

"Angry because he was kissing Vivian Partridge?"

"No," she said. "Angry because he called me an antidote and said my hair was an untamed mane. I am only revealing these lowering comments to you, because I think you don't mind so much how I look."

Romulus rose up at once and hugged her waist. "My darling Allegra, you are spectacularly beautiful. Great heavens, has no one ever told you? Why do you think I've been beating Niall off with a stick?"

"You are very kind to say that, but I think it is only because you care for me."

Romulus shook his head vehemently. "Even if I wasn't top-over-tail in love with you, I'd still have to acknowledge that you are a paragon."

"You," she stated firmly, "have not seen my sister. She was well named Helen. That lady from Troy had nothing on her for looks. She is quite beautiful. And she is never shatterbrained or hot tempered."

"She sounds like a dull lot to me, Allegra."

She sighed. "I do so like it when you call me Allegra. Being named Diana is all very well, if one is an alluring huntress with long legs and a noteworthy bosom."

"I think your bosom is quite worthy of note," he said slyly.

"I am much more an Allegra than I will ever be a Diana. But see, you have distracted me from Beveril."

"I certainly hope so."

She wrinkled her nose at him. "After he and Lady Vivian left the dock, I was determined to march right into the ball and end my engagement. But then the boat came loose. I wasn't so afraid at first—until I met you I thought I knew all about navigating the river. But there was only one oar—"

"Very bad for rowing," he remarked.

"Then, well, you know the rest. The bump on my head, falling into the water, being rescued by a tall river god—"

"What?"

"That's how I thought of you at first. I was quite dazzled, you know."

"Daft is more like it."

"Oh, and who is resisting compliments now?" she chided him. "You were so tender with the cygnets, and so wise about so many things. I had never met a man like you, Romulus. My father is very kind, but in an absentminded way. And the gentlemen of the *ton* are more concerned with their shirt points and their watch fobs than with living, breathing things."

Romulus watched her in silence for a bit.

She shifted on the grass. "What is it? You've grown so quiet."

"You won't be part of the *ton* if you marry me. You must understand that. My father was a river warden, a commoner. I know little of my mother, but I assume she was of his class. I've never been out in society. Except for my friends in the regiment, I have never hobnobbed with the gentry."

"I have no love for the *ton*, Romulus."

"It's not only the *ton*, sweetheart. Your family will not support you in marrying me. They may very well turn their back's on you—you need to think on that before we are wed. Doors will be closed to you that you now take for granted as being open."

Diana knelt down beside him. "The only door I need opened to me is the one to your heart. My father will accept you, because he loves me. Helen and James may be upset at first, but I know they will come to care for you. James desires a seat in Parliament . . . it might even please him that I am marrying a man who works to earn his bread."

"The common touch, eh?" Romulus sounded doubtful.

"You are not common in the least," she said with great conviction as she cupped his cheek. "So now that you know the entire story, do you forgive me for lying to you?"

He sat unspeaking for a moment. "I'm still not sure I understand why you needed to keep up the pretense. You'd already made up your mind to jilt Beveril—you could have gone home the day after you recovered from your fever and had it out with your family."

"What, and never see you or hear from you again? I knew the longer you let me stay on, the more chance that I could make you love me. I *was* suffering bridal nerves, Romulus—to use your wretched expression—but Beveril wasn't the groom in question."

Romulus sighed. "And there I was, holding back my feelings, thinking you couldn't possibly love a man like me. I don't know which of us was the more foolish." He added as an afterthought, "I gather you never really believed I was keeping you with me to spite Beveril."

Diana was glad he couldn't see her guilty blush in the darkness. "I only said those things to provoke you. I couldn't have borne it if you'd sent me away without telling me how you felt."

"Oh, you provoked me, right enough." He tipped her head back, his fingers tracing along the pulse in her throat. "I've never come nearer to throttling a woman. I hope you're not going to keep up this tendency to lie once we are wed."

"Just a few small lies," she said with a grin. "To keep things interesting."

"Oh, I doubt that will ever be a problem," he murmured as he let his mouth follow the trail that his fingers had blazed along her neck. With a moan she lay back in the grass as he worked his way up to the soft recess behind her ear. He raised his lips from her skin, leaving behind a shimmering heat.

"Can we go back to the camp now, Rom?" she asked.

"Why, sweetheart? Are you getting sleepy?" He brushed the hair gently back from her face.

"No," she said intently. "I want to dance with you. River gods can dance, can't they?"

"Only with water witches, my love. And only in Gypsy meadows, under a waning moon."

Chapter 10

Diana and Romulus danced for what seemed like hours. They ate roast pig, and steaming potatoes straight from the fire. Diana drank wine from a goatskin, spilling a good deal more than she managed to get into her mouth, laughing in delight when Romulus kissed the sticky traces from her face. The stately balls and formal cotillions she had attended in London paled beside this Gypsy revel, and she thought she must be a changeling to be entranced by so simple an entertainment. Romulus had called her untamed and unfettered, and Diana felt the truth of those words for the first time.

She and Romulus had settled their future as they'd walked back across the field to the caravans, and so there was no longer any need for her to keep hidden away. Once they reached the gathering, Rom never left her side and openly declared his affection for her with every look and gesture.

When the revelers at last began to drift toward their respective homes, Niall took Romulus aside and handed him the reins to his piebald stallion. "Allegra's too weary from dancing to walk, Rom. Take her to the river on Roibin. You need only slap him on the rump and he'll come back to me, just like a spaniel."

Before Diana could protest, Romulus had swung her up onto the horse's bare back. Then Niall cupped his hand at Rom's knee and sent him vaulting up behind her. Diana had never envisioned Romulus on horseback. As he skillfully turned the unruly stallion in a circle and then urged him into a gallop, she realized that she needed to reassess his title. Her river god, it appeared, was part centaur.

He held her close before him, as the wind whipped at their hair, sending a tangle of black and russet flying behind them. The trip to the river was all too short, and Diana was breathless as Romulus slid off the beast and lifted her down.

"Kiss me again, Rom," she pleaded, once he had sent the stallion skittering away.

"No," he said, as he traced her bottom lip with his thumb. "The next time I kiss you will be on my island. On the porch where I kissed you in anger. This time I will not, I swear, make the same mistake."

"And tomorrow?" she asked, needing to hear him say the words again.

"Tomorrow," he said fondly, "we will journey north, to your father's home. Where I will ask for your hand properly. Though I daresay it will be the first proper thing about this courtship."

Diana grinned. "And you're certain Niall won't mind keeping an eye on the swans while we are away?"

Romulus nodded as he tugged the dory up to the slip and tied the bow line of the punt to its stern.

"What about your skiff?" she asked, anxiously peering down-river. "Is it all right to leave it unattended?"

"Right as rain," he said. "I asked Niall to row it over in the morning."

"Speaking of rain," Diana said as he handed her into the boat. "Did you feel a drop?"

"Probably the dew falling," he said, looking east to the lightening sky. "It's nearly dawn."

He rowed across to the island, and brought the dory alongside the river slip. Hand in hand they made their weary way up the incline toward the path.

Romulus was the first one to see the light glowing through the trees ahead of them. He pushed Diana back as he ran forward. "Stay!" he called urgently over his shoulder. "Stay down by the boats!"

Diana, as always heedless of his commands, followed on his heels. She was to regret that imprudence for a good long time.

As she came out of the trees, she saw with a pounding heart that there were five men gathered in the front yard of the house. Lanterns sat at their feet, the wavering yellow light lending their faces an eerie, frightening aspect. They had formed a semicircle around Romulus, who stood facing them, hands fisted, arms curled at his sides. His whole posture was one of barely contained outrage.

Diana called out, "Romulus!"

He spun to ward her off. "No, Allegra!" he cried. "Go back!"

She flew toward him, her own temper flaring.

If these villagers thought they could oust Romulus from his island by sheer force of numbers alone, they had reckoned without her. As she neared Romulus, and the men who loomed before him, she saw her mistake. Though two of the men looked to be villagers, three wore Beveril's livery of gray and gold. Which was not surprising, since Beveril himself was now stepping down from the front porch of the lodge.

Her forward motion brought her right up to Romulus. He put one arm behind him, holding her back protectively, though his voice was laced with anger and regret as he muttered, "You've washed it now, my witch."

She grasped his arm between her trembling hands. *Sweet Jesus, she had run right into danger.*

"This is a pleasant domestic scene," Sir Beveril drawled as he came forward toward them. "The lord and his lady come home for the night." He leaned closer to Romulus. "Or should I say the baseborn knave and the woman he abducted."

Romulus threw his head back. "Does it look like I've been keeping her here against her will?"

Beveril sneered. "I can see that you've beguiled her—just as you beguiled Lady Vivian."

Diana's heart skipped a beat. What could Beveril mean? Had Romulus been dallying with the beautiful widow before he met her? If it was true, it certainly explained the enmity between the two men, the rancor that now fairly sizzled in the air.

Romulus gave a harsh laugh. "There has never been anything between Lady Vivian and me."

"And what is between you and this chit?" Beveril made a curt motion toward Diana.

"I am going to marry him," Diana stated as she tightened her hold on Rom's arm. There it was, out for all the world to hear.

"Yes," Romulus said with narrowed eyes. "She is to be my wife."

"Devil take you, she is not. She is promised to me. Do you think Mortimer will stand by while she marries a mongrel like you?" He jabbed the leaded tip of his riding crop into Rom's chest. "She is still underage, Perrin. And will do as her family bids."

Rom's eyes darted to Diana in mute appeal. She nodded bleakly. "Not twenty-one for another three months," she whispered hoarsely.

"Then we will wait," Romulus bit out. "Until she is free to make her own choices."

Beveril sneered openly. "She'll be my wife by then. And you will be rotting in a jail cell."

With an inarticulate cry, Romulus threw himself at Beveril, sending him reeling back toward the porch. Beveril held him off with one arm as he barked to his servants, "Take him, damn you!"

The three men closed rapidly in on Romulus. Too late, he thrust a hand into his rucksack, groping for his pistol. They knocked his hand away, and grappled with him until he was forced to his knees, his arms twisted behind his back. He uttered a raw cry which was echoed by Diana as she ran toward him. The two villagers stepped forward and blocked her path.

"Let him go!" Diana pleaded, turning to Beveril. "This is Rom's island. You have no right to be here!"

"I have more right than you, my sweet." As he spoke, he reached out and stroked Diana's hair.

Romulus snarled, "Get your festering hands off her!" He was trying to rise up, but the three men forced him back down to the grass.

"Shut him up," Sir Beveril said brusquely to one of the villagers.

Argie Beasle stepped forward and quickly back-handed Rom across the face. "Ain't so cocky now, are ye, my fine fellow," he taunted, rocking back on his heels.

Rom looked past the little poacher, his eyes blazing up at Sir Beveril. "Not man enough to do your own dirty work, eh, Hunny-cut?"

"I wouldn't sully myself by laying hands on you," he muttered.

"A fine excuse for cowardice."

"Again, Beasle!" Sir Beveril ordered.

As Argie drew his arm back, Diana spun the little river rat around by the shoulder, shoving him with all her strength away from Romulus. He staggered back, and then was about to lash out at her when Beveril barked, "Enough, Beasle! You may hit Perrin as often as you like, but this lady is still my intended."

"I am not!" Diana said between her teeth. "I will never marry you. Now order your men to set Romulus free, or I will tell the world what you have done here tonight."

"What?" he sniffed. "That I have rowed over to my aunt's island and apprehended the madman who abducted my fiancée?" He tsked gently. "I have the law on my side, Diana. This vermin—"

He nodded abruptly toward Romulus, "—has forfeited all his rights by keeping you here."

Diana leaned forward. "Listen to me, Beveril. Romulus has committed no crime. He did not abduct me, nor did he keep me here against my will. He saved my life when I was drowning. He nursed me when I was ill. You should be thanking him that I am still alive."

"That will be the day, that I thank this river scum for anything. And as for whether or not he has committed a crime, that is for a magistrate to decide. I fancy a few weeks in a jail cell waiting for trial may serve to cool his ardor for you."

"No!" Diana cried. "You must not!"

She knew Romulus would be destroyed if he was ever returned to prison. His spirit would wither away into dust. She flung away from Sir Beveril and ran back to Romulus. The men had dragged him to his feet and bound his hands behind him with a cord. He now stood with his head thrown back, his eyes dark and hollow as they regarded her.

"What should I do?" she pleaded. "Oh, my love, tell me what I should do."

He shook his head. There was a trickle of blood on his mouth from Argie's blow. "You can't do anything now, Allegra. It's over."

"No!" she keened, reaching out for him. The men who held him dragged him back, away from her hands. "I'll go to Lady Hamish," she said urgently, trying to offer him some hope.

"My aunt left for London today," Beveril remarked evenly from behind them. "She has a complaint of the digestion and needed to visit a specialist there. I doubt if she will return before a fortnight has passed."

Diana glared at him. "She will not let you put Romulus in jail."

Romulus rallied slightly. "She has a point, Hunnycut. Lady Hamish will not like it that you have usurped her power."

Beveril snorted. "My aunt has tolerated a great deal from you, Perrin. Your unsavory associations, and your freakish behavior. But I guarantee she will not be so forgiving when she learns of your latest outrage. Not that it matters. You will be long gone from here by the time she returns."

Diana's eyes implored Romulus. *Tell me*, they begged. *How can I help you?*

"Go home, Allegra," he whispered hoarsely. "Make your peace with your family. Beveril knows there's nothing I can say in my own defense. . . . I did keep you here long after I knew where you belonged. God help me, how could I not?"

Her heart was lurching in her breast. She couldn't believe Romulus was telling her to go.

"They can't harm you," she cried softly. "You have done nothing wrong."

"I forgot my place," he said bitterly. "In your world that is unforgivable. Go now, Allegra. For once in your blasted life obey me and go home."

She turned from him in numb confusion. Beveril was holding out one hand to her.

The strained silence of that moment was broken by a loud, shattering crash. Argie Beasle had pitched one of the lanterns through the nearest window of the house, into Rom's bedroom.

Seven pairs of eyes watched in stunned shock as an orange tongue of flame licked its way up the frame of the window and then quickly spread to the rest of the room.

Without a second's hesitation, Diana darted toward the porch.

"*No-o-o!*" Romulus bellowed in primal fear when he saw where she was headed. He kicked out at his captors, fighting now like a man possessed. The cord that had bound his wrists had come undone, and he quickly laid about him with his fists. As the men fell back from his fury, he staggered forward toward the house, crying, "Allegra!"

At Beveril's command, one of his men ran forward and struck Romulus on the side of the head with the butt of a pistol. He fell heavily to his knees. Again the pistol descended. The last thing he saw before the darkness engulfed him was his water witch disappearing through the front door of the burning building.

"*A-l-l-e-g-r-a!*" The anguished cry never left his lips.

Sir Beveril was hard on Diana's heels as she crossed the sitting room. He reached for her, but she twisted out of his grasp and ran for the storeroom.

"*Are you insane!*" he raged, thrusting aside the tea table as she darted through the storeroom door ahead of him. Already the smoke from the bedroom was billowing in behind him. Beveril batted his way through the door in Diana's wake.

She felt his arms close around her. "No!" she choked, striking at him with her fists. "Let me go!"

"I won't let you kill yourself over that man, Diana."

"I'm not trying to kill myself," she gasped hoarsely as she broke free. "I am trying to save these birds."

She swung the top crate off the stack, but could not manage the second one. She held the cage out to Beveril in mute entreaty, but he attempted to knock it from her hands. She quickly drew it back and cried thunderously, "For the love of God, Beveril, these are your aunt's swans!"

His eyes narrowed at first in confusion, and then he nodded his comprehension. He hoisted the first crate under one arm, and then caught up the top of the second one in his free hand. For the first time Diana was grateful that he was such a large, strapping man.

"Now get the hell out of here!" he barked.

She raced through the house toward the front door, coughing and choking in the fog of smoke. Flames were licking into the sitting room from the hallway. In desperation Diana plucked up the largest of Rom's books and heaved it through the window. She scrambled out over the sill and tumbled onto the lawn, and then watched as Beveril's men helped him climb out, taking the crates from him to hasten his exit.

Diana rolled away from the burning house, and then lay still, gasping for air and trying not to swoon. She saw Romulus, lying facedown in the grass, and crawled to where he lay. One arm was stretched out, as though he were still reaching toward the house. She tugged him onto his side and tenderly wiped the blood from his mouth with a corner of her skirt. His face was pale, waxen in the light of the fire. She laid her mouth upon his cheek, murmuring of her love and of her grief over the pain she had brought to him.

Mere hours ago she had lain with him in a Gypsy meadow and kissed him until they were both dizzy with passion. Now . . . now the world had shattered into small pieces and would never be put right. She felt the tears on her face . . . and on her neck and on her hands. It was raining. But the house behind her was burning, and all the tears of heaven could not douse the fire. She put her head down and wept in truth. For Rom, for his house, and for herself, who had brought this foul vengeance down upon the man she loved.

Sir Beveril knelt and stroked her hair.

"Get away from me," she snarled, scuttling away from his touch with a loud hiss. "You have done a wicked thing tonight. A truly wicked thing."

"Not wicked, Diana, just. The knave was too full of himself, by far. How dared he raise his eyes to a lady of gentle birth. Prison's too good for him, but it will have to suffice."

Diana heaved herself up onto her knees and threw herself against Beveril's chest, clutching at the lapels of his driving coat. "No," she breathed, her eyes wide with panic. "You mustn't! Promise me you'll not put him in prison. I'll do anything you want. I swear it."

Sir Beveril covered her hands with his own. "Anything?"

Diana grit her teeth. Rom's sanity, his very soul, was at stake. "Yes," she said hoarsely. "Anything."

"You'll marry me now? Before the week is out?"

She nodded numbly. "If that is what it takes, then, yes, I will marry you."

"Then I promise you Perrin will never see the inside of a jail cell."

Argie Beasle had sidled over to them; he stood tapping the flat side of the ax he carried against his bony shin. "I scuttled his boats as you ordered, sir."

Beveril rose and thrust the poacher roughly from his path. "I told you to sink the boats, Beasle. The house was not to be touched."

Argie shrugged sullenly. "I owed him."

Diana rose slowly to her feet. Mindless of the pelting rain, she walked as one dead past the liveried men who stood gaping at the fire. She longed to turn around, to see the last of her blessed haven, but she knew she would crumple, to see it engulfed in flames.

Kneeling down beside the crates, she swung open both doors. The cygnets clambered out and gathered around her. With a harsh motion she drove them away from her, knowing they would be safer on the river than among these swan-killing ruffians. Peeping in bewilderment, they scattered along the edge of the grass, heading in the direction of the river. Diana watched until they disappeared from sight.

The smoke was getting worse now, burning her eyes and her throat. Through the billowing haze, she looked for Romulus. He was gone from the front yard, and two of Beveril's men with him. She hadn't even been allowed a brief farewell.

Beveril took her by the wrist then, and hauled her unprotesting from the yard. As they passed the path that diverted off to the river slip, she looked down through the wet foliage. The dory and the punt lay below her, half submerged in the dark water. Argie Beasle had done his work well.

She now knew where Argie and Wald Chipping had gone in the ferry boat. They hadn't gone upriver after pheasant or rabbits. No, they had rowed to Hamish House and brought Sir Beveril to Rom's island. Hoping to find her there alone, no doubt. And when they discovered she was no longer on the island, they had waited. She and Romulus had walked blithely into their trap.

"What of Romulus?" she asked in a remote voice.

"Gone," Sir Beveril replied tersely. "My men will take him to Richmond."

"What then?"

Beveril scowled. "They're to put him on a coach for London. If he's smart, he'll stay well away from here. But if you make any attempt to locate him, Diana, or if he tries to reach you, I'll see that he rots in prison for a good long time."

He will come for me, Diana whispered to herself. He wouldn't stay away, not after the promises he'd made in the Gypsy meadow. Not that it would serve any purpose. She was as good as wed to Beveril now.

A long, low sob escaped her. It was impossible to keep the wracking torment from tearing at her heart.

At the inlet two rowboats were beached on the shingle—one of Beveril's men waited in the smaller boat. Diana let herself be lifted onto the seat, and then sat in silence as she was rowed across the river to where Beveril's carriage was now waiting.

As she climbed from the boat, pointedly avoiding Beveril's outstretched hand, she ventured one last look at the island. Through the teeming rain she saw the red lick of the fire over the trees, and the billows of smoke sketched against the dawn sky. Argie Beasle and the other villager, the man called Wald Chipping, had cast off in the second boat, and were now rowing upstream. She wondered how much money Beveril had given them for betraying Romulus. What was it worth, she mused wretchedly, to bring a man's dreams crashing down around his head?

It was over now. The heron and the cygnets were gone. The keeper of the swans was also gone from his world. And she was in permanent exile from the island where she had first learned to love.

Chapter 11

Diana spoke to no one when she arrived at Mortimer House, pinch-faced, hollow-eyed, and covered with soot. She had no words for Helen, who bustled her upstairs to her bed, with a taut expression on her beautiful mouth, or for James, who hovered in the hallway, with a look of concern on his long, dour face. Helen had allowed Sir Beveril into Diana's bedchamber once she had been dressed in a night rail and tucked under the covers, but she merely turned away, burrowing her face into the pillow.

Someone had left a candle burning on her nightstand, even though it was full daylight by the time she was put to bed. She gazed at the wavering flame and thought again of the house on the island. Fire was a cleansing thing, her father had told her, when, as a child, she had wept as a local farmer set his fields ablaze. The wheat had been infected with a fungus, he'd explained, and the field needed to be made clean.

But the fire that destroyed Rom's house had been an evil thing. Brought about by evil men. And the worst of it was, she had promised to marry one of those evil men. Within the week.

When Helen came to look in on her later that morning, Diana decided it was time to have her say.

"Hello, Helen," she said hoarsely. The smoke from the fire had left her voice weak and scratchy.

"Diana!" Her sister knelt beside the bed. "Thank God you are unharmed. I wanted to call for the doctor last night, but James said you were probably only exhausted."

"I'm sorry to have worried you, Helen. And James. I hope you got my note from Wilfred Bailey."

Her sister nodded. "He brought it here himself. Though it was the strangest message I've ever seen. But at least we knew you were still alive. How could you have run off like that, Diana? And then have stayed away for so long?"

"I fell in love," Diana answered simply.

Helen grunted in a most unladylike manner. "Sir Beveril mentioned a river warden who had been keeping you on an island. But what nonsense is this? This is one of your odd starts, isn't it?"

"It's not an odd start, Helen. He rescued me from the river, and then he took care of me when I was ill."

"Nanny Perkins took care of you when you had the measles, and you didn't fall in love with her."

Diana nearly smiled. Sometimes the prosaic Helen was quite amusing in spite of herself.

"Romulus doesn't look anything like Nanny Perkins," she proclaimed. "He looks like a god, Helen. Tall and broad shouldered, with the most beautiful eyes, and hair the color of beech leaves."

Helen stood up. "I think you do need a doctor—you must be feverish. Sir Beveril said this Romulus person was a great scarecrow of a man, a freakish fellow that the villagers run from in fear."

Diana sighed. It was pointless to even attempt to convince her sister of Rom's sterling qualities. Not after Beveril had poisoned her thoughts.

"It doesn't matter what he was like . . . now," she uttered sadly. "I am going to wed Sir Beveril before the week is out. I promised him and so I suppose I must."

"Well you needn't look so Friday-faced about it, my girl. You should be on your knees thanking the Lord that Sir Beveril still wants you, after . . . well, after your unfortunate situation."

"Why not say it out loud, Helen? I was compromised. There, it's not difficult to say. And there is another word I am not afraid to say—greed. For it is greed alone that is prompting Beveril to marry me."

Her eyes widened. "What do you mean? James has dowered you well, but you are hardly an heiress."

Diana said, "The night of my ball, I overheard Beveril tell Vivian Partridge that, in addition to my dowry, James has agreed to pay off all his gambling debts."

Helen's brow puckered. "James has said nothing of this to me."

"An arrangement between gentlemen, perhaps," she suggested slyly. She saw that Helen was rattled by the thought that James hadn't confided in her, especially in a matter that involved her own sister.

"Beveril is a gamester and deeply in debt," Diana stated. "Thousands of pounds in debt, I shouldn't be surprised. He ought to offer James a ministry at least, for such a boon."

Helen still said nothing, but her face had gone pale.

"And speaking of Lady Vivian, I don't suppose you were aware that she is Beveril's paramour?"

"Diana!" Helen squealed, raising her hands to her cheeks. "Ladies are never to speak of such things."

Diana glared up at her. "So you did know about her."

Helen walked to the window and stood a moment, pleating one of the draperies. "There are some things a woman must learn to accept about her husband, Diana," she said without turning. "A man shares his home with his wife, his wealth and his stature. In return, she must, at times, look the other way."

"Bosh!" said Diana with a scowl. She was rewarded when her sister's shoulders quivered noticeably. "Romulus would never place me in such a humiliating position."

With a sigh. Helen returned to her bedside. She laid one hand on Diana's shoulder. It was the first even remotely comforting gesture she had offered her sister. "I will speak to James about Lady Vivian, if you like. He can insist that Beveril forego that lady's . . . ah, companionship, if it will ease your mind."

"And what of his gambling? And don't tell me that gentlemen will have their little pursuits, and that I should look away. He'll continue to bleed James, I'm sure of it. At least until he receives his inheritance. Do you remember the squire in Bothys? His gambling beggared his whole family, including his own brother."

"I'm sure Sir Beveril is not in that league," Helen proclaimed.

"He's probably worse," she muttered. It occurred to her that her practical sister was more out of touch with the reality of things than Diana had ever realized. Practicality, it appeared, did not go hand in hand with worldly wisdom. "Helen," she said into the strained silence, "Tell me—do you love James?"

Her sister looked startled. "Love him? Why, he is the soul of kindness and generosity to me. To both of us, Diana. More so now, if he is willing to clear Beveril from debt for your sake."

"But do you love him?"

"I don't put any stock in romantic love. But I am very fond of James. I have a true affection for him."

"And before you were wed? What were your feelings for him then?"

"I admired his ambition. And as I have said, he was very kind to me."

"But what if you knew him to be a man beneath contempt—a bully, a wastrel, a man who dallied with another woman, practically under your nose. What then, Helen? Could you marry such a man?"

Helen shifted her eyes away from Diana. "James was none of those things, as you very well know."

"Ah, but I am not being asked to marry the admirable James. It is Beveril who awaits me. And he is all those things. If you have a care for me, Helen, if you have any sisterly affection at all, you will help me find a way to break my promise to Sir Beveril."

"Why?" she said sharply, heedless of Diana's plea. "So you can marry some water-stained river person?"

Diana closed her eyes. "No," she said. "I had one shimmering night with Romulus, and that is clearly all I am to be allowed. Beveril has sent him away, and if he returns, he will face prison."

"And so he should!" her sister snapped. "I only pray this 'shimmering night' you speak of didn't include the loss of your virtue. Beveril won't have you if he suspects that to be the case."

Diana had a moment of weakness, wondering if she dared lie to Beveril and tell him that Romulus had taken her virginity. After all, she hadn't had any compunction about lying to Rom. But in her heart she knew she couldn't sully his honor with such an untruth.

She wished he had taken her virtue, wished he had given her a child. Then, even if she never saw him again, she would have some token of his love. She was weeping now; she felt the hot wetness splattering down on her hands. All the promise she had seen in those golden eyes . . . now swept away forever.

"No," Diana said thickly. "Romulus did nothing outside the bounds of propriety. He . . . he was the most honorable man I've ever known."

Diana never gave up hope that Romulus would risk prison and return to rescue her. But she knew that unless he came for her before the end of the week, it would be too late.

Plans for her wedding went forward, but she was a mute, disinterested spectator. The wedding was to be a quiet affair at Mortimer House with only Diana's family members present. Beveril had objected politely but adamantly when James suggested summoning Lady Hamish back from London for the occasion; he claimed she was too unwell to travel even so short a distance. After the wedding, Beveril intended to take her to Yorkshire, where another ceremony would be performed with her father in attendance. She'd be twice married to Beveril, Diana thought bleakly, when she didn't even desire it the once.

Late at night, as she lay sleepless in her bed, Diana often wondered why Niall had not come to see her. Perhaps he blamed her for what happened on the island. Perhaps he was right to do so. She thought of running off to live with the Gypsies, but that notion only reminded her of how close they had come the last time to falling under Beveril's wrath.

No, she saw no way out of her predicament, short of throwing herself into the Thames. But the river lately had been calm in the extreme. She'd have had to weight her pockets with stones to do the deed.

Two days before her wedding Diana was sitting in the garden, trying to focus on the book in her lap. Beveril had ridden over to see James that morning, so she had escaped from the house and sought refuge in the trellised garden folly. She had barely said a word to Beveril since that night on the island, but it didn't seem to bother him any. Her dowry was doing enough talking for the both of them.

She saw him ride off eventually on his bay hack, and thought she might walk down to the river. That was as far as she was allowed to go on the estate—to the edge of the breakwater and to the back of the garden. At Helen's behest, James had warned all the servants, both inside and outside the house, to keep watch over Diana. Even now she saw two gardeners eyeing her from behind a lilac bush. Her sister was not going to give her another opportunity to bolt. She was nothing more than a prisoner in a pretty cage.

As she set down her book, she noticed someone approaching from the direction of the stables. The two gardeners started forward, until they realized it was a woman. No threat there, they reasoned, not from a lady in a dashing green silk gown. Diana saw that a gauzy veil trailed down from the front of the woman's wide-brimmed straw bonnet, obscuring her face.

"Miss Exeley," the visitor called out to her. "Please, if you would spare me a moment of your time."

She watched in bewilderment as the graceful specter approached her. She rose from her bench as the woman came closer, and then gasped as the veil was drawn back. It was Lady Vivian Partridge.

"I am so glad I found you out here," the lady said a bit breathlessly. "I've been waiting in the lane in my carriage for over an hour, hoping to catch you alone."

"Sir Beveril has just left," Diana said stiffly.

"Yes, I know. That was why I waited. I didn't want him to know I'd talked to you. You are shocked to see me here . . . No, I don't blame you. Not good *ton* for a man's mistress to come calling on his fiancée."

"What do you want?" Diana asked sharply. She found civility a bit beyond her at that point.

Lady Vivian gave her a reassuring look. "I want to help you," she said in a throaty voice. "No, that's not quite true. I want to help both of us. I love Beveril, you see. But your brother-in-law has made him promise to stop . . . um, seeing me, once he marries you. I cannot bear the thought of losing him, Miss Exeley."

Some vague pity stirred in Diana. She knew all to well how it felt to have the man you loved warned away. "I have no desire to wed Sir Beveril," she said with complete candor. "But I must marry him, to keep Romulus out of prison. Beveril hates him, but I expect you know that."

Lady Vivian looked down and toyed with the cuff of her embroidered glove. "Not to diminish your own charms, Miss Exeley, but I believe I am the reason Beveril so detests your Mr. Perrin. Even before Beveril began to court you, I started paying rather noticeable attention to the river warden. I knew there was no surer way to rouse Beveril's jealousy than by casting out lures to a man he already disliked."

"What's sauce for the goose," Diana said, echoing the words Lady Vivian had spoken on the dock. Romulus must have been the "rascally knave" Beveril had spoken of that night.

The lady nodded. "But I had no idea Beveril would carry his vendetta to such an extreme."

Diana drawled, "You mean the fact that he burned down Rom's house, sank his boats, knocked him unconscious, and threatened him with prison?"

"There's more to it than that, Miss Exeley. A great deal more."

"What more could there be?" Diana bit out. "Romulus has nothing left for Beveril to destroy."

Lady Vivian nearly started back at the force of Diana's words. "Indeed there is something more. Beveril told me of his intention to send Romulus to London, and implied that it had been carried out. But the river warden never left the grounds of Hamish House."

Diana found herself clutching one of Lady Vivian's gloved hands. "Tell me, and quickly."

The lady drew a breath. "One of Beveril's coachmen is courting my abigail . . . he let something slip to her only this morning. Romulus is being held prisoner on the estate."

Diana gasped. "Sweet Jesus, this cannot be. Romulus was never to see the inside of a prison."

Lady Vivian frowned. "He's not in prison, per se. He's being kept under guard, not inside the house obviously. The coachman didn't know exactly where they were keeping him."

"It makes no sense," Diana muttered. "Beveril wanted Romulus gone. Why would he hold him here?"

"So he doesn't carry you off before the wedding, perhaps. Beveril is surely in a pelter to marry you."

"His creditors are doubtless clamoring for their money," Diana said archly, as she paced across the floor of the folly. She spun back to her visitor. "You needn't fear to lose Beveril, Lady Vivian. I will never marry him now. He has broken his promise to me. A prison is a prison, whether it's Newgate Gaol or an outbuilding on an estate. He lied, and now I am free. I . . . I only wonder that you can love such a man."

Lady Vivian gave a graceful shrug. "I know he has a great many faults, but when has that ever stopped a woman from loving someone. He might yet marry me, once you are beyond his reach."

Diana said without intentional cruelty, "There are heiresses aplenty in the *ton*, Lady Vivian. You forget that he is still deeply in debt."

"I'd sell everything I possess to aid him."

"Yes, I expect I'd do the same for Rom," Diana said softly. "And now I must ask you for one more piece of information, Lady Vivian. Have you any idea where Lady Hamish might be staying in London?"

She thought a minute. "Beveril keeps only bachelor quarters in the city, so she wouldn't have gone there. She has a close friend who lives in Grosvenor Square—Sir Robert Poole's sister, Lady Seaton."

"It might serve," Diana murmured. "It is a beginning, at least."

As her visitor turned to go, Diana shook herself from her frantic planning.

"Lady Vivian, I haven't thanked you for coming here. You betrayed Beveril to help me save Romulus. I don't think he deserves you, but as you have pointed out, we can't always choose where we love."

The lady took her hand. "Romulus Perrin is lucky to have found you, Miss Exeley."

Once she had gone, Diana ran to her room and changed from her morning dress into a plain dimity gown. It was nearly one o'clock, and she knew her sister and James would be in their rooms dressing for luncheon. She crept across the lawn toward the river, keeping to the shadows of the trees. The boathouse was locked, but she had pilfered the spare key from the butler's pantry.

The interior of the boathouse was dim, the ceiling prismed with pinpoints of light. A rowboat floated beside James's pleasure barge. This one had two oars, Diana was pleased to note. She was untying the line, when the door behind her banged open. The two gardeners stood there, backlit by the sun.

"Miss Diana!" the elder one called as he ran toward her. "You must come in now."

She quickly undid the line, scrambled into the boat, and pushed away from the dock.

The men leaned far over the side, reaching for her. "Miss Diana, please! We have our orders!"

Fighting back her panic, she drew the boat up beside the outer doorway and hefted the wooden rod that held it closed. The door swung outward, just as the younger groom pitched into the water beside her boat. In seconds she was out on the open river. She began rowing determinedly for Treypenny, moving with the current. If Mortimers' servants chose to follow her on the river, they had only the pleasure barge, and it required six strong men to row it. She knew she was safe from pursuit for the time being.

Let Niall be in the Gypsy camp, she prayed. He was her only hope of contacting Lady Hamish.

As she neared the water stairs, a group of cygnets floated past, unaccompanied by an adult swan. Were these some of Rom's babies, she wondered, stroking so boldly over the water?

"He's coming back," she called softly as they swam past her. "I promise you he is."

After she had grounded the boat beyond the village, and hidden it in the reeds, she hurried through Treypenny, making sure to avoid the Waterthrush. She was breathless when she reached the Gypsy camp.

Niall saw her as she came along the lane and ran to meet her. "*Allegra!*"

She threw herself into his arms.

"Ach, lass. No, don't cry. There now. That's better." He wiped her eyes with a large red kerchief.

"Oh, Niall," she wailed. "I am so happy to see you. I thought you had forgotten me."

His eyes darkened. "Not a bit. I came to see you the day after Romulus was taken. Argie Beasle was bragging in the 'Thrush over his part in the dirty business, so I knew what had happened. But they wouldn't let me see you. Mortimer's butler threatened to have me flogged if I didn't leave. I came back three days in a row. I even left a note with one of the gardeners, but I gather you never got it."

"No," she said sadly. "And I'm not surprised. I was not allowed any reminders of Romulus."

"I've been looking after the swans," Niall said, holding her in the crook of his arm. "I found Rom's skiff near the village and knew he wouldn't mind me using it. I've been spending time on the island, sifting through the debris from the fire. I found this in his trunk."

He had pulled a medallion from his pocket and now offered it to Diana. She turned it over in her hand. It was a commendation for valor engraved with the Prince Regent's own seal.

"May I keep it?" she asked, trying to restrain her tears. "He might want it back again."

"If he ever returns," Niall said crossly. "I can't believe he's stayed away so long. It's been nearly a week since they took him off to London."

"He never got to London," Diana said darkly.

Niall's eyes widened. "But Argie said—"

Diana shook her head slowly. She then told him what Lady Vivian had discovered from her abigail.

Niall gripped her arms. "Beveril's holding Rom on the estate? We've got to find him, Allegra!"

"No," Diana said intently. "It could take days to locate him in a place the size of Hamish House."

"Then I'll snatch Beveril off his horse, and torture him until he tells us where Rom's being kept."

Diana grinned. She liked his bloodthirsty plan. Except then it would be Niall who ended up in jail.

"No," she said with more calmness than she was feeling. "We've got to find Lady Hamish in London."

After she'd told him about the woman in Grosvenor Square, Niall whistled for his stallion.

"When you locate Lady Hamish," Diana said urgently as he vaulted onto the beast, "tell her she must return here at once. Tell her about Romulus, Niall. She will come then. I know she will."

"Stay here," he said. "I'll likely be back by nightfall. But I promise I won't return until I've found her."

She watched him gallop off, a prayer on her lips. Every instinct compelled her to row across to Hamish House and accost Beveril herself. But she feared to show her hand. He could move Rom from the estate and then they might never find him. But it was killing her that he was imprisoned so close by, and that she had no way of freeing him.

She made her way to Gisella's caravan. The old woman clucked over her, fed her, and then tucked her up on the padded bench beneath a colorful woven comforter and ordered her to nap. Diana didn't want to sleep, couldn't imagine she could ever sleep again until Romulus was set free. But when she stirred awake at last, she saw that the sky outside the open door of the caravan was quite dark.

Find her, Niall, she prayed. *Find her and bring her home.*

Romulus knew he wasn't back in the French prison. There was some solace in that.

The voices he heard in the less clouded part of his brain were definitely speaking English. But he didn't like to dwell for long in that place of lucidity—for that was where he saw an endless vision of Allegra running into a burning house. It was easier to sink into the black nothingness, where he could convince himself that she was still alive, that the woman he had loved beyond all thought and all boundaries had not perished in the blaze. That the cygnets he had been fostering had not been burned to death, trapped in their crates. That everything that had meaning for him had not been reduced to ashes.

But with the immutable logic of a fevered brain, he knew for a certainty that all those things had come to pass. Still he called out her name, over and over, pleading with the fire not to take her.

"The woman's gone," a particularly whining voice responded with great relish. "Dead in the fire."

Before that revelation, Romulus had thrashed about, his disordered dreams flaying him into resistance. But now, now that he knew she was in truth gone from him, he lay as one dead.

The men who hovered over him slapped at him sometimes, and prodded him to force him awake. Buckets of water were dashed over his head, until he swam up into consciousness. But then the memories came crashing back—the reminders of all he had lost, of the blue-eyed, black-haired witch he had loved so fiercely—and he quickly submerged again into the beckoning abyss.

Days passed. He knew it by the shift of light on the wall of the rude building where he was kept. But even when his eyes were open, his mind stayed shut to any external intrusions. He neither ate nor drank, though his jailers often carried food and water to his mouth.

"Told you he was mad," the whining voice pronounced, after another fruitless attempt to rouse him.

"He's in shock," a deeper voice countered. "From the blow on his head, no doubt. See that he's kept warm, Beasle. I'm paying you and Chipping a pretty penny to watch over him. If he hasn't stirred by tomorrow, I'm afraid I'll have to call in a physician."

"You don't want no doctor sniffing around here, sir. How would it look for her ladyship's nephew to be keepin' a man locked up against his will?"

"We'll be accounting to more than doctors, if he dies."

Not going to die, Romulus wanted to reply. He would have welcomed death—his only conscious desire was to find his way across the void, to the woman who surely awaited him on the other side. But he knew he was a long way from that blessed release.

After the man with the deep voice had gone away, the whining man began to lash at him with a switch. "Wake up, ye bloody begger! Wake up, I say!"

Romulus felt the harsh sting of the limber wood upon his arms and his body, and then, when the whining man had worked himself up to a frenzied pitch, upon his face and throat.

Fine, he thought. Anything to help him along toward oblivion.

Chapter 12

S ir Beveril opened the door to the shed slowly.
   His prisoner was lying in exactly the same position he had
been in last night. Beveril stepped forward and prodded his leg
with one booted toe. The man on the ground groaned softly. Beveril knelt then, and raised his head from the straw. Though the
swelling on his mouth had gone down days ago, there were now
raised welts on his throat and on both cheeks.

"What's this?" Beveril called sharply over his shoulder. "What
are these marks on his face?"

The little man standing behind him shifted his shoulders uncomfortably. "I was only tryin' to rouse him a bit. I feared you
would be bringin' in the doctor."

Damn you, Argie Beasle! Beveril swore to himself. He should
have known better than to let the man anywhere near his prisoner.
A smattering of remorse swept over him as he gazed down at the
marked face. Beveril had only wanted to see Perrin brought to his
knees—because he had dared to keep Diana from him, because he
had befriended his aunt, and most of all, because he had cast his
eyes on Lady Vivian. For all his self-love, Beveril was truly enamored of the beautiful widow, and it was a measure of his desperation that he had agreed to James Mortimer's edict that he give
her up.

He laid one hand upon Rom's brow. It was clammy to the touch.
Jesus! He'd wanted to break Perrin's insolent pride a bit. But
this man, whose head lolled back in the crook of Beveril's arm, appeared to have had a deal more than his pride broken. Beveril
looked down again and saw that his prisoner had opened his eyes.
At first they were unfocused, but then as recognition dawned,
Romulus smiled grimly and rasped, "Both gone to perdition, have
we, Hunnycut?"

Beveril's relief that Perrin had at last regained some form of consciousness, was short-lived. From outside the shed there came the sound of carriage wheels and the jingling of harness. And the thud of rapid footfalls as Argie Beasle made a hasty retreat.

He lowered his prisoner onto the straw and went to the doorway. With a sinking heart he watched as Lady Hamish's barouche drew up on the cart track that edged the field. Behind it rode the black-haired Gypsy boy. He swung down from his lathered horse as Lady Hamish descended from her carriage.

"*Beveril!*" she cried in a ringing voice that set the hair on the back of his neck on end. "What in God's name is going on here?" She crossed the space that separated them until she was standing directly before the shed. "What have you done with Romulus?"

He shifted to one side, trying to block the sight of the unconscious man from her vision. "This is my own affair, Aunt. It's nothing you need trouble yourself over."

She disregarded his words and brusquely pushed past him. He heard her gasp of shock as she recognized the man lying in the corner of the shed. She sank to her knees on the dirty straw, heedless of the elegant carriage dress she wore, and lifted his head into her lap. Beveril watched in stunned disbelief as she tenderly stroked the damp hair back from his brow.

Gad, was every woman he cared about beguiled by this red-headed rogue?

"I wouldn't believe it when the Gypsy boy told me," she said softly, almost to herself. "I refused to believe you could do such a foul thing." She looked up at him, her eyes now blazing with contempt.

Beveril took a step back. "Please, Aunt Estelle!" he cried. "It's not what you think. He . . . he was keeping Diana with him. There on that accursed island. Now she fancies herself in love with him. I-I planned to set him free once she and I were wed."

"And what of these?" Her fingers were tracing above the raised weals that marred Rom's face.

"One of the villagers did it. He had a score to settle with Perrin. I didn't condone it, Aunt. As God is my witness, I meant him no real harm."

She rose slowly to her feet. "You have done him irreparable harm, Beveril," she uttered in a searing voice. "He was in a French prison for six months, did you know that? He managed to escape with eight of his men, got them across France and home to England. But I doubt that would have weighed with you."

Beveril was shaking his head in disbelief as he fell back before her wrath.

"He was a hero, Beveril," she continued as she advanced on him. "He was commended by the Prince Regent himself. I brought him here to heal, because he was scarred and damaged by his time in prison. Damage it has taken him ten months to get over."

"You never told me any of this," he protested.

"It wasn't my story to tell. But you had only to meet the man to know how fine he was, how noble."

"He was . . . a-above himself," Beveril sputtered. "He cozened you, Aunt, could you but see it."

"No," she breathed. "You cozened me. I've learned a great deal about you today, Beveril. I knew of your gaming debts, and your liaison with the Partridge woman. But I did not know until this moment what a gutless, self-serving coward you are."

She turned away, calling to her driver. "William, please, would you carry Romulus to the carriage?"

Before the driver could climb down, Beveril had moved forward and lifted Romulus from the straw. He walked past his aunt with the lifeless form of the river warden in his arms. As he neared the carriage, he staggered slightly. Niall rushed forward and caught Rom's legs, and together they laid him on the seat.

Beveril turned then, weaving slightly on his feet. "I am most sorry, Aunt Estelle."

She swept past him and climbed into the carriage. She took up one of Rom's hands and began to stroke it. "Home, William," she said without so much as a glance at her nephew. "And when we get there, you must send immediately for Dr. Harley."

Beveril watched the carriage drive away. Niall had remounted his horse and sat gazing down at him.

"I didn't know," Beveril repeated in a hollow voice. "Not about the prison. Not that he was a hero."

"Neither did I," Niall said grimly. "And I'll wager neither did Diana, at first. But we cared for him all the same. As your aunt said, you only had to meet him to know how fine he is."

Niall kicked his stallion into a gallop and set off across the wide field toward the spot where Argie Beasle was attempting to extricate himself from a thicket of nettles.

Sir Beveril Hunnycut walked numbly to where his own horse was tethered. After one last look at the rooftop of the great house, whose gray slates showed in the far distance, he mounted and rode off in the direction of Vivian Partridge's home. He knew he was no longer welcome at Hamish House. And he knew he had no one to blame for that banishment but himself.

The following morning, there was still no sign of Niall. Diana fretted and fussed, striding back and forth between the caravans, muttering to herself and wondering where the devil the boy had gotten to. The Gypsies gave her a wide berth—she reckoned they thought her a fitting mate for the redheaded madman.

When Niall came galloping into camp at last on his wild-eyed horse, she expected to see some sign of victory or defeat on his face. But it was set and stony, offering her no clues. He slithered down from the horse's damp back—still wet from their swim across the river—and took her firmly by the arms.

Her heart stopped for an instant before he spoke, for she saw defeat now, clearly written in his eyes.

"He's been found," he said quickly, ending her suspense. "Lady Hamish found him this morning and had him brought to her house. But he is very ill, Allegra. Something I've never seen before. I sat with him after the doctor left, stayed there talking to him, trying to reach him. But nothing I did seemed to rouse him."

"Is he unconscious?"

Niall winced and shivered. "No, that's the damnable part. His eyes were open the whole time. But it's as if he just isn't there."

"I must go to him." She tried to shake off his hands. "He needs me!"

"No," the boy said evenly. "Listen to me, sweeting." He cupped her head between his two hands and gazed into her eyes. "It will shock you—do you hear me, Allegra?—shock you horribly, to see him like that. Trust me—I'm still reeling from it."

Her mouth quivered. "Wh-what did Beveril do to him, to m-make him like that?"

"Kept him locked in a shed—since the night he was taken from the island, I gather—and placed him in the tender care of Argie Beasle."

"Ah, no."

"Yes, though we've probably seen the last of that river rat. I left him screaming for help in a patch of nettles." Niall's mouth tightened. "He'd beaten Romulus with a switch, and left him covered with welts."

The tears were flowing unheeded down Diana's face. "H-he

h-hit Romulus that night on the island," she stammered. "Hit him while he was being held down by three men." She drew a shuddering breath. "They've broken him, haven't they, Niall? That's what you're afraid to tell me. Sir Beveril and Argie Beasle have crushed all the spirit out of him."

Niall looked away over the green field. He was damned if he was going to cry in front of Allegra.

"Who can say?" he answered softly. "Lady Hamish told her nephew that Rom had been imprisoned by the French for six months. I take it you knew that much about his past."

Diana nodded. "It nearly broke him that time. That was the only reason I agreed to marry Beveril—to keep Rom from being imprisoned again. But Beveril lied to me."

"His star is not very high with his aunt right now. She laced into him like an avenging angel. Didn't think you gentry folk had it in you."

Diana nearly grinned. How like Niall to make her smile when her heart was breaking.

He caught up one of her hands. "There's nothing you can do for the present. Lady Hamish is looking after him herself. She cares for him enormously, Allegra. You should have seen the look on her face when she saw him lying there on a filthy pile of straw—"

"Niall, don't. I can't bear anymore."

"Then let me take you home. There's still your family to face. Though they should be used to you running away by now. Seems to be a weekly occurrence."

She did grin then. For his humor and his friendship and for the fact that he—the lowly Gypsy boy—had been the instrument of Rom's deliverance.

Niall rowed her back to Mortimer House in the boat she had appropriated. They sat in silence, Diana gazing down at her hands, sniffling every so often. She didn't see the taut expression that pulled at Niall's face as he passed the southern boundary of Hamish House. He tried to look away, but something compelled him to turn his eyes to one darkly shadowed patch of riverbank.

Argie Beasle had screamed for help, just as Niall had told Diana. But it hadn't been because the nettles had caught him. It had been a quagmire, which lay hidden beneath those dark, low-limbed trees.

Argie had fought his way clear of the nettles when he'd seen Niall approaching across the field, but before Niall could apprehend him, he had taken off toward the river. He'd managed to squirm into a dense thicket of grass and reeds, and as Niall rode up, he heard Argie's shrill cries and the sound of loud hissing. By the time Niall got his horse around the tangled growth, the damage had already been done.

A large swan, most likely a male, had been guarding his cygnets in that thicket. He had chased the intruder onto the innocent-looking patch of riverbank. All that remained of Argie Beasle was one quivering, bony arm reaching up toward the sky from out of the sucking mud.

The swan was standing back from the quagmire, observing the man's death throes with a lordly disdain. He hissed loudly one last time before he turned and made his stately way back to his nest. Niall watched, unmoved and unmoving, until the last fingertip disappeared beneath the turgid surface.

The law of the wild, much like Gypsy justice, was not ordained by the courts of the land. But it was swift and it was thorough.

Diana walked boldly through the front door of Mortimer House, holding Niall at her side, one insistent hand at his wrist. The footman stumbled with the candelabra he was carrying, and the stout butler forgot to suck in his belly, as was his wont when guests entered his domain. She found Helen and James in her sister's sitting room. Helen's face was tearstained, and James looked, with his tousled hair and disarrayed neckcloth, more boyish than Diana had ever seen him.

"Diana!" they cried out in unison. Then Helen pointed to Niall with a shaking finger and cried, "I left orders that this person was not to be allowed in the house. How dare you disobey me?"

So much for her warm welcome, Diana thought wryly.

"He's not 'this person,' " she declared to her astounded relatives. "His name is Niall Yanni."

James took one look at the strikingly handsome youth and turned to his wife in confusion. "I thought the fellow she's in love with was called Romulus Something-or-other."

"Romulus Perrin," Diana said patiently. She placed one hand on the Gypsy's shoulder, giving him a slight squeeze of encouragement. Not that he appeared to need it—his eyes were as fearless and bright as ever. "This is Niall, my friend. I stayed with his grandmother last night, in case you fear I have compromised my-

self again. And as long as I am allowed to live here, I expect that
he will be allowed to visit me."

"He is a Gypsy," Helen protested, looking to her husband for
support. James seemed uncertain of what course to pursue and
took refuge behind his wife's writing table.

Niall shrugged. "It's not a crime," he said evenly, "being a
Gypsy."

"For your information," Diana stated, "Niall helped Lady
Hamish to rescue Romulus this morning . . . from Sir Beveril. I
fear my intended will need to quit these parts for a while."

Helen began to moan softly. "I knew she would undo everything," she cried, clutching a handkerchief to her mouth. "Oh,
James, I am so sorry. She has been the soul of ingratitude, and after
all you've done for her. I think we should send her back to Yorkshire, before she has us hounded from the *ton*."

"Hush, Helen," James said tartly, as he moved from his refuge
and approached Diana. "What do you mean he rescued Perrin from
Sir Beveril? The river warden was sent off to London; Hunnycut
told me so himself. I was relieved to hear it, actually. Didn't want
the fellow showing up here and making trouble."

"My fiancé," Diana said with a long and very meaningful glance
to her sister, "lied to you. He lied to us both, James. Romulus has
been imprisoned on Lady Hamish's estate for the past five days."

James Mortimer digested this news slowly. He saw his hopes of
a parliamentary career begin a downward slide. Not only because
Beveril would no longer back him as a candidate once his finan-
cially advantageous marriage to Diana was called off, but also because James had publicly allied himself with Hunnycut whenever
possible. With a man he had discovered to be a gambler, a roué,
and now—the last straw—a deceitful cad.

He looked across to his wife, wilting on her chaise, and to his
sister-in-law, who was waiting with anxious eyes for him to make
a judgment of some sort.

"I don't know what to say," he responded honestly. "Except that
I think I must forbid you to marry . . ." He paused for effect. "Sir
Beveril Hunnycut."

Helen's moans grew louder as Diana's eyes lit up. "And do I
have your permission to marry Romulus?"

James humphed a little. "He'd best ask me that question in person."

"He's a bit indisposed at the moment," Niall interjected. "But he's the man for Diana, I can tell you that. He, at least, manages to find her when she runs away, which is more than I can say for the two of you."

He grinned across at James, who found himself smiling back.

"You'll like Romulus, I think," Diana said soothingly to James. "He was a captain in the artillery. And a decorated hero." Through the fabric of her skirt she touched the medal that lay in her pocket.

"A hero!" Helen cried in a disparaging voice. "This *is* one of your odd starts, Diana. Why on earth would a military hero waste his time looking after a lot of silly birds."

Diana smiled. "Because that's what heroes do, Helen. They look after things."

She knelt beside her sister and patted her consolingly on the shoulder. "It will all turn out, you'll see. And who knows, when Romulus has recovered, perhaps James can back *him* for Parliament."

Diana stood in the hallway waiting to be announced.

She had been in many fine homes since coming to stay with her sister, but Hamish House surpassed them all. From the classic lines of the red brick exterior to the understated richness of the interior furnishings, it was a place of exquisite and restful beauty.

Diana knew the baroness had inherited both title and property in her own right—a rare occurrence in the aristocracy. But it was clear the lady had used her power to good effect. Her estate appeared prosperous in the extreme. It was a pity that her only close relative, the one who stood to inherit this flourishing property, was the loathsome Sir Beveril. Diana had a sudden insight—if she had married him, Hamish House would have one day become her home. It sparked her imagination for all of three seconds, until she recalled the only home she'd ever wanted lay in charred ruins on an island in the Thames.

As Diana came into the drawing room, the elegant woman on the brocaded sofa rose and beckoned to her with one hand. "Miss Exeley."

"Lady Hamish," she said, trying to still the trembling of her voice. Though her expression certainly appeared welcoming, the white-haired woman conveyed a distinct aura of power and authority. Diana had made her curtsy to the Queen of England without feeling so intimidated.

"Come in, child. I won't bite."

Diana was not even halfway across the room before she burst out, "How is he faring, Lady Hamish?"

The older woman came forward with a soft rustle of silk and took Diana's hand. Her brown eyes were sad, Diana saw, with gray smudges of weariness beneath them.

"Tell me," Diana repeated. "I must know."

"He is not well, I'm afraid. No, no—" She held fast to Diana's hand as she tried to tug away. "You cannot see him. Not just now."

"But I—" Diana's eyes had filled with tears and she brushed them impatiently away. She was done with weeping. She drew a steadying breath. "I know I came here today uninvited. And Niall warned me that Rom was still not well. But I've waited two days, and I couldn't stay away another minute."

The woman stroked her hand. "Don't trouble yourself over it. I've been wondering when I would finally get to meet you. I am only sorry that it is under these trying circumstances. It is very difficult . . . seeing Romulus in such a state and not being able to relieve him."

"Is it true then, that he will not respond to anything?"

The lady nodded. "It was true until last night. He seems now to have roused from that state. Though I'm not sure his current condition is much of an improvement. He is raging around in his room like a man beset by devils. This morning he tossed my footman out into the hall when he carried in his washbasin."

"Perhaps a fever is making him behave so strangely."

Lady Hamish shook her head. "I wish it were that simple. Doctors have physics for such things. But Dr. Harley offers me little hope. I fear that what ails Romulus cannot be put right with medicine."

Diana bit at her lip. "I might be able to soothe him." She thought back to the night of the thunderstorm, when Romulus had found comfort in her arms.

"He has no idea of where he is, or of who any of us are. It's as though he's lost all memory of his past."

Sweet Jesus! Diana nearly cried out the words. Was it possibly true? Had Romulus suffered an actual loss of memory? What cruel irony then, after the foolish game she had played with him.

"He can recall nothing?" Diana asked bleakly.

"There is one thing," Lady Hamish said haltingly. "Though I don't like to tell you, my dear, knowing what you feel for him. He has some wild notion that a woman named Allegra was burned to death in the fire on the island. Someone from his past, no doubt, who has come to haunt his disordered brain. He called her name incessantly, even when he lay unmoving in his bed."

A relieved smile had lit Diana's face. "Lady Hamish," she exclaimed softly, "*I* am Allegra. Romulus watched me run into the burning lodge. He must think I was trapped inside. Oh, my poor Rom."

The lady shot Diana a dubious look. "Why would he think you were called Allegra?"

She responded with a blush. "It's a rather long story." She sank to her knees on the carpet and raised her eyes to the older woman. "But Romulus will recognize me, Lady Hamish. I know he will."

The baroness touched one hand to Diana's hair. "Love heals all wounds, hmm? I believed that myself once, very long ago. Perhaps it's time I learned to believe it again."

"Let me go in alone," Diana whispered to her hostess outside Rom's bedroom door.

She was surprised to discover that the room he had been given was one of those that hostesses usually reserved for favored guests—the spacious chambers at the front of the house. The baroness had certainly not stinted where Romulus was concerned.

Lady Hamish nodded. "I trust you know what you are doing."

Diana winced as she opened the door and slipped into the room. She wasn't sure of anything anymore.

The draperies at the front windows were open only a few inches, and since there were no candles lit in the chamber, the room was full of shadows. She looked first to the bed. The covers were rumpled, but the bed was empty.

She took two steps into the room.

A surly voice called out from an alcove on her left. "Who the devil let you in here?"

She turned with a tiny gasp.

He was there, less than five feet from her, standing before an ormolu screen, which fronted the alcove. He wore a dressing gown of some rich, heavy fabric that seemed to hang on his painfully thin frame. That was all she could make out—his face was obscured by shadows.

"Romulus," she whispered.

His eyes, hollow and stark, darted to her face.

"More bloody ghosts," he snarled as his eyes met hers. He

raised both hands as if to ward her off. "Go now, there's no longer any use in haunting me." He took another step closer. His fist shot forward and slammed against the door frame beside her. "Do you hear me!" he raged. "Get out!"

She could see his face all too clearly now. It looked almost cadaverous, the skin taut over the once-elegant bones. Whip marks crisscrossed both cheeks—Argie Beasle's cruel legacy, she recalled. Nearly a week's worth of dark, bearded stubble covered his chin. It only added to his fearsome appearance.

She was appalled by the change in him, and yet she couldn't tear her eyes away. There had once been such beauty in that face. And such loving warmth in his golden eyes. Now as he gazed back at her, those eyes glazed with suspicion and simmering rage, she feared that he truly was mad.

Diana planted her feet and refused to give in to her clutching fear. This was Romulus . . . this was the man she loved. She longed to stroke her fingers across his pale skin, and soothe the anger and the fear from his haunted eyes and from his taut, narrowed mouth.

"Romulus," she said again. "It's me. It's Allegra."

A violent spasm twisted one side of his face, pulling up both lip and cheek. She cried out then, not in fear, but in recognition. This wasn't madness, it was the same affliction he'd suffered when he returned from France—the uncontrollable tics and twitches. But how like a madman it made him appear.

At the sound of her cry, Romulus had staggered back against the screen. "No more ghosts, I say!" His hands scrabbled against the carved wood behind him, as though seeking an entry through the solid barrier.

She reached out to him, to halt his wild-eyed retreat. He scuttled away from her hands, moving with a lurching motion that was painful to watch. This man who had taken such sure strides over the grassy paths of his island, now moved like a lame beggar. Niall was right, Diana thought, it was horrifying to see him this way. But she shook off her horror. He was ill and he needed her.

He was nearly to the window, when she called out softly, "Come back to me, Romulus. You vowed you would come to me, any time, any place. Come back to me now, from wherever it is you have gone."

He spun to her, his eyes now wide with shock. "Allegra," he gasped. His fevered stare seemed to pass right through her.

"Where are you? Don't leave me here alone. Not without you. Christ in heaven, not without you." He slid slowly forward to his knees, his trembling hands fisted over his face.

She ran to kneel before him. There was such tension in his body, it vibrated in the air between them.

"Not alone, Romulus—" She whispered the litany as though she had spoken it only hours before. "Not alone any longer, my love."

She coaxed his clenched hands away from his face, letting her fingers drift over the sharp planes of his cheekbones and the gaunt hollows beneath them. Gently, slowly, she drew him up onto the bed, sliding herself onto the mattress beside him. Holding his head cradled beneath her arms, she murmured tenderly, "I'm here with you, Romulus. Your Allegra is here."

She lowered her head and kissed him softly on the mouth, letting her lips linger on his, trying to warm his icy flesh.

"There," she murmured as she drew back. "Did that feel like a ghost's kiss to you?"

He lay there beneath her, his eyes full of strange wonder. "I watched you die a thousand times," he whispered. "Am I now in my grave, that I have you here beside me again?"

She touched his brow with her lips. "The prison sickness made you think I was dead. But you are not in prison any longer. You are safe now, among those who care for you and love you."

His fingers drifted over her face, caressing her skin. He buried his hands deeply in her hair, tugging at it gently until all her hairpins came loose and it billowed down over her shoulders.

"Allegra," he sighed, raising one dark tendril to his lips. "Stay with me."

She watched his face relax, saw the pain and rage drift away from his haunted eyes. She lay there for a long time, her body entangled with his, as though they were lovers in truth. She knew it when he slept at last, felt the easy cadence of his breath against her cheek.

Only then did she slip away from him. He moaned slightly, and reached a hand out, groping for her. She took it and continued to bide there beside him, holding that hand against her heart until he slept again.

Diana sent a brief note to Mortimer House explaining that she intended to stay on and care for Romulus. Her family had at last relaxed their hold on her, and James had even become an unexpected ally—for the last two days he had managed to keep the still-fuming Helen out of Diana's path.

Lady Hamish sat with Romulus that afternoon while he slept, relieved that his slumber showed every sign of being relaxed and natural. When she emerged from his room, Diana could see that the dark circles under her eyes had already begun to fade. Lady Hamish pronounced that all he required now was some nourishing food, and enough time for his nervous condition to subside. Diana smiled in agreement, nearly giddy with relief that he was truly on the road to recovery.

Their collective joy was shortlived.

When Diana returned to Rom's room later that afternoon, carrying in a tray of soup and bread, she was met by a stranger. No longer one who did not recognize her; rather, one who refused to acknowledge her.

He was sitting in a chair near the window, gazing out through the partially open draperies. When he saw who had entered his chamber, he abruptly twitched the drapes shut, got up from his seat and lurched into the alcove, where he promptly disappeared behind the carved screen.

"I don't want you here," he called out hoarsely, his voice brimming with hostility.

Diana stood with her mouth agape, and nearly dropped the tray.

"I've brought you some broth," she said evenly, trying not to let her fears rise up again.

"I don't want broth. I don't want anything." He sounded like a peevish child.

"I'm not interested in what you want," she replied tartly, in a tone that would have done Nanny Perkins proud. "Now sit in your chair and swallow this broth . . . or I will ladle it down your throat!"

His voice lowered a notch. "Your bedside manner is a bit lacking, Miss Exeley."

Well, at least he knew who she was, even if she misliked his use of that particular name.

"And your manners are totally lacking, Mr. Perrin," she responded. "Now come out from there."

"No!" he growled.

Diana set the tray down on his bedside table and went to peer behind the screen. Even in the near darkness she could see the plaintive, guarded expression in his eyes. He looked like a stag brought to bay. He flung one hand toward her, as if to thrust her away. That hand shook uncontrollably, as it hung there in the air between them. Diana wanted to cry out at the unfairness of it—that he should be so dreadfully afflicted—but knew she dared not express her anguish.

He seemed to sense her dismay anyway, and abruptly curled both shaking hands to his chest, so that the cuffs of the dressing gown obscured them. That childlike gesture of vulnerability pierced her heart.

"Come to gawk, have you?" he muttered. "Gawk at the cripple." He turned his head into his shoulder. "Leave me a little dignity, will you, for Christ's sake!"

"I only want you to eat." She added softly, tenderly, "I've had some experience getting stubborn creatures to eat."

If he recalled those words, the ones he had spoken to her that first night on the island, he gave no sign of it. Diana realized then the dilemma she had placed him in. If he fed himself, he had to sit before her, and attempt, with his palsied hands to carry the food to his mouth. Or he could allow her to spoon the food into him as though he were an infant. Either scenario would have repelled a man as proud as Romulus Perrin.

Diana sighed. "Very well. I will leave the tray. But when I come back for it in an hour, I expect to see that you have eaten every bit."

He said nothing, and so she went from the room, still trying to fathom this strange illness. One thing was clear to her, however. In spite of all that she and Rom had shared, regardless of all they meant to each other, he still insisted on shutting her out of his pain. There was almost a selfishness to it she could not comprehend. She dreaded to tell her hostess that, although Rom's memory might have recovered, his spirit was still deeply troubled, so she hid in the rose garden until it was time to remove the tray from his room.

She knocked this time. And allowed him a chance to retreat behind the screen. As she feared, he was nowhere in sight when she entered. She went to the bedside table, relieved to see that at least he had eaten most of his soup and all of the bread.

"Would you like one of the footmen to come up and shave you?" she asked without turning around.

"Where's the point?" he asked crossly. "I doubt I'll be riding out to pay calls on all my friends. And if you would cease barging in here, I'll be happily rid of my only visitor."

She longed to heave the soup bowl at the screen. "This isn't working, Romulus."

"Thank God you've realized it." His curt, disembodied voice came welling across the chamber. "I don't require a bleeding nursemaid! I'm sure you can find some other poor soul to plague with your charity."

"Oh, bosh!" she said with great feeling. "I wasn't talking about myself, you insufferable man. I meant this hiding business isn't working. I am not going to flee in horror, just because you've developed a bit of palsy. I am not one of those superstitious fools from Treypenny."

"It's not only the . . . palsy. I . . . I don't want to see you, or speak to you. Can't you get that through your stubborn head? I don't have to explain myself to you—suffice to say that my feelings for you have changed. *I* have changed."

Diana gripped the edge of the table. She was proud her voice didn't waver as she called back, "Then come out from there, and say those words to my face. Like a man, Romulus. Not like some craven—"

"I am a craven!" he muttered fiercely as he staggered into the dim light. He raised his trembling hands toward her, entreating her. "It's not this damned affliction." He thumped at his chest with one fist. "It's what is gone from here, from my heart. I feel nothing. Nothing but rage, nothing but hatred."

Diana closed her eyes briefly. "I don't blame you for hating them, Romulus," she said quietly. "What Beveril and Argie did to you was indefensible."

"It's not them!" he cried raggedly. "I don't hate them. Christ, I don't even think about them. It's me . . . it's myself that I hate. You're right, I am no longer a man . . . nothing but a worthless, spineless craven."

He came toward her, and though his steps were unsteady, his eyes looked straight into hers. "I wanted to die . . ." he breathed. "I prayed to die. There wasn't an ounce of fight left in me. I let Argie Beasle whip me and never raised a hand to stop him. There is nothing in this world that can take that blight from me. Not you, not anyone." He gave a harsh laugh. "Not that there is anyone else. They're all gone. My father, my friends." His face twitched noticeably, as he said in a frighteningly matter-of-fact voice, "My mother abandoned me, did you know that? My father never admitted it, but I heard the peasant woman who looked after me in

Rome relating the sorry tale to a neighbor. Francesca forgot I was fluent in Italian." All the glibness left his voice as he bit out. "Even my own mother couldn't bear the sight of me."

"No, Romulus," Diana wailed softly. What she most feared had come to pass—his ghosts had risen up again to taunt him, and clearly a new one had been added to their ranks. The pain in his voice when he spoke of his mother had chilled her to the core. "You can't know why she left you."

"Good thing she did. It saved her discovering what a worthless coward she had whelped."

Diana knew with shuddering certainty that this ailment was far beyond her feeble powers to cure.

"I love you, Romulus," she said in a small voice. "For what it is worth."

His mouth tightened as he narrowed his eyes. "Don't. Don't love me, Diana. Don't waste it on a man who will never be able to love you in return."

"You did love me . . . once."

"No," he said dully. "I never did. It was just another sort of madness."

He dragged himself back to the screen then, back to the shadows that obscured his traitorous body. There was no barrier on earth, however, that could have obscured his broken, wounded soul from Diana. She went toward the doorway, her face white, her hands clutched to her breast. If Romulus had been watching from his refuge, he would have seen her stagger and almost fall as she neared the doorway.

As the door shut softly, the man behind the screen put his trembling hands over his face and wept.

Chapter 13

Lady Hamish was in the lower hallway, arranging a bouquet of tulips and early roses in a Delft bowl. She looked up expectantly as Diana came down the stairs.

"He is still lucid," Diana said, her tone giving little away. She lowered her eyes, trying to disguise the bleak despair that had settled there. "But the nervous condition he suffers . . . has made him uncomfortable with visitors."

Lady Hamish saw at once the distress on Diana's face, heard the raw edge of pain in her voice.

"If you don't mind," Diana continued, "it might be less taxing for Romulus if I alone looked after him."

To Diana's relief the baroness agreed, albeit sadly. "I will do whatever you think best."

Diana spent each afternoon with Rom, trying to break through his frightening reserve. He barely acknowledged her presence in his room and, though he'd stopped hiding behind the screen, he made a point of always sitting at the window, his face averted from her. She read to him from the books of mythology she loved—she'd found several in Lady Hamish's impressive library—but the tales of Olympian gods with their very human flaws, left him unmoved. She spoke to him of her life with her scholarly, invalid father in Yorkshire, and of the school she had started there. All the bits and pieces of her past that she had been unable to share with Romulus on the island, she now offered to him. He made not one comment.

It was like trying to batter down a wall of diamond-hard, impenetrable ice. But she kept on regardless—because she would not let her own sense of futility defeat her. But every night, when she went wearily to her bed, she let the tears of frustration rise up and spill out.

Niall came to visit Romulus three days after Diana's arrival and would not be turned away. She stayed out of the room, hovering near the doorway while Niall was closeted with him. There were sharp words and muttered curses exchanged, and when Niall emerged, his face was flushed with anger.

"He *is* mad," he uttered balefully. "He called me a filthy Gypsy, and told me if he'd wanted the room fouled, he'd ask to have some swine brought in."

Diana blanched.

"He's turned into bleeding Beveril," Niall stated, and then grinned. "Don't look so mournful, my sweet. A man who's up to those insults at least isn't fading away. That's what I most feared. Anyway, I got a bit of my own back. Told him he looked like a flea-bitten billy goat."

Niall's scathing criticism must have fazed Romulus—over tea that afternoon, Lady Hamish informed Diana that the patient had rung for a footman and asked to be shaved. It felt like a small victory.

The next day Niall returned, carrying a covered wicker basket. "This," he said, handing it to Diana, "is just what he needs. The man never could turn his back on a foundling."

The basket contained a fat cygnet. Crowing with delight, she lifted the creature from its bed of straw. Then her eyes clouded in dismay. The baby swan had an odd-looking leather boot on one leg, attached with a harness over its back. "Oh, Niall, what's wrong with his foot?"

"Snapping turtle got him, it looked like. I found him bleeding on the shore of the island the day after the fire. He was nearly done in, poor creature. I've been keeping him there, in the pen. He's one of your brood, I suspect."

"This is very clever," she pronounced, after examining the false foot. "Can he swim?"

"Like falling off a log," the boy assured her. "He's been swimming in the pond for days."

Diana carried the cygnet into Rom's bedroom and set it on the floor near his chair. It made a beeline for Rom's legs and began to hop about, eager for attention.

It has to be one of ours, Diana thought. *He clearly remembers Romulus.*

The man in the chair looked down and frowned. Then he reached down and lifted the cygnet onto his lap. His shaking fingers, once so deft, prodded cautiously at the leather boot. "What foolishness is this?"

They were the first words he had spoken to Diana in four days. "He was bitten by a turtle and lost his foot," she explained. "Niall made him the little shoe—you know how skilled he is at leather working."

Gently, Romulus set the cygnet on the floor. "He should have let him die," he said morosely. "Some things we shouldn't tamper with. Poor beast will never have a normal life."

"He's not a poor beast," Diana said, bristling. "He is called Remus." The name had only just occurred to her, but she thought it most apt. Romulus looked up at that, his brows knit in distemper, but Diana ignored his scowl. "And as he gets older, Niall can make him a larger shoe. He swims very well, you might be interested to hear. *In spite of his affliction.*"

With that pointed statement, she went from the room. She made a great show of walking down the hall, letting her feet thud on the floor. Then she crept on tiptoes back to his door, which she had purposely left open a crack. Sure enough, there he was, leaning from his chair, talking to the baby swan. She couldn't quite hear his words, but they were soothing, reassuring.

The great sham! she thought with fond fury. So he wasn't beyond all feeling. He wasn't beyond love. He'd just lost his way, lost his faith in himself. But he'd find his way back and learn to value himself again. A man who could croon to a baby swan was a long way from being completely lost.

After five days of being kept from Rom's presence, Lady Hamish decided it was time for a reckoning with Diana. Though she had continually questioned the girl about her patient, her questions brought no satisfactory answers, so that morning she mentioned she would have a look in on Romulus herself. The dismay in Diana's eyes was all the answer she needed. She drew the girl into the small morning room.

"Tell me," Lady Hamish said gently, but adamantly. "Tell me everything."

To Diana's credit, she didn't prevaricate. She regaled her hostess with every bitter, angry comment Romulus had hurled at her that first day, and every hurtful, silent snub he had offered her since. She railed at those who had left their mark on him—the mother who had callously abandoned him, the French who had imprisoned him, Beveril Hunnycut who had plotted his downfall, and Argie Beasle who had whipped him like a cur. She feared, she said with a sob, that everything in his past had conspired to destroy his sense of self-worth. And if that weren't enough, there was his never-ending guilt over the death of his comrades in prison.

Lady Hamish worried her lip. "He carries a fearful weight on his shoulders, that one," she murmured. "All that needless guilt. A man's pride is so easily damaged, Diana. And I don't need to tell you, Romulus Perrin is prouder than most men."

"He is in purgatory, Lady Hamish," Diana wailed softly. "Alone and without hope. That is why I didn't want you to see him. It would rend your heart."

Lady Hamish smiled slightly. "I am tougher than you give me credit for. Now let me think on this—there may be something I can do to restore Rom's faith in himself."

Diana looked doubtful. "Forgive me for saying this, Lady Hamish, but how can you help him? He has turned his back on me, who loves him without judgment. How can another help him to heal?"

"Perhaps the beginning of a cure," the lady replied cryptically, "is to discover the source of the illness."

Lady Hamish waited until Diana was abed before she went to her jewel case and drew a folded paper from a compartment hidden at its base. Then taking up a small bottle of cordial and two glasses from her dressing table, she went out into the hall. The trip to Romulus's bedroom, only three doors from her own chamber, was the longest walk she had ever taken.

She knocked once and then entered. His eyes widened when he saw who his late-night visitor was. He quickly threw down the book he was reading and was halfway to his hiding place when she spoke out.

"No, Romulus," she said quietly. "There is no need to hide from me. Nothing I see in you could ever displease me." He stood wavering before her, clearly unsure of what to do. "Sit," she said, pointing to his chair. "And I will sit here, just beside you."

She set the glasses on the table that stood between them, and then poured a generous amount of the deep amber liquid into each one. Romulus watched her the whole time with puzzled eyes.

"I see you are recovering nicely from your recent internment," she said in a level voice. "The twitches are far less pronounced than the last time."

His eyes brightened slightly.

"No, you didn't know that, did you?" she said. "It took you weeks to get the use of your hands back the last time, as I recall, and look at you now, holding your glass with hardly a tremor."

He knocked back his drink with a single motion, and Lady Hamish refilled his glass. "Yes, this is a very good cordial," she observed. "Smuggled, I don't doubt. My butler gets it from the publican in Treypenny."

The baroness rarely babbled, but she knew she needed a bit of time before she got down to business. She carried her own drink to her lips, wishing her heart wasn't beating so erratically.

"Lady Hamish," he said slowly, "I wish you would stop tossing pleasantries at me, and get to the point. You haven't bothered with me this week past, and I wonder that you should trouble yourself with me now."

The lady took this surly outburst in stride. He had always been fractious, she recalled fondly.

"Our resident dragon has kept me away from you, thinking to protect me, I suppose. Until today, she's led me to believe that you were merely a little out of sorts." Her voice deepened. "She neglected to tell me that you have been sitting here for nearly a week, festering with guilt and self-pity."

"Madam!" Romulus uttered, as he staggered to his feet. "Don't make me abuse your hospitality."

"How? By telling me to mind my own business? You are my business, Romulus Perrin. Though it's taken me twenty-five years to come around to it."

Romulus shuddered as he fell back in his chair and laid his head wearily against the cushion.

One of them he could fight. Barely. But if they were both going to have at him, Allegra *and* Lady Hamish, then he'd best take his leave of this place. If he had anywhere else to go, that is. Maybe he could return to the hospital in London. At least there a man was not badgered by women who thought they knew what was best for a fellow.

Not to mention that it was killing him in slow increments to see Allegra every day, and to hold himself aloof from her. To keep trying to convince her that his love had been nothing more than an unfortunate lapse. She was a damned, stubborn chit, but he'd never thought of Lady Hamish as stubborn. High-handed, perhaps. And resolute. But now he saw that she was as bone-headed as Allegra.

"I fear you have left me in the dust, Lady Hamish. What have you waited twenty-five years to do?"

As she took a paper from the pocket of her gown, he saw that her hands trembled worse than his did.

"There is no good way to say this, except right out. I haven't told you before now, because it was clear you were making your way in the world without me. I almost told you last year, when you came to the island, but again, your spirit prevailed over your illness, and I saw that you still had no need of me."

Romulus made a feeble attempt to forestall her. "I need nothing."

She waved away his protest with an impatient flick of her fingers. "You need to hear this now," she said intently. "You need something to jolt you back into life. I'm telling you not only for your sake, but also because I cannot bear to watch that sweet creature who loves you lose bits of her soul a day at a time." She stopped and drew a breath. "Romulus, I am your mother."

There was a long, strained silence in the chamber.

"*My mother?*" Romulus echoed in a ragged whisper. He felt as though his heart had stopped beating. His breath was trapped in his lungs, like that of a man who has stayed too long underwater. Disbelief and anger at her startling admission warred immediately in his heart with hope and incoherent relief.

Lady Hamish reached out and cupped the side of his cheek. He felt it twitch beneath her palm.

"Don't look at me so, my dearest Romulus. It breaks my heart."

"I have no mother," he said tersely, pulling back from her touch. Disbelief and anger had come to the fore. "She left me as a babe, in Rome. Jaunted off without so much as a backward glance."

"Yes, I left you," she said, regret lacing her voice, even after so many years. "But only because another sort of duty called me away."

"I don't want to hear this." He crossed his arms over his chest.

"But you shall. You must. Your father and I had gone to Rome, so that we could be together. For the three years we lived there, we were happier than any two mortals had a right to be, especially after you were born. Then my father's health began to fail; he pleaded with me to come home, to help with the running of the estate. But your father, Jeremy, would not come with me. He feared there would be a scandal, and that it would kill my father if he found out."

"What—that you had born a bastard to a commoner?" he asked, not caring how harsh his words sounded.

Lady Hamish smiled wanly. "No, that I had married the man I loved, however below my station, and had a child with him."

"Married?"

She smoothed out the creased, yellowed sheet on her knee before she handed it to him. Rom's eyes widened as he read the words on the faded marriage license.

"Jeremiah Perrin was my husband, Romulus. You are my son, my legal son." She waited a moment for the meaning of her words to sink in. "And it distressed me beyond words to leave you. But it was only to be for a time, until my father recovered and I could return to Rome. But Papa's illness grew worse—he suffered for four years. I stayed on and nursed him—as you nursed Jeremy while he was dying."

Romulus nodded brusquely. His eyes were shuttered from the woman who sat opposite him.

"After Papa died, I wrote to your father, begging him to come to England, to bring you home to me. I had taken up the reins of Hamish House while my father was ill, and I knew I had an obligation to the people who lived here which made it impossible for me to return to Rome. But Jeremy refused to come back. He was a proud man, Romulus—perhaps too proud—and he had no use for my wealth or my title. He wanted you to be raised as he had been, to work for a living, not to become an idle society sprig. Jeremy said that he wouldn't take his place at my side in England, that he loved me too much to see me made a byword in the *ton*. And he declared he wouldn't have our child torn between two worlds, that you were content living as a river warden's son. I saw the wisdom of that . . . though you might not see it."

"I was still made to live in two worlds!" The words erupted out of him as his voice rose plaintively. "I was the son of a laborer, a man of indifferent education and few refinements. And yet I was given tutors and sent off to university. What was I to make of that? Which path was I to follow, madam?"

Her head had lowered at his words. "Your father wanted you to learn what he believed were the true values in life—industry, not idleness. Compassion, not indifference. He wrote to me a month before he died to tell me that you had become everything he desired. A worthy child, he called you. *Our* worthy child. He wanted you to be educated, Rom, not to place you between two worlds, but so that you would have the advantages of knowledge and wisdom to aid you in life."

Romulus stirred restlessly. "Now I know where the money for my education came from."

Lady Hamish sighed. "I was more than willing to support you both, but Jeremy would only accept enough money to ensure your future."

"My future?" he echoed harshly. "What sort of future can I have now, when everything in my past has been a lie? My father lied, letting me think you had abandoned me. You lied, using false friendship to keep me close to you, just so you could ease your own conscience. And Diana lied; over and over she lied to me."

She reached for his hand. "Sometimes loving a person makes lying unavoidable. Just as you are lying to Diana, telling her that you no longer love her so that she will go away and not see you in such pain."

"It's not a lie," he hissed. "It was a foolish mistake, what I felt for her."

"Why, because you believe she is so far above you?"

"No," he snarled. "Because she represents everything my father taught me to mistrust." His voice lowered and grew distant. "While I was at school, I shunned the company of the other students, because they too were of a class I had been warned to avoid." He turned to her. "How could my father have loved you, Lady Hamish, when he disliked the gentry so intensely?"

She shook her head slowly. "I never knew the answer to that. He loved me for years before he declared himself. He was my father's bailiff and lived on the island—he built that lodge, you know. I haunted him every day, from the time I was seventeen, pestering him about the birds and the river. I must say, your Miss Exeley is a deal more expedient than I was. She won a declaration from you in less than a week."

"I have told you," he stated curtly. "Miss Exeley is no longer an issue."

"Oh, bosh!" she said, sounding exactly like the expedient Miss Exeley. "You and I both know you are in love with her. And I couldn't be more pleased. She is a rare and wonderful girl."

Romulus finished off his drink and then set the glass down with a dull clink. "You think this revelation will somehow change things? That I will fall weeping into your arms and have my soul cleansed?"

Lady Hamish surprised him by laughing outright. "Dear Lord, you are so like your father sometimes. He could be the most lugubrious old thing. And no, I don't expect you to fall weeping into my arms. I expect we will go on as we have done, which is to say, we will be good friends to each other. But I think it is time I acknowledged you. I have longed to name you my son before the whole world. It is you, Romulus, who shall have the running of Hamish House and not my lamentable nephew."

Rom's eyes grew even darker. "I would never ask you for such a thing."

"I would give it to you, though. Your proud, stubborn father made me swear that I would not leave the property to you—so that you would never be corrupted by wealth. And I thought myself still bound by that promise. But I see now that he was wrong. You needn't dwell between two worlds any longer, Romulus. This house is your birthright, as much as the honor and integrity your father bequeathed to you."

"And what of Beveril?" he asked, turning his gaze to her. "He loves me little enough as it is."

She fisted her hands in her lap. "Beveril has forfeited any claims on me. Were he a better man, I might forgive him his actions against you. But he has proven himself unworthy of any consideration."

"He saw me as a threat, Lady Hamish—rightly so, it now appears. You might temper your harsh judgment a bit, when you reflect on that."

"Still turning the other cheek? Lud, there's more charity in you than I'd have been able to muster. But if you feel pity for Beveril, then it will be in your power to aid him—*if* you accept your birthright."

Rom's face was unmoving except for a tic that fluttered under one eye. "The birthright my father disdained? What use is it to me now? It will not change the past, my past." His voice grew ragged as his eyes bored into hers. "Why did you let my father prevail, madam? Why didn't you insist on keeping me with you?"

She took a moment to answer. It was a question she had asked herself countless times over the past twenty-five years. "I was very indulged as a child, Romulus. Raised to be prideful and arrogant. My younger sister was much the same, and you can see how her nature has been reflected in her son. Until I met your father, I doubt I gave a thought to anyone's comfort but my own. I tried to change for him, to become more . . . selfless. I tried even harder once you were born. But then I was called home to England. I was torn, Romulus. So torn that you cannot comprehend how I suffered. But your father assured me we would be together soon. And so I left Rome believing I would be separated from those I loved for only a short time.

"But by the time Papa died, I alone was overseeing Hamish House. And I wanted to continue on in that role. It was my duty—a noble duty, I reasoned. But Jeremy said he wouldn't be my consort, lording it over other mortals, and that if I wanted to see you, I had to give up my life here. I almost hated him then, for being so unbending. But I knew his nature was strong, where mine was weak, and so I did not fight to get you back. He was the parent you needed, the one who would invest you with his strength and his compassion."

"Was it compassionate to keep a child from his mother? I think it was bloody pride. He gave me a rare dose of that, as well as his other qualities."

Tears glittered on her lashes. "Then I must ask your forgiveness. For letting logic set my course, rather than listening to my own heart. But heed me, Romulus—every day of my life since I received Jeremy's letter telling me he would not be returning to England, I have strived to become the sort of woman who would deserve her son's love. I have practiced charity and philanthropy wherever I found people in need. I did change my nature, but by then you were both only distant memories."

Romulus whispered gruffly, "Perhaps it was best left as a memory, Lady Hamish."

She rose slowly and set her drink down. "I don't expect a miracle, Romulus. I know there are dark things inside you that no one else can grapple with. I only wanted you to know that I am here for you, that I love you and always have. And that you have a home at Hamish House, for all time. Your father had his own demons, you can be sure. But when he was with me, when we were together, there was a light in that dark place. Even when we were no longer together, I knew from his letters that the light remained."

He gazed up at her thoughtfully. "I always thought it odd that he never seemed angry, as I did, at the loss of my mother. . . . But perhaps he never did lose you."

"No," she said, letting her hand drift to his marked face. "And I never lost him. Not as long as you were in the world." Her hand clasped his shoulder then, her fingers firm and compelling. "Don't turn your back on the world now, my dearest boy. Don't flee away from love and from light."

Romulus rose and started to move away. He needed time to sort things out. His universe had shifted and he felt himself teetering above some uncharted abyss. No, not an abyss, he realized suddenly, but a shimmering valley that offered peace and reconciliation. His soul twisted about inside him, trying desperately to flee the coils of guilt and pain that held him captive.

He turned back with a wrenching cry, reaching for her, for this woman whose benevolence he had never understood . . . until now. He wrapped his arms around her, needing the comfort, needing the healing contact. And as she welcomed him gladly into her arms, he knew that she needed it as well.

For twenty-five years they had dwelled apart, all because of one man's stubborn pride.

Something broke inside him, shattered into a million tiny pieces. His own false pride, his needless guilt, all his wretched fears. All he could feel at that moment was a blinding joy.

"M-mother," he stuttered. "I still cannot believe it."

"Believe it," she said, reaching up to kiss his brow.

He leaned into the warmth of her cheek. "Yes . . . yes, I must believe it. God, it feels so utterly right."

She pulled back from him, her hands sliding to his wrists. "There is still doubt in your eyes, Romulus."

He nodded slowly. "I am still afraid, Mother. I have found you, it is true, and it is a blessing I never expected in my lifetime. But what of Allegra? I have nothing to offer but this broken, empty husk."

"Foolish boy," she said tenderly. "There is a great deal you have to offer her. Your strength and your kindness. And your courage—you are so very brave, Romulus, if you only knew it. But that is the way with honorable men. They, more than any, think themselves lacking." She smiled. "I once told your father that if he'd lived two thousand years ago, they'd have made him a blasted prophet. He was well named Jeremiah."

Romulus almost grinned. In truth, his father had had the air of a Biblical holy man—pious, outspoken, unyielding in his convictions—and yet brimming with goodness and full of concern for everything in his care. Including his son. He had loved this woman, enough to marry her and give her a child, but not enough to forego his own bitter prejudice and remain at her side.

He regarded his mother now with open affection. He saw in her face a distinct echo of his own features. The shape of the eyes, the wide mouth, the jutting cut of nose and chin.

"Speaking of names," he said, "I've always wondered how I

came to be called Romulus? It's an odd name, surely, for two English people to choose."

Her eyes danced. "Your father would have agreed with you. He wanted to call you Tom. But I wanted you to have a grand name, a bold name. The name of someone who would do great things with his life. And you have, my son. Very great things. And if you can manage to hold on to that remarkable young woman, I don't doubt you will continue on that path. She has never stopped believing in you."

"I know," he said ruefully. "And I've cursed her for it. Not that it ever does any good, where Allegra's concerned." He drew his hands wearily over his face. "I have a great deal to answer for."

Lady Hamish cocked her head. "Ah, now, don't start adding her to your list of guilty woes. She knows what she's about, that one. I let your father's stubborn convictions draw us apart, fool that I was. But your Allegra would brave anything, I think, to stay with you. Even your not inconsiderable temper."

Romulus nodded as his eyes brightened. Once his head stopped spinning, he could decide what course to follow, but whatever his future held, he knew it would include Allegra.

"I'd rather you didn't reveal any of this to her, just yet," he said. "I'm not sure I'm cut out to be lord of the manor. Keeper of the swans was hard enough work."

"Oh, but people are so much easier to manage than swans," Lady Hamish remarked sagely. "Your father should have taught you that."

She left him then, after seeing him tucked into his bed.

"Like a damned sprat," he observed to the cygnet.

Remus, who had slept through all of Lady Hamish's startling revelations, heard his voice and came lurching over to the bed looking for attention. Romulus lifted him onto the comforter. "You shouldn't be able to walk," he said, flicking the leather boot with one finger. "And you certainly shouldn't be able to swim."

But apparently, some things that looked to be beyond all mending managed to heal. And if they didn't he reckoned, then you just damn well had to make the best of them.

Romulus fell asleep with the baby swan tucked under his chin.

Chapter 14

In a storybook, the next day would have dawned bright and fair. But this was England, after all. A fierce wind had come up and, though the wind had not brought rain with it, the sky had turned a sour gray-green and a tattered cloud mass hung low over the whole district.

Diana came into Rom's room as usual, carrying his breakfast tray. He sat, as usual, in his chair near the window and did not look at her. She set the tray upon his lap, turned away, and was almost to the door, when he called out, "Allegra."

Her eyes lit up. So, she was no longer Miss Exeley. She turned slowly. "Yes?"

"Would you keep me company while I have my breakfast?"

She moved cautiously back to his chair. He was gazing at her with open adoration.

She frowned. "I think you must be feverish," she pronounced dubiously. "Your eyes are smiling at me."

He grinned crookedly. "And my mouth, as well."

Then a spasm twisted his cheek upward. His eyes hardened in dismay as he raised one hand to cover his face. "No," he said, as if to himself, "it's nothing."

"Indeed, it is nothing," Diana exclaimed softly, as she sank to her knees at his feet and drew his hand down. "It is the merest nothing. Less and less each day."

His face relaxed then, and the anxious expression in the golden eyes softened.

"But what of here?" she asked, venturing all, as she placed one hand over his heart. "What of the emptiness here?"

"My heart is full, Allegra. More and more each day. Ah, don't cry, my witch. Haven't you cried enough over me? No more now, I say."

She was in his arms then, his breakfast tray pushed hastily to the floor, where Remus was delighted to cannibalize three poached eggs.

"Why?" she entreated him, holding him away, her hands at his shoulders. "Why have you suddenly stopped snarling at me? And more to the point, how can I be sure you won't start up again? Too much starch in your pillowcase . . . too much pepper in your soup. Anything could set you off."

"Only one thing will set me off," he murmured, his lips against her hair. "If you ever leave me. I would bind you to me, Allegra, for all time, if that were possible."

"Ah, but I am a wild thing, untamed and unfettered," she reminded him.

"Yes," he said, drawing back to gaze into her bright eyes. "And wild things must always return to their true home. Where is that home, my sweet witch? Where does this wild thing belong?"

She whispered against his lips, "With you, Romulus Perrin. Wherever you dwell, is my home."

He returned her kiss, holding her tight against his chest, unmindful of his trembling hands. He couldn't tell whether they trembled from the palsy, or from the warm, supple feel of Allegra melting in his arms.

"Can you ever forgive me?" he crooned. "For loving you in such a wrong-headed way? For turning away from you? I learned last night that there is no honor in drawing back from one who loves you."

"Last night?" She blinked in confusion.

"It's not important now. I tried to make you go away, Allegra. Because it's damned hard having you see me like this, and . . . because I couldn't believe you could want a man who . . . who let a skulking river rat humiliate him. But you don't care, do you? None of that matters to you."

"No," she stated, "it doesn't. You were delirious when Argie beat you. You had been for days, the doctor said. You'd have broken the switch over his head if you'd been in your right mind."

"That wasn't the only reason—the delirium," he said softly. "I thought you were dead. Argie Beasle, blast his hide, told me you were. And without you, Allegra, I had nothing to live for. No reason to fight off a vengeful poacher. . . . No reason to fight for anything."

She pondered this a minute. It was certainly flattering to hear that without her, Romulus had lost the will to live. But she needed to make him see how unrealistic that sort of love was.

Diana the dreamer was about to give a lecture on practicality.

"Romulus, even if I had died in the fire, you still had other reasons to live. Niall, for one, and Lady Hamish, and all the creatures on the river who depend on you. I will be as much a part of your life as a woman can be . . . but I can't be everything."

"No," he said softly. "I wanted . . . I needed something to fill up my soul . . . because ever since I returned from France, it's been so very empty. But I'm afraid even a water witch hasn't that much magic."

"Then what has made this change in you?"

"I think I found one answer last night. I can't explain it just yet. I . . . I can only say that I feel whole again. And I couldn't be with you, or love you, until that occurred."

"And now?"

"Now I am complete. Well, except for one part—my heart is no longer my own." He tipped her head back and gazed into those gentian eyes that had haunted his dreams since the night he pulled her from the river. "It is in your keeping, Allegra. For all time, if you will have it."

"For all time," she echoed.

They spent the morning together, free at last to give voice to the feelings that had lain unspoken in their hearts for the past week—and trying, fruitlessly it turned out, to keep a safe distance between them while they talked. The instant either of them got anywhere near a piece of furniture, they were both, in short order, entwined upon it in the most improper manner. Rom's chair, her chair, the chaise beside the dressing room. Every place but the wide bed, which, by mutual consent, they stayed well away from.

For a man just out of his sickbed, Diana thought with a sigh, her river god was surprisingly agile.

Lady Hamish came peeking into the room while they were sharing their luncheon—and Rom's chair. She beamed at them, said, "Lovely, lovely," with her hands raised in a fluttery benediction, and then quickly withdrew. Diana saw Romulus trying to hide a blush behind his hand.

Something was up between those two, Diana sensed it in her bones. And it had to do with Rom's abrupt change of mood this morning. But she didn't have the heart to ply him with questions just then.

By early afternoon, the wind storm had increased to gale pitch. Rom's eyes were troubled as he stood and watched the willows and oaks on the front lawn bending and tossing in the wind. "This isn't good," he observed to Diana, who was sitting on the carpet teasing Remus with a piece of string.

"The river's risen," she said, craning up to look out the window. "Will it affect the birds, do you think?"

"I cannot say. I've never seen such a wind, even in the Channel. But tonight there's a full moon and, since the Thames is tidal until it reaches Hampton Court, there's bound to be a storm surge along here."

"What is that?" Diana had risen to her feet and was gazing out the window past his shoulder.

"The tides from the sea will be enormously high, and all that water will come inland, carried here by the Thames. Look—" He tugged her in front of him, held her close with one arm, as he drew back the drapes to reveal the full vista of the river which ran along the entire front of the property. The water was moving even more rapidly than the night she had been trapped in the one-oared rowboat. But something was very wrong, she realized, as she saw a tree branch race by in the direction of Mortimer House.

"Sweet Jesus!" she cried in shock. "The river is flowing backward!"

Romulus let the drapery drop. "The surge has started. The tidal flood is running all the way up past Richmond. I believe something like this happened once before, years ago. But not in my lifetime."

"I want to see it up close," she said, enthusiasm lighting her eyes. "Something to tell our grandchildren."

Romulus leaned to place a lingering kiss on the back of her neck. "If you get caught in the surge, my intemperate witch, you won't have any grandchildren to tell."

Diana was about to make some pert response, when Lady Hamish came hurrying into the room.

"Romulus," she said breathlessly. "There is a man downstairs who insists on seeing you. He rode here in this awful windstorm."

Joe Black came pounding into the room in her wake, a protesting footman still clinging to his back like a barnacle. "Leave off there!" Joe cried, at last able to brush the man away. "Mr. Perrin, sir," he said as he rushed forward. "I know you haven't been well. But you are the only man who can help me."

"He is not yet fully recovered," Diana interjected fretfully.

"I know it, miss." His worried eyes shifted to Romulus. "I see how thin you are, sir, and how washy. I'd thrash that Argie Beasle within an inch of his life, if he hadn't taken himself off to God-knows-where. I'd not bother you with this, but it's my family. My little girl and her cousins."

"What is it, Joe? Tell me, man. If there's anything I can do for you, I will."

"It was the swans, sir. A nest of them on that narrow island downstream from yours. We saw them yesterday, me, an' my wife, an' our little girl when we rowed across from Treypenny to visit my sister's family. We had taken Wald Chipping's boat—he's another one who's scarpered off, sudden-like. Four boy cousins, my Bessie has, an' each one more trouble than the next. They stole that boat this mornin' sir, to go see the swans. And they took my girlie with them."

"No." Rom said the word as if by merely pronouncing it, the children's theft would be undone.

"Indeed they did. Rowed it over to that island. And there they be, with the water rising, and them stranded. It's killing my wife and my sister to see it, sir. To see their own babbies trapped like that. They're only seventy feet from the shore, but they might as well be on the moon."

Rom was pacing about the room now. Diana and Lady Hamish darted alarmed glances at each other.

"What's happened to their boat?" Romulus asked in a clipped voice.

The publican shrugged. "If I know my oldest nevvy, he never thought to tie it up. There's no boat there now, not that anyone can see."

"Maybe the island won't get covered over," Diana suggested hopefully.

Romulus turned and touched her hand briefly. "Unlike my island, that one does have a name. Hereabouts, they call it the Sinker."

"Oh," she said weakly.

He went to the window and gazed out. His eyes gauged the current height of the river. "The island will be underwater inside of an hour. Maybe less."

He tugged off his dressing gown and tossed it onto a chair. Beneath it he wore a cambric shirt and dark broadcloth breeches—courtesy of Lady Hamish. A pair of gleaming top boots stood beside his bed. He sat down and quickly pulled one on.

"Romulus, no!" It was Lady Hamish who had cried out.

Diana was surprised she wasn't the one protesting. But she knew this call to action was one Romulus couldn't refuse. Not without imperiling his still tenuous self-esteem. This was exactly the sort of thing he thrived on. He was a rescuer, as she had good cause to know—he would no doubt be answering someone's cry for help long after they were in their dotage. She told herself she'd just better get used to it.

"You're not taking a boat out—" Lady Hamish clutched his arm. "You're still ailing, Romulus, and the river is a deathtrap."

"You'll not get far, sir, if you set off from here," Joe Black concurred bleakly. "The water's reversed its flow, it's coming down from London. I thought we could ride north to Richmond, find a boat there. Then you'd be headin' with the current."

"There's a boat near that island," he told his astonished audience, and then winked at Diana.

"Of course," she breathed. "Mortimer's rowboat."

"It's beached on this side of the river—north of the Sinker." As he spoke he thanked the Providence that kept him from burning the boat, and the river sense that had made him drag it far above the waterline.

Diana ran to crouch before him, "Can I do anything to help?"

He shook his head. "No. Best keep out of the way."

"*Romulus* . . ." she muttered, leaning forward with a set, mutinous expression on her face.

"Sorry," he said wryly, "I forgot that you rarely take no for an answer." He rapidly ticked off a list of items. "I'll need a coach, and rope—two hundred feet, should do it. A grappling hook, a knife, blankets, and as least four strong men. Can you gather those things in the next five minutes?"

"Like falling off a log," she said briskly as she started for the door. She glanced behind her as she reached the entryway, noting the worried faces in the room. Her river god was the only one who looked calm and untroubled. She ran back and kissed the side of his face. "I love you, Romulus Perrin," she whispered. And then she bolted from the room.

"Oh, and two sets of oars!" he shouted after her.

After he had tugged on a coat of melton cloth he went striding from the room with Joe Black and the footman hurrying after him. Lady Hamish went to her room to fetch a cloak, and one for Diana. She had no intention of letting Romulus go off alone into danger, and she suspected the girl would be of the same mind. She then ordered up her barouche, thanking God her horses were not flyaway highbreds, but more passive plodders. It wouldn't do to take flighty cattle out in such a tempest.

As she stepped from the rear of the house, the howling wind

caught at the hood of her cloak and sent it billowing behind her. The sky had gone yellow, the color of soured buttermilk, and the wind shrilled like a banshee over the top of the tall house. In all her fifty-two years she had never seen the like.

As Diana came out through the stable entrance, dragging an unwieldy coil of rope behind her, she saw Lady Hamish standing silhouetted against the dark kitchen doorway. She marveled at how regal the woman appeared, like Elizabeth Tudor about to send her fleet against the Spanish armada.

Lady Hamish came resolutely across the cobbled yard, and after throwing the cloak over Diana's shoulders, she helped her carry her burden toward the coach that awaited Romulus. Lady Hamish waved away the driver's offer of assistance, and the two women hauled the rope into the coach's interior. The footman came listing around the corner then, his narrow frame buffeted this way and that by the gale, as he juggled the four oars he had fetched from the boathouse.

Rom came out of the stable, still issuing instructions to the four grooms Diana had recruited. The grooms climbed into the coach, stepping over the rope that lay coiled there, like a long, braided serpent.

Romulus gave Lady Hamish a swift hug. Her eyes were wet with tears when she released him. He turned to Diana then. "Thank you," he said into the wind. "Thank you for not being afraid."

"I'm petrified," she called back, holding her hair away from her face with both hands.

"So am I," he said, as he bent her back and quickly kissed her. "Be brave, my darling. Stay with Lady Hamish—she will need you if anything goes wrong."

And with that curious pronouncement, he climbed into the coach. The driver pulled out, whipping his horses into a gallop once the coach had passed from the stableyard. The barouche, its canvas top up, drove into the stableyard in the coach's wake. Diana tugged open the door and aided her hostess up the steps. She tumbled in after her, the wind sending her cloak flying about her like a shroud.

Lady Hamish's eyes were liquid with fear. "Can he save them, do you think?"

"He can, if anyone can," Diana stated, as she settled herself on the opposite seat. A cold, trembling hand reached across the space that separated them. Diana took it and squeezed reassuringly. "Romulus knows the river," she said stoutly. "And I do believe, my dear Lady Hamish, that the river knows him."

*   *   *

He'd seen it done once, in Tuscany, while he and his father were living there.

The rivers of that Italian province were ancient; they had carved deep gullies into the ruddy landscape. For the most part they were placid—slow moving and serene. But occasionally, when there was too much rainfall high in the Apennines, those rivers became raging torrents. Villages which had stood for centuries were carried away before the tons of water that were unleashed from the mountains.

A farm family had been trapped on the roof of their barn by such a flood. The swollen rive raged on either side of the barn, making it impossible for a boat to reach them without being carried away by the plunging water. But the Tuscan farmers had figured out a way to combat the current. They had attached two lines to a rowboat, fore and aft, and then launched it upstream from the beleaguered family. Once the boat was in the river, one group of men held the stern rope, keeping the boat stationery in the water, while another group went downstream and manned the bow line. After the boat had been rowed across the flooding water and the family rescued, the second team quickly hauled the boat to shore, working with the current. It had taken all of ten minutes to accomplish, and Romulus had never forgotten the sight.

He had also not forgotten that the only difficult part had been getting the boat across the current to the stranded family. The man who had worked the oars that day was a giant of a fellow. And he had taken another man with him, to push away the tree limbs and wooden planks that were borne along by the racing water. Romulus knew he could organize the rescue, but wondered if he had the strength to get the boat across to the island. He was, however, probably the only man fool enough to try.

When the coach reached the bank opposite the Sinker, Romulus saw that a group of people had gathered there—two tearstained women among them. The mothers of the lost chicks, no doubt. He looked across the white-capped water, saw the children clinging to the lower limbs of a pitching maple tree, their hair and clothing whipped by the wind. The river was already lapping partway up the trunk of their refuge. Another clutch of villagers stood on the opposite bank, braving the fierce wind to discover the fate of the stranded children. There was nothing like human drama to draw folks from their homes, he knew, even in the worst weather.

He leaped from the coach and struggled through the underbrush to where the Mortimer's rowboat lay, its camouflage now blown away. He breathed a prayer of thanks that it was still there, as he swiftly righted it and then attached the two ropes, for and aft. He cursed as his shaking fingers refused to do his bidding. There was so little time. Already the river was licking at his boots.

He sent the grooms to their respective stations, watching as the two men who were to stand opposite the downstream end of the island waded through knee-keep eddies along the bank. His mother had chosen her servants well, he saw. Not a weak-hearted fellow in the lot.

He climbed into the boat, set the oars, and was about to push off into the maelstrom, when Joe Black came huffing up to him. "Let me come with you, sir. To push away the debris." He motioned as a large, deadly-looking piling shot past. Romulus wondered wryly if Joe Black had any Italian blood.

"Climb in, Joe." He passed him one of the spare oars to use as a gaff, and then cast off.

The current caught at the craft as though it were made of paper. Rom felt the abrupt tug of the stern line, the twang of the rope as it caught and held. The two men upstream labored at the shore, knees bent, feet digging into the muddy bank, keeping the boat stationary in the water. Rom put his back into the oars, feeling every muscle protest as he set off across the current. It was like pushing against a wall of stone.

Joe Black leaned over the side and fended off a tree limb the size of a pony. "Sweet bloody blazes!" he cried over the wind. "I'm going to have my nevvy's hide for putting us through this."

Rom said nothing. From his vantage point, the island seemed to be miles away. There was no way he'd get the boat across. But he kept on rowing, in spite of his aching weariness. The distance to the island slowly decreased—he could see the children in detail now, desperation evident in their numbed faces.

Now that he had his quarry in sight, Romulus rowed with renewed intent, stretching every sinew to the limit. But his overtaxed body, still depleted from the five days in the shed and weakened by his wretched nervous condition, began to fail him. His arms were trembling now from exertion, and he felt as though his heart would burst. With one last mighty heave, he brought the boat to within ten feet of the tree. Joe Black quickly stood up and hurled the grappling hook over the nearest stout branch. He then reeled the line in until they were directly below the maple. Romulus looked up at the five frightened faces.

"Crikey, it's the bogey man!" one of the younger boys cried out.

"You, Mikey, you shut your gob," Joe admonished his nephew. "Mr. Perrin risked his life to save you."

The first four children slithered down the tree and into the boat. The last, a wideset youth of perhaps sixteen, was making his way down when Romulus called out, "Stop! The boat can't take any more weight."

Already the water was lapping dangerously near the gunwales. He thought he'd be able to easily carry five children in the boat, but Joe Black's nephews were all strapping specimens. Rom knew he hadn't the strength to make another trip across and he doubted Joe had the skill to make the crossing on his own. Without conscious thought, he climbed from the boat and settled himself on one of the tree limbs.

"Go on, lad." He motioned downward. The youth quickly lowered himself from the branch he'd been clinging to. Joe Black looked up at Romulus. He said nothing. But what he was thinking was written clearly on his somber face. He ordered the child in the bow to give two tugs on the downstream line and, as if by magic, the boat began moving into the current, rapidly angling across the water toward the shore.

"Thank you, sir!" Joe Black shouted out.

Romulus watched as the two men at the downstream station helped Joe Black and the children from the boat. The boys and Bessie clambered up the bank to where their mothers waited. Farther upstream, Lady Hamish's barouche was drawn up near the edge of the water, and Romulus could see the two cloaked figures who stood there, their arms entwined. His mother and Allegra. He wondered how long they had been standing there, and thanked God he couldn't see their faces.

The water was swirling around his boots now, brown and full of silt. As he shifted to a higher branch, the tree canted noticeably. Undermined by the force of the water and by the weight of all those strapping children, his haven was no longer secure.

"Romulus!"

He heard the voice over the wuthering of the wind.

"*Rom-u-lus!*"

It was Niall, calling from the opposite bank. He was trying to force his stallion into the water, but the horse, wise creature, was having none of it. As Niall slashed at him with the ends of the reins, the horse reared up. Niall threw himself off its back and waded out into the water.

Romulus cupped his hands around his mouth. "No, Niall!" he cried out. "Don't do it!"

Niall stopped and looked up. Across sixty feet of water their eyes met.

Rom's gut twisted. He'd said unforgivable things to the Gypsy, to drive him away. But like Allegra, Niall was not easily daunted.

"I'm sorry," Romulus mouthed. Niall nodded once, and then drew slowly back from the water's edge.

The tree creaked and tipped a bit farther to one side. Romulus held his breath. There were times in the past year, when he wouldn't have minded dying in the river. But not now, not when he had so much to live for. It was damnable to think that he would perish before he had a chance to reclaim his life. To seize the joy that had always eluded him before he met Allegra, before he knew he had a mother who loved him.

It had made all the difference to his wounded soul, to discover he was the son of that intelligent, capable woman. A woman who had learned, as he had, how painful it could be to place duty before love. His torment had melted away at her revelation. He saw then that neither of them was infallible—that life sometimes offered choices where there was no positive outcome.

She'd had to choose between responsibility to her father, and allegiance to her husband and son. He'd had to choose between staying behind to nurse his dying friends in prison—for that was the one thing he had never revealed to a single soul, that three of his comrades had still been alive when he left—and abandoning them, so that he could aid the men who were well enough to escape.

He accepted that choice now—that he had chosen to serve the living—without any lingering guilt.

And because of that acceptance, he had at last been free to set his mended heart before Allegra.

He'd made his decision that morning, as he'd held her in his arms. He would claim his birthright and take the place in the world that should have been his from infancy. Not that he regretted the years with his father—they had made him the man he was. A man capable of selflessness and deep commitment to those he loved. But now he wanted to use those strengths, the ones that had made him a healer and a rescuer in his life on the river, in a broader setting. He would oversee Hamish House with the same concern and integrity that he had brought to his swankeeping. And Allegra would be his touchstone—she, who drew everyone to her, would be his guide for learning to get on with others. Together they could fill Hamish House with love and with light . . . and perhaps even bring his mother back into the world she had foresworn so many years ago.

Yes, he would have done all those things, he mused bleakly, if he wasn't stranded in this tipsy tree, facing a damned watery death.

Diana stood shivering beside Lady Hamish, fighting off despair as she cursed the river that was swirling below Rom's perch. Already he was into the thinner branches of the tree, which now hung perilously close to the racing, white-capped water. As she watched, it lurched a bit more to one side.

The wind had died down somewhat, enough so that you could hear yourself think. But she didn't want to think. Not when all her thoughts led to the same fearful conclusion.

It was unthinkable that she should lose Romulus now—she'd only just gotten him back! If only she were not so weak, she could have rowed the boat back to him herself. She wondered if she dared ask one of the grooms to risk his life. Or the publican. But although the wind had lessened, the water still fretted and plunged. It wouldn't be fair to ask it of them. She feared only an act of God could save Romulus now.

"He's moving," Lady Hamish cried softly, her fingers holding tight to Diana's shoulder.

Diana's eyes darted up. Sure enough, Romulus had shifted on his branch and was reaching cautiously below him. His fingers found the submerged grappling iron that was caught on one of the lower limbs and he coaxed it away from the tangle of sodden leaves. He leaned forward, well out from the tattered green canopy above him, and flung it over the water. It caught in the branches of another tree some fifteen feet from beyond him. He tugged on the line, securing it, and then slid off his branch into the roiling water.

"No!" Diana cried out.

The top of his head was all she could see—his wet hair the same color as the dark, muddy water.

Lady Hamish's arms drew around her. "He's trying to save himself." Her voice broke. "Praise God, Diana, he's fighting back!"

As they watched with anxious eyes, the man in the water drew himself toward the distant tree. The current snatched at him and carried him out beyond his goal. Twice his head disappeared beneath the surface. Both times Diana had to look away. Hand over hand, with agonizing slowness, Romulus pulled himself toward safety. When he reached his goal, he clung, unmoving, to the slickened trunk of the tree. After some time, he dragged himself up onto one of the lower branches.

Diana turned to the baroness, holding her by both wrists. "Tell me, Lady Hamish," she implored. "Why does he mean so much to you? I see it in your eyes, I feel the fear for him pulsing in your veins. You are right—he is fighting back now. Yesterday he would have let the river take him. What did you say to him, what did you tell him, that has made such a difference?"

She sighed. "He didn't want me to tell you yet . . . but it's foolish to hold back now. Romulus is my son."

Diana reeled slightly. "You are his mother?" And then she smiled. "I should have guessed. It all makes sense now. He . . . he told me he found his soul last night."

"Is that what he said?" The baroness smiled. "I wasn't precisely sure he took it as good news."

There was a commotion behind them as a rider came clattering up and reined his horse beside the barouche. Sir Beveril Hunnycut dismounted and came striding toward them.

"Beveril!" Lady Hamish cried.

He gave her a cautious glance. "Vivian's cook heard about the children trapped on the island, from a traveller who took refuge in her kitchen. I thought I'd come along . . . see if there was anything I could do."

"The children are safe," Lady Hamish said.

"Well, that's a fine day's work." He cocked his head. "But then why are the two of you still here?"

Wordlessly, Diana pointed to the group of trees at the center of the island.

"Good lord!" Beveril exclaimed when he saw Romulus clinging limply to a branch. He turned and quickly drew Lady Hamish into his arms.

"There wasn't enough room in the boat," she whispered hoarsely into his shoulder. "And now he's the one who is trapped."

Beveril assessed the situation, saw even from this distance that the man across the water had used up his last reserves. And he saw at once what needed to be done. He may have been a self-serving glad-hander in Parliament, but he knew his way around the ordering of men.

"You there!" he called to his aunt's grooms. "Drag this boat down-river, er, upriver. I'm going across."

He tugged off his fitted riding coat and helped the men pull the boat up onto the shore. They hauled it over the bracken that edged the river until it was well above the island. Lady Hamish came running up just before he pushed off.

"Forgive me, aunt," he said without looking up from the oars.

"I'll forgive you anything, Beveril. If you bring him back to me. He is—"

"I know," he said as he met her eyes. "I think I've always known."

Diana brushed past the baroness and scrambled over the gunwale. She was clutching one of the extra oars to her chest.

"Well, what are you waiting for?" she said as she sank down on the stern seat.

"No!" Beveril and Lady Hamish cried out in unison.

Diana stuck out her chin. "I need to do this, don't you see. If I have to stand here one minute longer unable to do anything, I shall go mad. And besides," she pointed out to Beveril, "you won't make it across if you are broadsided by a log. Now please row!"

He cast off then, rowing boldly for the island. The water pushed the boat back a few feet for every stroke he took. Diana wondered how Romulus had been able to make the first trip, as ill as he had been.

Though the wind continued to buffet over their heads, and the chill water sloshed over the sides of the boat, she felt no fear. Her only focus was the man on the island. She nearly didn't see the jagged length of timber that came bearing down on the boat like a missile. Just before it crashed into them, Diana scrambled to her feet and fended it off with her oar. It caught in an eddy, thudded hard against the stern, and then went racing away. She whispered a prayer of thanks—the river gods were still with her.

Romulus watched in disbelief, as Beveril and Allegra came doggedly toward him over the surging water. Beveril brought the boat directly beneath the tree, and then gazed up into Rom's disbelieving eyes.

"You needn't look so shocked," Beveril said blithely. "I did a bit of rowing at Oxford. Well, aren't you going to come down . . . cousin?"

Romulus pried his trembling fingers from the tree limb and tumbled into the boat. Diana immediately threw her arms around him, hugging him fit to break a rib.

"Steady on, witch," he said softly. "I'm only just out of my sickbed." He saw the expression of stunned relief on her pale face, the stark fear only now beginning to fade, and all his levity fled away.

"I thought . . ." he uttered hoarsely. He couldn't seem to find the words. "I was . . ."

"I know," she answered, reaching up to stroke the wet hair back from his face.

He set his hands on her shoulders, his golden eyes full of reproof. "Don't ever frighten me like that again, Allegra. There was no need for you to place yourself at risk."

She wrinkled her nose. "You're a fine one to talk," she chided. "Next time *you* wait on the shore with your heart in your throat, and see how you like it."

"My heart was in my throat. That blasted plank nearly carried you both off."

"I'll make a trade with you," she said. "I'll stay off the river when it's in flood, if you promise to restrain your heroic impulses for a few decades. At least long enough to meet your grandchildren."

"I'll have other things to keep me busy," he murmured, leaning forward to kiss her.

With a little cough, Beveril remarked, "I hate to break up this touching reunion, but I think we should get back to shore—the boat seems to have sprung a leak."

He tugged twice on the bow line as Diana settled Rom on the stern seat. They were swiftly drawn back to the shore, which was a good thing, since the boat was rapidly filling with water.

The grooms ran forward into the river and pulled them from the sinking craft. The man who was helping Romulus to shore was quickly supplanted by Diana, who wrapped both arms around his waist as she coaxed him up the slippery bank to where Lady Hamish was waiting.

He reached out to his mother with both hands.

"Romulus," she whispered, a catch in her voice, as she rushed forward and clasped him in her arms. Her pale face was glowing with relief as she tenderly drew a blanket over his shoulders. "Come to the coach now, my dear. We need to get you home."

He nodded, but then caught sight of one of the grooms, who was about to sever the line that held the listing rowboat to the bank. Romulus took a step back toward the water and waved him off.

"Don't!" he called over the wind. "Don't give it to the river. I'm very attached to that boat." He looked down into Diana's face. "It tossed a black-haired water witch at my feet."

"I'm still there, Romulus," she said, grinning up at him as her hands plucked at her drenched skirts. "Well, perhaps not at your feet, but just as waterlogged as the day you found me."

He tucked her under his arm as the three of them made their way toward the coach. Beveril stood beside the open door and guided his aunt up the steps. He turned then and laid his hand on Rom's shoulder.

"You've got grit, Perrin," he declared. "It's hard to dislike a man with grit." His voice deepened. "And you've also got . . . my most sincere and humble apology." He held out one hand.

Romulus took it, though his eyes remained wary. "I forgive you, Hunnycut. But I wonder if you will forgive me. For taking what you once thought was yours."

"Not mine any longer," Sir Beveril said gruffly. "Never was apparently." His gaze shifted to Diana. "Neither the house nor the girl. I wish you joy of her—she's a rare handful."

Romulus tugged her against him. "That she is." His mouth twisted into a wry smile. "But then I'm no day in the park, either."

They watched as Beveril went striding over to his horse.

"Will your mother make things right with him?" Diana asked. And then bit her lip.

His eyes narrowed. "So she told you about that, did she?"

Diana nodded slowly. "Yes, though I feel a fool for not having realized it sooner."

"Mmm. Not half as foolish as I feel. But I'll see to Beveril, even if she doesn't. He had . . . an unfortunate upbringing."

"You don't hate him any longer, then? For what he did to you?"

He studied her a moment. "This seems like as good a time as any for starting over. The old scores are evened now, I think."

"Yes," she answered. "And I even got to repay you for rescuing me . . . well, a little."

"Ah," he said, setting his hands tight at her waist. "But you've got to be careful who you rescue from the river, Allegra."

"Oh, I know all about that," she said. "They don't always pay you back in kind."

"Did I say that?" he responded with a grin, just before he bent her back and kissed her hard upon the mouth.

Chapter 15

It was definitely not good *ton* to run off from your own wedding party.

But Diana had received enough congratulations and felicitations to last her a lifetime. She slipped through the French doors of Lady Hamish's drawing room, lifting the skirts of her pale amber gown as she flitted over the velvety green lawn. The river drew her, as it had the night of that other party, the one she had fled from in heart-sick doubt.

The sky was darkening overhead, the western horizon shot with fingers of scarlet and gold as she stood upon the granite breakwater, gazing across the silvery Thames. She thought back over the past three weeks, and to all that had transpired since the day of the windstorm.

After his ordeal on the river, Romulus had slept for two days straight. Diana had fretted over what his state of mind might be when he awakened, but when he at last roused from his slumber, he had hoisted her onto his bed and proceeded to kiss her with such vigor, that she knew her fears were groundless.

She had returned to Mortimer House that same day, sure in her heart that Rom was mended, and knowing, further, that he needed time to be alone with his mother.

"Wise Allegra," Romulus had called her, as he saw her off. Wise, perhaps, but dashed lonely. Even if Romulus had driven over to visit her nearly every day, his visits were monitored by Helen and James.

Diana gazed back at Hamish House, alive with light and music and a host of wedding guests, and sighed wistfully. Even now, now that she was wed to her swankeeper, there still seemed to be no private moments between them. She wished that the lodge on the island was still standing—it would have been a perfect honeymoon cottage, remote, secluded and gloriously private.

Diana kicked at a loose stone in distemper and heard it thunk into the river. She felt as though she were a public exhibition, on display for people to gawk at. Everyone seemed to be watching her with a knowing expression in their eyes. It was unsettling to say the least.

Lady Hamish had insisted on holding the wedding at her home, a fitting venue now that she had publicly acknowledged Romulus as her son. Her lawyers in London were busy preparing the papers of investiture, and if the *ton* had seized on the scandal, no one at Hamish House was any the wiser. Wedding guests had been arriving all that past week, and the baroness had made the transition from recluse to accomplished hostess with her usual grace.

Diana's father had traveled down from Yorkshire for the wedding, in the solicitous care of James Mortimer. Romulus and her father soon discovered they were kindred spirits, their appreciation of literature creating an instant bond between them.

Beveril had attended the morning service, but had then gone off with Lady Vivian to his estate in Surrey. Lady Hamish had settled a generous allowance on him and had paid his gambling debts, and he had sworn to stay well away from the gaming tables. Diana truly hoped he could keep that vow. If she knew Vivian Partridge, that lady would certainly make every effort to distract him.

Niall had acted as best man for Romulas, wearing a fine suit and a merry smirk. He'd looked likely to make every woman in the chapel swoon with desire. Well, every woman but Diana, who only had eyes for her tall, auburn-haired groom. Romulus wore his own dress clothes with studied nonchalance, unaware of how the sight of him standing beside the altar made her pulse race as she came down the aisle.

She drifted toward the boathouse, wondering how long it would be before her new husband noticed her absence and came after her. He would always come after her, she knew. And she needed him, needed to be alone with him without dozens of curious eyes prodding at her. They'd had such an easy communion when they were alone on the island, and she prayed they could find a way back to that state.

She stopped at the boathouse, turning her eyes again to the water. Two swans drifted past, paddling lazily in the direction of the island. Perhaps it was the same pair she and Rom had seen the night he had taken her on the river. Newlyweds, she had called them. Just beginning their lives together.

Together. The word sang in her heart, her happiness beyond measure. But then a little tremor of fear rippled through her at the thought of her approaching wedding night. Fear and delicious anticipation.

"Not thinking of taking out a rowboat, are you?" Romulus said softly from the shadows behind her.

She grinned to herself in the fading light. "Mmm. The thought had crossed my mind."

"What? And leave all your well-wishers behind?"

Diana sighed. "I *wish* they would all go away."

Romulus chuckled softly. "Not until the last wine bottle is emptied and the last morsel of food is consumed. I'm afraid my mother has taken this hospitality business to an extreme."

He stepped forward and handed her the flute of champagne he had carried from the house, and then touched his glass to hers. "To you, Allegra. To us."

She sipped at the frothy liquor. She'd already drunk enough to float a ship-of-the-line, but it didn't seem to be affecting her. Her senses were swimming, but not from anything she had imbibed.

Romulus was standing a little away from her, leaning against the side of the boathouse. Except for the chaste kiss he had given her in the chapel, he had not made any other overtures toward her. Unlike Niall, who had kissed her at least a half dozen times in the course of the day. She wondered if perhaps Romulus was also feeling a bit shy. But then she saw how his eyes were watching her, with heat and barely contained hunger, glowing gold in the fading light. Her breath caught in her chest, and a tight shiver of desire knotted in her middle. He had looked at her that way in the gypsy meadow, as though he wanted to devour her.

She threw her head back and met his gaze boldly.

He grinned slowly, in unhurried appreciation of the clear message shimmering in her eyes. "I suppose we could throw them all out. Now *that* would be a scandal."

"No," she said, taking his hand. "I have a better idea."

The interior of the boathouse was cool and shadowy. Rom left her for a moment, went forward along the catwalk to swing open the wide door, so that the lambent light reflecting off the river flowed inside. Then he guided her down the steps to Lady Hamish's pleasure barge and settled her on the padded seat.

"Now," he said, settling beside her, "I believe this should be private enough to suit you." He lounged back on the cushions and watched her through half-closed eyes.

She leaned in close and hissed softly, "If you don't kiss me this minute, Romulus, I'm going to throw myself into the river."

He drew back. "Kiss you, Allegra? I hardly think it seemly to be kissing my wife in a boathouse."

"*Romulus!*" Her blue eyes flashed dangerously.

In answer, he reached out to lace his fingers through her hair, plucking out the pins that held up the intricate coiffure that her abigail had labored on for nearly an hour. "If I kiss you," he warned softly, as his fingers drew the heavy mass of curls down over her shoulders, "I doubt I will stop at that."

"Lord, I hope not," was all she had time to murmur before he swung her onto his lap and captured her mouth with his own. His lips explored hers, slowly and with infinite tenderness. Diana arched up to meet his kiss, twining her arms about his neck. He tasted of champagne, and honey cake, and of warm, simmering passion.

Romulus nuzzled her bare shoulder, his breath tickling against her ear. "I taste you in my dreams, Allegra," he murmured as though he had read her thoughts. "It's the damnedest thing. I wake up hungering for your mouth and your body. One night in a meadow was all it took for you to fill up my senses. But this, this is more than mortal man can stand."

"Or mortal woman," she said with a husky sigh. "Lord, I've missed you, Rom." His arms tightened around her almost painfully. "Being alone with you, just the two of us. Will it ever be that way again?"

He traced a finger over her cheek. "I wager we'll find a way to steal a few minutes every day."

"A few minutes," Diana groaned. "I am beginning to wish you were still just a swankeeper . . ."

"No, you don't," he said as he drifted his mouth across her chin. "And neither do I. I was hiding away on that island until I met you . . . You, my witch, are what drew me back into the world."

Diana sighed again, this time in delight. He hadn't called her his witch in what felt like years.

"And now?" she said, pulling back from him slightly.

"Now I have life in my grasp again. And responsibility. Which is not a bad thing."

She nodded against his shoulder. "But it frightens me a little, this new life we're to have."

"I know," he said gently. "But we'll do good things, Allegra. We can make a change in the world. It's what my father never could see—that money and a title are not inherently evil things. My mother came to learn that, and in spite of what she thinks, I believe she was the stronger of the two."

"We will be strong together, Romulus," she vowed. She added in a fierce whisper, "We *will* be united."

"Oh, yes," he breathed as his hands stroked along her sides. "We will most assuredly be united."

He caught her up against him, his resolve to behave with gentlemanly restraint now fled away. God knew, he'd kept his distance from her as long as he'd been able during the interminable wedding party, passing from guest to guest and watching the clock's painfully slow progress. He'd seen Beveril slip away with his lady and had resented his cousin's freedom. Rom knew he had to stay behind and do the pretty to the wedding guests. But he was done with them now. They could drown in a vat of brandy for all he cared.

His mouth sought out Allegra's in the near darkness, his hunger for her at last given free rein. She shifted beneath him, moaning slightly, which only fretted his blood to a keener pitch. He rasped his chin over her throat, thrusting her down with both hands, as he angled his body over hers.

Her hands tangled in his hair, her breath coming in little sobs, as he deepened his kisses, delving his tongue into her mouth, over and over. The fire in his belly sizzled and flared as her tongue danced against his. He was gasping, sighing, as his head spun and his loins clenched. It was exquisite agony.

He shrugged out of his coat, casting it from him without a thought, and then tugged at the elaborate folds of his neckcloth. She grinned at his muffled curses and in the next instant her deft fingers had the cloth unbound from his throat. She replaced her fingers with her lips, letting her cool mouth trail along his parched skin, kissing and biting at him until he cried out.

"Now your shirt—" she pleaded, her fingers plucking at the fine lawn. He had it off in an instant, reeling back as her mouth skittered over the sleekly muscled skin of his chest.

"Ah, Rom," she sighed, "this is heaven."

"Now your gown," he purred. His hands danced along her back, thwarted by the tabs. "I should have insisted you be married in a gypsy gown," he muttered into her shoulder and heard her chuckle.

"Here," she said, sitting up so that he could have access to the fastenings.

He stroked his mouth over her throat while he freed her from the stiff satin gown. Beneath it she wore only a gossamer chemise. She might as well have been naked, he thought, with only that whisper of fabric between them. He coaxed her back into his arms, sliding one hand beneath the lace bodice. She was simmering velvet under his palm, round and firm. He lowered his head, tasting her through the sheer lace.

But it was still not enough, not nearly enough. He slid the straps of her chemise from her shoulders and then drew the delicate fabric down to her waist. The wracking sigh that struggled up from his throat was echoed by the soft groan she uttered as his fingers closed over her breasts.

He threw her back onto the padded seat, taking her mouth now in a frenzy of kisses, as his hands discovered every sweet contour of her body. Breast and thigh, hip and belly, he cradled her and caressed her. Naked beneath his hands, naked beneath the skirts of her gown, she rose up to meet him. He explored her, gentled her, and then as his mouth lowered to her breast, he fired her anew.

"Sweet Jesus!" she cried out, thrashing in his implacable hold. Romulus was not daunted by the strident tone of her cry. He knew his witch now, understood her hunger, and relished her fierce appetite. There was no fear in her, only the yearning for a completion that he alone understood.

She clung to him, shivering with unspoken need, as he rucked up her skirt and petticoat and traced his fingers over one rounded knee. His restraint was perilously near its end, but her mouth, open and eager on his throat, was driving him far past the point of caring. She groaned as his hand moved along her thigh.

He started to pull back, but she shook her head. "I'm not afraid, Romulus."

"I fear I will hurt you." He whispered the warning against her ear.

"No," she cried, her fingers digging into his arms. "You cannot ever hurt me."

But he did. He heard the startled gasp of pain as he entered her—the swift, sudden intake of breath. And then the slow, tentative gasp of pleasure as he eased himself a little farther into her. He kissed her gently, his lips a tender pledge upon her half-open mouth. "Let me free you, Allegra," he crooned.

"Yes," she breathed. "Oh, please . . ."

He moved inside her slowly at first, the moored barge rocking beneath them in stately counterpoint to his tentative thrusts. But then as his body increased its tempo, it felt as though the whole world was shifting wildly beneath them.

Allegra was gasping now, her legs drawn up to couch him, as he plunged against her. She was quicksilver, precious and molten, flowing around him, her heat engulfing him, drowning him in liquid fire.

He called out to her softly and then more urgently. "*Bella*," he cried. "*Dolce, dolce, bella.*"

"Rom!" she responded breathlessly, tugging his head down to her mouth. "Oh, Rom . . ."

He felt her passion begin to crest, the shuddering tremors lifting her up from the seat. He gave a ragged, piercing cry against her mouth as he felt his own control slip away. There was nothing between them now but heat. And then for an instant there was a blazing recognition, as he pulled back and lost himself in her bottomless eyes. Damn the promises they'd made in a musty chapel—this was what bound them together, love and desire and all the wonder of shared bliss.

She shattered then, crying out as passion carried her over the brink of innocence into the realm of earthly delight. And so, having at last set her free, his wild, untamed water witch, Romulus gave in to his own need, rising and soaring with her in the final act of loving completion.

Diana stretched her arms over her head, dislocating Rom's elegant coat, which he had drawn over her. Not that she needed his coat to keep her warm, she thought, with his body so close beside hers on the barge's seat. He twitched the coat back over her, letting his hand drift to the rise of breast, which she had only recently restored to some semblance of modesty by tugging up the tattered remains of her chemise.

They were in a shameless state of disarray—Rom's shirt was off, his breeches only half fastened, and the bodice of her gown was pooled about her waist. It was a wonder they both hadn't ended up in the water, she thought wickedly. She'd never felt better in her life, buttery and content and singingly alive.

"I've always wondered," she murmured lazily against his chest, "why these are called pleasure barges."

He tickled her ear with a stray lock of her hair. "And now you know?"

She grinned up at him. "Yes, though I do think ecstasy barge would be a bit more accurate."

"Not to mention florid. So I take it you were not . . . um, displeased."

She scrunched up her mouth thoughtfully, and he had a gripping desire to kiss the foolish expression from her face. "No," she said after some reflection. "Though it's not fair to judge after only one . . . experience."

"Oh, lord," he said as he tucked her head against his chest. "I can see it's going to be a very long night."

They summered in Italy. Under the relaxing, sensuous Mediterranean sun, Romulus soon recovered from the last traces of his nervous disorder. Diana fell in love with Rome, and understood now why Rom's parents had been so supremely happy in that ancient, sprawling city. The great river Tiber flowed beyond the windows of their villa, and it burgeoned with exotic birdlife. Diana regretted now that Rom had refused to take Remus with them—he had rolled his eyes at her suggestion, muttering that he would not be the first man in history to spend his honeymoon with a witch *and* a swan.

They returned to Hamish House just as the leaves in the beech trees were starting to turn. The morning after they got settled in, Romulus received a message from Niall, asking them both to meet him on the island. Neither of them had been back there since the fire, and Diana wondered if the sight of the charred lodge would stir up any of her husband's so-far dormant ghosts.

When they pulled up at the slip, Diana saw that Rom's skiff, which had been bequeathed to Niall, was already tied to the iron ring. Niall himself came down the path, his face lit with pleasure.

"Little mother!" he crowed, kissing Diana on both cheeks.

"How did you know?" she asked wonderingly. "Doctor Harley only confirmed it this morning."

Rom slipped an arm around her waist. "You know gossip on the river, Allegra. It travels like lightening."

"Didn't need a doctor," Niall replied. "My granty saw it last week in her chicken bones."

"That's lovely," Romulus drawled.

Niall grinned at his friend. "You're looking fit. I gather matrimony agrees with you."

"It's not so bad," Rom said dryly, avoiding his wife's elbow. "You might want to try it."

"Me?" Niall made a face of horror. "I'm still a sprat." He winked at Diana, who laughed back.

Niall started up the path, chattering nonstop about Remus and the progress he'd been making.

"If you're going to tell us how big he's grown," Romulus muttered, "I won't be surprised. I've seen how much you feed—"

Romulus had stopped speaking in midsentence and was standing stock still at the top of the path. Diana, who was trailing behind him, her hand in his, nearly ran right into his back.

"Rom?" She peered around him and her mouth dropped open.

The lodge stood in the clearing, dappled with autumn sunlight. It looked exactly as it had the day she ran off. The same red brick, mellowed with age, the same ocher trim adorning the window and doors. The herb garden was past its prime, but a few hardy lavender plants still poked their heads up to the sky.

"Well, I'll be damned," was all Romulus could manage.

"It's a miracle," Diana whispered from beside him, her fingers tight on his arm.

Niall stood a little in front of them, trying not to look smug. "The villagers did it," he pronounced. "To repay you for saving the children. Lady Hamish bought the supplies, but the people of Treypenny did all the work. And Beveril scoured every bookstore in London to replace all the books that were lost. Well, aren't you going to say anything?" He eyed them expectantly.

"I don't know what to say," Romulus replied, rubbing the back of his head.

"I know you are to have the big house eventually," Niall continued. "But I thought you might want a place to get away from things. Your own little haven."

Diana walked beside Romulus up the brick path toward the house, still in a daze. It was as though the fire had been nothing more than a bad dream. But without the fire, and it's wrenching aftermath, Romulus would never have made peace with his grief and his guilt. And his ghosts would have always continued to haunt him. Now, she knew, they had truly been laid to rest.

Perhaps her father was right—perhaps the fire on the island, like the one in the farmer's field, had been a cleansing thing.

Her revery was broken when a fat, nearly grown swan came scuttling around the corner of the house. As usual Remus made a beeline for her husband.

"Christ, Niall," Romulus muttered. "He looks like a pug dog,"

Unmindful of this allusion to his excessive girth, the swan began to peck entreatingly at Rom's leg.

"I think he looks beautiful," Diana exclaimed as she knelt to stroke the bird's long, white neck.

"He just needs a bit of exercise, is all," Niall said. "He's outgrown the lake at Hamish House, but I wanted to wait until you were back before I took him on the river. He's got a new boot now, and I've started on the next one, for when he's full grown."

Romulus turned to his friend. "You've got a rare skill, Niall. You should do something with it . . . something along medical lines, perhaps. There are veterans aplenty in London who could use a new limb."

Niall gave a hoot. "That's bloody likely. A Gypsy doctor."

Diana interjected, "Well, if a swankeeper can run for Parliament, I don't see why a Gypsy can't become a physician."

"Who's running for Parliament?" her husband asked with a flash of his golden eyes.

Diana put a hand over her mouth. "I wasn't to say anything until James had spoken with you. They need a representative from this district. Beveril said he would put in a word for you, if you were interested."

Romulus shook his head in amused resignation. "Back in England two days, and already hip deep in intrigue. I knew I would never be bored with you, Allegra, but have a little pity."

"I'm leaving now," Niall announced. "Before you two come to blows." He swept the swanling up in his arms. "Oh, by the way, my granty sent you a gift—it's on the porch."

He went off, whistling his usual tune, as Romulus handed Allegra up the stairs. There was a basket on one of the benches. She drew away the checkered cloth and then exclaimed, "Eel pie! Oh, Romulus, look."

"I am looking," he said softly, his eyes grown dark. He removed the basket from her hands, and then slid his arms along her waist. "And I am recalling a promise I made to you on the river stairs in Treypenny."

"You said the next time you kissed me, it would be on this porch," she recited.

"There's been a deal of kissing since then," he remarked.

"Aye," she said wickedly. "And not only kissing."

He gave her a wry look. "Yes, that too. But I think I still owe you that one kiss."

"Oh, very well," she sighed, as she closed her eyes and pursed up her mouth in a dutiful manner.

He let his thumb drift over the hard line of her lips, until her mouth softened and opened slightly.

"You are very glib . . ." he began.

"What?" she asked breathlessly, gazing up at him through half-closed eyes.

"For a woman . . ." he said, as he leaned closer and tangled his hands in her hair. "Who is about to be compromised on the front porch of a swankeeper's lodge."

"No," she said, trying not to laugh. It seemed she laughed a great deal these days. "I doubt you could manage it, what with the benches and the stairs and such."

"Like falling off a log," he said as he tugged her into his arms.

Niall stopped watching from the bushes right about the time Romulus finished kissing his wife and carried her into the house. There was now a fine walnut bed in the bedroom, another gift from the lady across the water. And the storeroom had been turned into a second bedroom, which was a good thing, what with the baby on the way. Well, two babies, actually. Twins. Just like Romulus and Remus in the storybook from Lady Hamish's library. But he'd let them discover that for themselves, he decided with a grin, as he caught up the swan and headed for his skiff.

They didn't need to know everything his granty saw in her chicken bones.

Author's Note

There really is an inhabited island on the stretch of the Thames described in my story. Eel Pie Island lies several miles south of Richmond and can be reached by a riverside footpath. It is currently home to a number of charming cottages and is connected to the mainland by a rickety footbridge that rises up over the water. I was also inspired by visits to two Thames estates: Ham House, with its elegant gardens and sweeping facade, and York House, with its fabulous fountain. I apologize to lovers of the Thames for any liberties I may have taken with its history—and plead imagination, my wayward consort, as an excuse.